MW00658739

No Price Too Great

Lee Solomon

This edition published by
Dog Ear Publishing
4010 W. 86th Street, Ste H
Indianapolis, IN 46268

www.dogearpublishing.net

ISBN: **978-159858-840-8**
Library of Congress Control Number: Applied For
This book is printed on acid-free paper.

Printed in the United States of America

Prologue

Their journey took them to the edge of the abyss; a Chinese woman and an American man. They gazed into the darkness below. This was a darkness borne of fear; a fear that chilled them to the soul.

Whether bravely or foolishly, they had decided they would never be together. Their passion and love for each other notwithstanding, they had made that decision. The decision made, with heavy hearts they had said a last goodbye.

And then silence.

Forty eight hours of silence.

Grief so overbearing that they could not sleep.

Too hurt to cry. Too hurt to think. Too scared to think about the future, they suffered alone.

They had to tell the girl. That is when the tears began to fall. The girl's tears would not stop. She cried all afternoon. Then late at night, still sobbing, she fell into a restless sleep. Her world fallen apart, her eyes so puffy she could no longer see. She lay there in the darkness with a broken spirit, wet tissues clenched in her hands.

The woman also cried now. Half a world away, the man shared their grief and their tears. Earlier, the girl had asked to talk to the man. The woman had said no. "He is hurting too," she said. "We are all hurting. We are so sorry. We don't want to hurt you. We don't want to hurt each other." "I never, ever want to go to America now," the girl had shouted at the woman, tears streaming down her face.

The woman sat in the darkness, deep into the night, mourning their loss. Her dark eyes had lost their sparkle. The long dark hair that spilled in curls from her head cast a shadow across her face as dim light from the moon crept into the room. She was a strikingly beautiful woman. Taller and shapelier than would be expected for a woman of her race, her appearance usually dominated when she entered a room.

Tonight, however, the woman was overcome with emotion. Her shoulders were slumped. Her breathing was shallow. Time stood still in her heart, while the minutes ticked surely by in the silent room. Shortly before dawn, with strength from somewhere deep within, the woman stirred. "This is not how we want this to end," the woman whispered to the exhausted body of the little girl.

The Road to Hong Kong

Chapter One

Startled by the sudden sound, the boy's skinny body shivered from the winter wind entering at will through the numerous cracks in the unheated old frame house. "It is three thirty," his mother called from the darkened door of the bedroom that the boy shared with his younger brother and sister. "Time to go to work."

The paint on the house had long ago surrendered to the effects of sun and rain, heat and cold, but even more to the effects of neglect. The boy was embarrassed to live there. The rundown house sat directly across the street from the elementary school that he attended. Some of the kids at school knew he lived in the old house. Most of them knew he just said "free" when lunch money was collected from the students for the week. This was another source of embarrassment for the boy.

The old man who owned the house lived in the basement. The landlord's mornings were typically spent walking to a local fishing hole. Along the way he would meet another old man who shared his passion for doing nothing except smoking unfiltered cigarettes, drinking beer, and hoping to catch a few small brim. The old man didn't even eat fish, but he always brought them home in the smelly wooden wicker basket that he carried on a strap on his shoulder. In one hand he carried the cane pole that he used for fishing. His other hand was usually busy with the ever present cigarette. The old man cleaned the fish as he sat on an old wooden bench under a tree in the back yard, Pabst Blue Ribbon beer heavy on his breath as the scales flew everywhere. The heads and guts were thrown to the ground, where feral cats who tolerated only the old man - and only when he was cleaning fish - pounced on the delicacies. The bones snapped in their mouths with a satisfying crunch.

His daily work finished, the landlord would walk up the steep concrete stairs beside the old house. Their work also complete, the cats would disappear into the bowels of the old house into a crawl space that no human could reach. The upper story of the house was at street level. The basement was partly buried in the sloping dirt below the upper story, while part of it was fully exposed because of the severe slope of the yard. The landlord gave the freshly cleaned fish to the cripple who sat on the front porch of the house, his crutches lying on the porch beside him. This was the boy's father. The boy, ashamed to be seen with his crippled father, often had to walk with him, especially when the weather was bad. It was the boy's job to help his father get back on his feet when he would fall. Block after block they would walk, along some of the busiest streets in the town. It sometimes seemed like everyone in town knew who they were and where they lived. "How is your father doing?" the boy was sometimes asked by total strangers. Shy and withdrawn, the boy would mumble a reply and look away.

"Come on, get out of bed. You're late." His mother's urgent tone brought the boy awake again with a start, and this time he climbed out of bed. No slippers waited for him on the cold wooden floor, so his feet endured the chill while he quickly pulled on worn jeans and shirt, socks and shoes. This wasn't easy for his mother either. She woke the boy each morning at three thirty so he could go to work, and then she would lay back down until five o'clock when it was time for her to dress for work. The house might be cold and rundown, but where else could she find a roof for their heads for $20 a month, she often thought. This was a hard life for her, but she felt sorry for the boy. A lot had fallen on his small shoulders. She also knew that he chafed at the humiliation he felt from his plight in life, and often marveled at his ability to escape those feelings by losing himself completely between the pages of a book.

Everything seemed to be a source of embarrassment for the boy, and his mother's job was another. She worked at the local garment factory, trying to support a family of eight, including her crippled husband. Neither the crippled man nor his wife had been educated beyond grade six, so the man stayed home and his wife earned what she could sewing clothes. Times were difficult during the best of times. But when the factory closed because of a lack of available work for a week or two at a time, which seemed to happen all too often, things were desperate for the family.

It was during these times that the six kids in the family were sent by the crippled man to dig through the barrels of discarded newspapers at the newspaper office that sat just off the town square about six blocks from their home. It was their job to find as many Wednesday newspapers as possible and locate the coupon for whatever was being given away free at the local supermarket that week. Sometimes it was a bag of marshmallows. Other times it wasn't food. If they were lucky it was a small loaf of bread.

When free food was given away in exchange for a coupon, the the crippled man ordered the six kids to run relays the two blocks to the supermarket. Once there they stood in line in bare feet or worn out shoes to claim the free item. In those days there was no purchase requirement in order to use the coupons. The managers at the store knew what the kids were doing, but they also knew about their family, so nothing was done to stop them from using as many coupons as they could find. The boy, able to run faster than the others, was required to run more than his share of the relays to the store. Knowing that people at the store knew why he was there, he tried to be as inconspicuous as possible.

The boy was the fourth child, but the older of the two boys in the family. Responsibility for working rested on his shoulders from an early age. Life was often an exercise in survival, but the boy had found a way to escape. The boy had learned that between the covers of almost any book was hidden treasure. The words inside the covers took him away from his troubled life, away from all the embarrassment that plagued him, and allowed him to enjoy a part of life that would likely never be his except in his dreams.

Now the boy slipped out through the rickety front door, catching the screen door so it would not slam shut behind him. He didn't understand why it was there. The screen had long since been ripped and torn, so it offered scant protection from flying insects when the front door stood open in warmer weather. The old house had no air conditioning either. Not even a fan circulated on the steamy hot days and nights of summer. The boy often lay in bed awake on those hot nights, his sweaty body stuck to the mattress. One day, he thought with childish innocence, I will leave this place for real, and not just in my dreams.

The cold night air cut through his thin jacket as he walked quickly through the dark streets. There were no streetlights along the side streets and alleys that served as his path to a little ramshackle building that sat on one side of Dickson Street. Dickson Street crossed College Avenue, the only four lane street in the town, on its way to the college campus that was sprawled on top of one of the hills in the town. Arriving at the building, the boy shivered again as he struggled to open the padlock on the door of the building. This time the shiver was borne of fear as much as from the cold, and he glanced around quickly, watching for any sign of someone coming.

This little building stood just two doors away from the local tavern that was frequented each afternoon by the landlord and his old fishing buddy. The boy could smell the lingering odor of piss and beer that permeated the weeds and dirt near the tavern. This place was looked down on by the townsfolk, but it still stood, just a block east of the railroad tracks where the train depot stood, also facing Dickson Street. Just across the tracks, and on the opposite side of Dickson Street, stood George's Lounge. This was the more reputable of the two taverns in town, and the one that was frequented by college students who were of drinking age or possessed a card that said they were.

With the door open, the boy reached inside and switched on the single bare light bulb that dangled from the low ceiling. Seeing that no one had broken into the building during the night, the boy stepped inside and found a book of matches. He leaned over the open heater, struck a match, and turned on the gas. Flames raced across the front of the little heater, trying to burn the asbestos that lined the back of the grates on the heater. Grateful for the warmth, the boy warmed his ungloved hands before stepping back into the darkness to pick up the two heavy bundles of newspapers and bring them inside.

Closing the door to the small building, the boy began rolling each newspaper and putting a rubber band around it. He worked quickly with practiced ease, enjoying the heat as the small building quickly warmed his body to nearly sweating temperature. This was only one of the boy's jobs. Each morning at this early hour, seven days a week, he came to roll the newspapers. Around five o'clock, the two college students who paid him to do this work would arrive. He would help them load the rolled newspapers in their cars, and they would set off to deliver the morning newspaper to homes across the small town. The boy would ride with one or the other of the college students and continue rolling newspapers while throwing them out his side of the car when they passed the house of a subscriber.

The job didn't pay much, but it was a job. More important to the boy, however, was listening to the college students when they talked about their classes, or about places they had seen, or about their plans after graduation. They were studying civil engineering. This was something the boy did not understand, but they talked about being able to earn $600 each month after graduation. "I would shovel shit with my nose for $600 a month," one of them would sometimes say with a laugh. How the boy yearned to one day follow in their footsteps, but he knew it was just a dream. No one in his family had ever gone to college. His family could never afford to send him to college.

And besides, even if his standardized test scores were eye opening for his teachers and school administrators, he had no time to study. After school each day he worked until well after dark at the bakery on Dickson Street, cleaning the floors. All day Saturday after rolling and delivering newspapers he worked at the bakery, helping the baker, and cleaning everything. On Sunday morning and Sunday evening his mother dragged the boy to church. There he learned about the Bible, learned the stories in the Bible, heard the fundamentalist preaching about fire and brimstone, and decided that religion wasn't for him.

"Ladies and Gentlemen, we are starting our descent into Hong Kong. The flight attendants will be coming through the cabin to collect any items that require disposal. If you need to visit the restroom, this would be a good time to do it."

The lawyer sitting in the very last row of the plane woke with a start at the sound of the intercom. It took him a moment to clear his head, leaving behind his dreams about his childhood. Hong Kong. Wow, he thought, after all these years I am going to be in Hong Kong again. With this realization he closed his eyes as the plane began its descent through the broken clouds of the early morning, his mind now remembering something far more pleasurable.

In 1968, he remembered, he had fallen madly in love for the first time. After reading all those books, and dreaming all those dreams, he had actually escaped his poverty stricken past. He had actually traveled to Hong Kong in 1968. Then he had gone through life knowing that he could never replace the young Chinese girl he had met there, who he thought at the time was the love of his life. They were only together for a few days, but he had never forgotten her. He let his mind take him back to her now.

He had joined the Marine Corps when he turned age 18. This was part of his trip through the back roads of life as he sought to claim his place in the world. While serving in Vietnam, Marines were given a week of rest and relaxation to spend in some country other than Vietnam. The now lawyer, then Marine, had arrived at Khe Sanh in South Vietnam in 1967 just in time to be guarding the perimeter on Christmas Eve night. At that time there were no wire, no land mines, no fighting holes, or anything else between the young Marine and the enemy except the thickest fog ever known to man. Scared? He was terrified, especially when the line he was helping guard was probed that night by the Viet Cong. When the bullets started flying and the grenades started bursting he had nowhere to hide, not even a low spot on the ground.

That was the beginning of the siege at Khe Sanh, and he was one of the Marines who dug the fighting holes and the connecting tunnels and filled the sandbags, using nothing but little entrenching tool shovels. He also helped set out the land mines and strung the barbed wire and endured months of being shelled by the enemy virtually every day and night. By the time the Marines at Khe Sanh turned the base over to the Army and went on the attack on Easter Sunday 1968, they were just happy to be alive. This gave them another chance to die going up the surrounding hills to attack the enemy soldiers who were dug in at the top, shooting and throwing ChiCom grenades down at them.

After leaving Khe Sanh, the young Marine and his comrades at arms fought battles for months in the I-Corps part of Vietnam, and then one day in the summer of 1968 there was an available slot for someone to go to Hong Kong for R & R. The young Marine got the slot. Since he got this slot at the last second, however, he hadn't planned ahead and didn't have much money available to take with him. Being as young and wild as most Marines, he spent almost all of his money within a few days of arriving in Hong Kong. Fortunately, the Marines were required to pay for their hotel and some of their meals in advance, so at least he had a place to sleep and something to eat.

The young Marine had been interviewed by a Marine reporter of about the same age after one of his unit's battles a few months earlier. The resulting newspaper article had appeared in the Stars and Stripes newspaper, and a tape of the interview had been sent to the local radio station in the Marine's home town. The young Marine just happened to be in Hong Kong at the same time that the reporter was there. The reporter asked the Marine if he wanted to go get a beer, and the Marine told him that he had spent his money and couldn't afford to buy a beer. The reporter told the Marine to come with him because he was buying. They got off the beaten path and away from the bars that catered to Marines who were on R & R from Vietnam.

The two of them sat in a small bar in the middle of the afternoon, mainly just glad to be alive, talking about going home one day. No one else was in the bar except the lady who owned it. After they had a couple of beers, the lady behind the bar called a couple of young girls to join them. These weren't the kind of girls they had met in the other bars. They were very shy and quiet, and very well-mannered.

The two young men knew that local custom would require them to buy these girls a drink if they sat with them. The girl sitting with the young Marine was very pretty, he always recalled fondly. He explained to her that he had spent all his money and that he was unable to buy her a drink. She said that was ok, that she would talk to him anyway. She bought him a beer, and after an hour or so she asked if he wanted to go to a movie. He told her that would be nice, but he still had no money. She said no problem, and told the lady who owned the bar that she was leaving with him to go to a movie. They left the bar, went to a movie (with English sub-titles), and then to dinner. The young Chinese girl paid for everything.

"Sir, can I take your cup"? The lawyer opened his eyes and handed the cup to the flight attendant. They sure are a lot older these days than they were when I flew to Hong Kong the first time, he thought. The plane bumped a little from the turbulence. "We are starting our final descent and should be at the gate in about twelve minutes," the pilot said over the intercom. "Please return your seats to their full upright position. Return all tray tables to their full upright and locked position, and stow any carry on luggage that you might have moved during the flight," added the lead flight attendant. The lawyer closed his eyes again, determined to enjoy the memories of his first visit to Hong Kong.

For the next three days and nights the young Marine and the young Chinese girl were inseparable. They made many promises to each other, knowing in their hearts that they couldn't keep those promises. Deep in their hearts they knew that they would probably never see each other again. It didn't matter. It was like finding an oasis in the desert. They were so in love with each other that the rest of the world didn't matter. Their lips were almost bleeding from kissing so much by the time he had to go back to the war. They cried and clung to each other all night the night before he left. Then all they had were the memories. She spoke broken English but didn't write or read English, so they knew they would never be able to find each other again.

Since those few days in Hong Kong with this beautiful young girl, the lawyer had always had a soft place in his heart for Chinese women. His thoughts turned now to how he had ended up on this plane.

In the building where his law firm was located, there was a deli that was owned by a Chinese woman. She was very nice, and she took the time to get to know many of her regular customers. She knew that the lawyer was divorced, and one day she asked him if he had ever dated a woman from China. He told her a shorter version of the story about the girl in Hong Kong.

Unbeknownst to the lawyer at the time, there was another story playing out on the other side of the world. This story began not long after he left Hong Kong as a young Marine, his heart full of love for the young Chinese girl.

In November 1969, around the time that he had finally left Vietnam as a young Marine, the third and youngest daughter was born to a Chinese family in Zibo City, Shandong Province, China. There were no boys in the family. Unlike what happened in many families in China, this daughter was welcomed into the family. She became the favorite daughter and was treated like a Princess by her father. She was fortunate because her family could afford to pay for her education, so she ended up going to college and obtaining a degree in Business Enterprise Management. She was also fortunate because she was blessed not only with intelligence, but with beauty and determination.

This young Chinese girl was named Ping. She followed the expected path into marriage at age 23, and had a baby daughter of her own at age 24. But then at age 25 she did the unthinkable at the time and divorced her husband. She also kept her daughter. She moved to Guangzhou, a key port city and the fourth largest city in China. For the next 12 years she worked hard and focused on raising her daughter with no further contact or support from her former husband. She became a manager in a large real estate development company, and then in another one. She bought a house and a car and helped provide for her extended family.

Ping knew she was essentially cursed in China, since she was divorced and had a daughter, so she let her career and her daughter fill the void in her life for the next 12 years. She took a vacation on Hainan Island in late spring of 2006, and went walking on the beach at night because she was unable to sleep. She thought about her life and knew that she had been successful with her career. She was happy with her daughter, but her daughter was now a teenager with friends of her own. Ping began to think about the future and she could see that one day she would be alone, and she didn't want to go through the rest of her life alone. As she walked in the sand with the waves lapping at her feet, she decided that she wanted to find a man and fall in love for the first time in her life. She had no idea how she was going to accomplish this feat.

Along the way, Ping had become the god-mother for the son of a Chinese woman who had married an American man and moved to Florida. Years earlier, this Chinese woman had become the god-mother of Ping's daughter. They were close friends, so Ping talked to her on the telephone about her night on the beach and her desires for the future. This woman told Ping that she was very happy with her American husband, and urged Ping to try to find a man in America by using the Internet.

Ping started looking on the Internet, but wasn't happy with what she saw. She also didn't feel comfortable with the process, so she talked with her sisters and her friend in Florida about it. They encouraged her not to give up. Meanwhile, Ping's friend in Florida had a friend in Houston. This friend was a Chinese lady who owned a deli in Houston. One day when they were talking, the subject of Ping came up. After hearing the story, the Chinese lady in Houston said that she knew an American man in Houston who was interested in meeting a Chinese woman. Sure, it could be luck. It might also be fate, the lawyer thought as he sat there, anticipating their first meeting.

As luck (or fate) would have it, they were introduced by the two Chinese ladies in America. Ping wrote an email to Lee and they talked to each other for weeks on end, just learning things about each other. They talked about families and friends and careers and cooking and housekeeping and music and books and everyday things about their cultural differences.

They also talked about holidays and plans and dreams for the future. Ping asked about holiday turkeys and wanted to know if the lawyer could share any anecdotal information about the Thanksgiving and Christmas holidays in America. She endured his stories about his childhood and why he had always loved eating turkey. She asked him if he would cook one for her some day. She learned that he was a high school dropout because he had worked since age 10 to help support a family of eight with a disabled father and a mother who worked in a garment factory. She also learned, however, that he was quite determined, and that his 10th grade education did not stop him from graduating first in his class from undergraduate school, and second in his class from law school.

The lawyer almost smiled as he remembered their early days. After writing many letters to each other, they began to share photos. The funny thing was, he thought, Ping was one of the most photogenic people he had ever met. She had incredibly good fashion sense, and always looked great in her photos. He now had hundreds of recent photos of her where she looked like she could have stepped off the cover of Vogue Magazine. And yet she sent not one of those photos to him until many months later. Instead, as an introduction, she sent him a simple photo of her standing in her home.

Ping could have been a housewife in America in that photo, he thought. She was completely unpretentious in the photo. She was wearing no makeup, no jewelry, had her hair pulled back to keep it out of her face, and wasn't even smiling very much. Sorry, but she couldn't hide from him, he later told her. He had just found the woman he had been searching for since 1968. Her beauty was astounding to him. The two of them continued talking and became ever closer, although they relied entirely on emails. It was as though they could see into each other's hearts when they wrote emails to each other. Neither of them even mentioned telephone calls or instant messenger as a means of communication.

Then one day, out of the blue, the lawyer received a cryptic email from Ping telling him that she wouldn't be able to talk to him for a while because of a family emergency. She said she would write again as soon as things had stabilized. He went for days not knowing what had happened or when or if he would hear from her again. Then he received an email telling him that she was back in Zibo City with her father because he had cancer and was dying, and that she wasn't where she could write to him every day because she was spending every night at the hospital with her father.

Ping asked him to please continue writing to her even when she did not write to him. He remembered all those letters that he wrote to her. He wrote to her every day, usually more than once. He eventually learned that she had her laptop at the hospital. She would write bits and pieces of letters to him, but was only able to send an email every 3-4 days. Their letters were not about love or falling in love or their future. Instead, they were agonizing in their letters about the terrible things that cancer did to people. They went through her father's surgery, and felt the elation when it was successful and the doctor said everything would be fine, only to have their celebration cut short when he began hemorrhaging and the doctor told the family he would die within 48 hours.

They went through the planning of the funeral, the purchasing of the clothing he would wear, the selection of the burial site, the grieving of the family, and the cremation of his body. Before he died, her father asked Ping to please take responsibility to ensure that her mother was cared for. Ping's mother had rheumatoid arthritis and required constant care, the lawyer had been told, and even though she was the youngest daughter, he knew that Ping has been the strength of her family.

Her father died worrying about his baby daughter being alone in the world some day, and the lawyer learned later that she wanted to tell her father about him and reassure him that she had finally found the man she had been waiting to meet all of her life. She didn't tell him, she explained, because she didn't know whether it would be received by her father as a blessing or not, since he would not be able to meet her newfound love before he died.

Now the lawyer could kick himself as he thought about the past. Ping knew he was very busy at the office, and she never asked him to join her in China. Thinking about it now, however, he knew that she wanted him to be there. He remembered feeling that it was just too early in their relationship for him to feel like he could impose his presence on her family. If I had known how she was feeling and what she was thinking, he thought now, I would have been there with her. He had many regrets now because he never met her father.

Ping was very, very close to her father, he had learned. She grieved like he had never known anyone to grieve over the death of a parent. Without telling him until much later, she purchased and contributed to the family a gift that the lawyer would have been expected to contribute as her father's son-in-law. She wanted him to have what she considered to be his rightful place in her family, even though at that point they hadn't discussed marriage or even met in person. She told the lawyer before he boarded the flight to Hong Kong that she did this because she knew he was the man she had been dreaming about. He in turn had told Ping the story about his long ago trip to Hong Kong, and how she was the woman he had dreamed about ever since.

"Flight attendants, prepare the cabin for landing and cross check," the voice intoned. Almost there, thought the lawyer dreamily. Almost there.

He remembered the books from his childhood. He remembered the young Chinese girl from years ago. But what dominated his mind was the thought of the beautiful Chinese woman he had come many miles to meet. He had read one of her letters so many times that he had almost memorized it. The words scrolled through his mind now.

My Dearest Lee,

I read your letter and that poem yesterday after work. I am so touched. I am glad that you opened your heart to me. I feel that your love for me is getting stronger everyday from your letters. My gut feeling tells me from reading your words that my choice is right, you really deserve all my love, you are the one that I can rely on for a life time.

Lee, I want to tell you my story which would help you understand me better.

When I divorced, Cici was just one and a half years old. And it was me who insisted custody of her. I did this although I knew that she would be a setback for me. I have to explain something here.

In China, men love their own kids so much, but that is not the case for raising other's kids. They don't love them; you can even call it hate. I love Cici so much and always worried that she would get hurt, therefore I stayed single and worked very hard to raise her without even getting a cent from her father. I always tried to give her the best.

I have spent all the time from my 27 years of age to 37 on Cici. I give her all my love and she is my moral support. And I could even say that her love has substituted for my craving for a man. She wrapped me to sleep every night. Cici was just an infant 12 years ago but now she has become a 13 year old girl. She is very much a good girl, and she is pretty mature for her age. She has begun to have her own world, her peer group, and has begun to insist on sleeping alone.

I know Cici is older and becoming more independent now. And I even know that one day she will leave me and have her own life. She loves me so much, but that is different. There was such a long time that I couldn't adapt to it, and I wondered how I would live the rest of my life. I was kind of lost and felt lonely and disappointed. I was even disappointed about Cici. I was always wondering if I would have to go on the journey of my life alone to the end.

I lived this kind of life for a while but I felt it was so tough. I began to long for finding an excellent man who could accept Cici and me, and bring me love. However I realized that it is such a tough task finding such a man in China. I did not trust Internet love, so that is why I listened when our friends introduced us to each other. I liked your photo, because you looked kind, friendly and sincere. I felt that you were an honest and trustworthy person. I believe in my judgment and gut feeling. I believe that you are the prospect of being my husband, my life partner.

Lee, please believe in your gut feeling and open your arms for your Ping. You should be confident that your Ping is an excellent woman and she is worth all your love. She will make you smile, and bring you a wonderful life. And there won't be any dull moments in your life. Lee, if we are together we will have a happy life, because we are the same kind of person who cherishes and will be faithful to one another. We have a lot in common, which makes us not only life partners, but soul mates as well.

I am glad to find that you want to come to see me. I have found out the information for you. You could take a flight to Hong Kong and at Hong Kong airport you could take the bus going directly to Garden Hotel in Guangzhou. It is very convenient. And you could have the bus driver tell you the arrival time and then ring me and I will meet and greet you in due time.

When you come to see me, at first I think you should stay in the hotel near me. I don't believe I should have you stay in my place when you first arrive. I hope you can understand. Chinese people who live near me come from old schools, and I have been living here for 12 years. Many people here recognize me, and if they notice that I bring a stranger home they would look down on me.

I think we should spend a few days and see if we really fit, and I can take you home when you commit to have me as your wife. After all I have many things to consider and I don't want to regret anything, therefore I must be cautious. I hope you can understand your Ping.

Dear Lee, can you feel my sincerity after this letter? Will you love me more? I will attach a few photos for you and one of them I like so much. I smiled nicely in it. I bet you will like it too.

Your forever love, Ping

The plane jolted as the wheels touched the runway. The big jet engines were thrown into reverse, causing the passengers to lurch forward against their seat belts. The lawyer opened his eyes, ready to step into the future. I wonder, he thought, if we will ever really be together? Will we even like each other when we meet in person? Why would this beautiful young woman have any interest in me? Is it really love, he asked himself, or am I just being used?

"Welcome to Hong Kong. Local time is 5:50 a.m."

Lost in China

Chapter Two

Lee cleared customs and immigration after arriving at Hong Kong International Airport. This was the new airport, not the one where he had landed all those years ago. The bus to Guangzhou took him past the old airport, and when he saw the mountain next to the airport, he knew in a flash that this mountain was the source of his recurring nightmare about being involved in a plane crash. The plane just couldn't gain enough altitude to clear the mountain, and each time he had the nightmare, he woke abruptly in utter terror. The dream was so real that he usually didn't know if he had been dreaming or if he was lying on the ground after the crash.

He could never remember where he had seen that mountain, but it all came back to him now. He had been sitting on the plane next to an off duty pilot when they landed. They had circled the mountain and the pilot had explained to him the difficulty of landing and taking off at that airport. "You have to gain altitude very quickly after takeoff," he had said, "or you will never clear the mountain." Why this was a recurring nightmare for Lee was a mystery. He had lived through some truly nightmarish events during the war, but none of those events came back to haunt him. The mind does some strange things, he mused, as he watched the road in fascination. He was sitting in the front of the bus and had a clear view of the road ahead. He could also see the surrounding terrain, though it passed him in a blur because he was tired and sleepy after the long flight.

Suddenly the bus pulled off the highway into what looked like a bus stop. Many buses had also stopped at this location. Lee didn't speak a word of Chinese, and he was the only non-Chinese person on the bus, but he could see that everyone was getting off the bus. He joined the other passengers, following them through the building. He saw that they were lining up at windows and showing their passports, much like one would clear security at an airport. He dutifully showed his passport, which was stamped by the official at the gate, and then he followed the other passengers back to the bus. They boarded the bus and set off again. Lee settled in for the two and a half to three hour ride to Guangzhou, but within ten minutes the bus pulled off the road again. He saw another bus station of the same type, except larger, and with more buses and more people standing outside the station. What the heck, he thought.

This time when they got off the bus all the passengers were retrieving their luggage. Unable to communicate with anyone, and not seeing any signs written in English, Lee did what everyone else was doing. This time they went through a similar process, but were required to place their luggage on belts so they could be run through x-ray machines. Lee was delayed because he was unaware that he needed to fill out some kind of arrival card. By the time he had done that, and cleared the security area, he recognized none of the people. How will I ever find my bus again, he thought. He walked outside and saw that many buses were arriving and departing, and he had no idea where his bus might be.

As he walked down the line of buses, a young Chinese girl in some kind of dressy uniform motioned for him to get on the bus next to her. "Garden Hotel," he said, hoping she could understand where he needed to go. "Garden Hotel, Guangzhou," he said. She responded in Chinese, but pointed to a circular decal that had been placed on his shirt near the collar when he bought his ticket at the airport in Hong Kong. Then she motioned for him to put his luggage on her bus and get on the bus. Ah, very clever, he thought. They put a tracking device on my shirt so they can make sure I get where I need to go. Suddenly more comfortable, he found a seat on the bus. When the bus was nearly full, the young girl who had helped him came through the bus offering bottles of water to the passengers. He took one, grateful for the drink.

The final arrangements had been that Ping would meet the bus from the airport at the Garden Hotel. She knew the scheduled arrival time for Lee's flight, and they had guessed at his approximate arrival time at the hotel. "I will be there at 11:30 a.m. and will wait there until you arrive," she had told him in her email. He was carrying her cell phone number as a backup, but it was still a little unsettling to land in a country with about 1.3 billion people, hoping to find the one person in that country who knew who you were. What if she isn't there, he thought, watching the landscape unfold before him.

It was Sunday morning so traffic was light. Farmers worked in rice paddies alongside the road. Rundown dwellings sat well back from the road, reminding him of those he had seen in Vietnam. He watched the billboards along the road, sometimes seeing advertisements from companies that he recognized. Most everyone else on the bus was asleep, he noticed. He was too tired to sleep. Too excited to sleep. Too emotional to sleep. Have I lost my mind, he wondered? Would anyone in his right mind fly 8,000 miles to meet a Chinese woman who is 20 years younger than him? He had read the stories. He knew the scams. He knew the failures, the frauds, the liars, the cheats. But he knew it worked both ways. Women from China and other third world countries were also taken advantage of, lied to, mistreated, by men from Western countries. This is crazy, he thought. I should get off this bus, turn around, and go back to Houston. But he had been drawn to her like a moth to a flame.

My dearest Lee,

Sorry for my late reply because I went shopping with Cici.

Lee, I thought of you all night last night. I read your letters over again from the first one to the latest one. I can feel your affection, which deeply influences me. Although we just met a short time ago, I feel like we have loved for a life time. Maybe we were a couple in our previous life and in this life we picked up our love again. Lee, do you also have this feeling?

I don't know why but I just love you so much already. I really, really want you and need you. I really want to be together. I want you to hold me in your arms. I want you to touch me softly. I want to close my eyes and feel your lips on my ear, feel your breath, and feel your temperature. I think I will get very excited, my body will be burning and I will feel a flow of electricity run through it. I will be so intoxicated and lean on your hug. Lee, can you feel it?

Lee, I think I can be sure that I am the same kind of person as you. I also work hard and play hard. Reading your passionate words, I wish that I were with you now. I want to hug you, watch the sunrise and sunset, and enjoy our wonderful life together. I am looking forward to seeing you and your family soon. I think I will like them so much.

I am glad that you will come to see me in China, and I have told Cici this exciting news. I will happily introduce you to my family and my friends so that they can share our happiness. But Lee, I want to ask you if you really love me? Is it from the bottom of your heart? Do you want me to be with you all your life?

If you do, you will get a great reward in return, which is that Ping will love you forever and always be faithful to you and be your woman for a life time. I am sure that you won't regret your decision because you will have a beautiful woman named Ping to be with you for life.

Lee, I really want to hear your sincere reply. I hope you will love me forever.

Your deepest love, Ping

When he received this letter from Ping, he already shared her feelings, but he couldn't bring himself to express them to her. Not yet. Not the way he wanted to. Maybe never. Something caused him to hold back. He thought he knew what it was. "If something is too good to be true, then it isn't true," he remembered his grandmother telling him. She was a half blood Cherokee Indian, less than five feet tall, strong as an ox and just as hard working. "As the old sayin' goes," she would say before espousing another bit of her homespun wisdom. She believed black silk threads worn around the neck had powerful medicine in them. Her Indian heritage influenced the way she felt about a lot of things in life. How would Grandma feel about this beautiful young Chinese woman if she were alive today? Lee wondered.

Lee loved to go visit his grandparents when he was a boy. It rarely happened, since his family had no car, and his grandparents lived out in the country at Round Mountain. Their land was so rocky that it took both mules to pull a plow through it. Old Red and Old Blue, they were called. Ornery as they come, one time Old Blue unloaded a kick on Lee's grandfather, breaking his leg. Lee watched him crumple to the ground and he went running to get his grandmother. He saw how strong his grandmother was that day, as she lifted her husband, who usually stood more than a foot taller than her, and carried him back to the house.

They had no telephone, so she couldn't call the doctor. They also had no running water, no indoor toilet, and no electricity. Their four room house was heated with a single wood stove in the living room. She cooked on a wood burning stove in the small kitchen. There was no better food in the world, Lee had thought as a child, than eating breakfast cooked on that stove. One time his grandmother fried a dozen freshly laid eggs for him in bacon grease on that stove. He ate every bite, sopping up the yolk with the biscuits she also cooked in the little side oven of the stove. He sure could use some of those eggs and biscuits about right now, he thought, his stomach grumbling at him a bit.

The huge billboard with Chinese writing brought him back to the present. All this thinking about food caused him to remember the first time he had tried Chinese food. He had rebelled at the very thought of eating it. But Bob and Barb insisted he at least try it. Or Mr. and Mrs. B, as the help called them. "One bite," they said. "Just try one bite and if you don't like it, you don't have to eat it." They owned a restaurant, B&B, they called it. Mr. B was an engineer by training and had once worked for a large engineering company, but now he dabbled in many things. They had located their little restaurant on the side of a steep hill on the bypass that wound up the hill, past the square, at which point the name changed to College Avenue, and then ran past Dickson Street and then Lafayette Street where Lee had grown up in that rundown old house. Archibald Yell Boulevard, the bypass was called. I can picture Ping sitting in that restaurant with me, Lee thought. I wonder what she would think about it. I wonder if she would enjoy taking a walk through my childhood if I took her to my hometown.

The bypass was named after the first Congressman from, and the second governor of, Arkansas. At the onset of the war with Mexico in 1846, he had volunteered as a private in a company of Arkansas volunteers, but at the mustering in he was elected Regimental Colonel. He had a colorful and not entirely positive image, but he had called this town home and this street was named after him. The land on which B&B stood was actually land that belonged to some distant relative of Mr. & Mrs. B, but over time, through adverse possession, it became their land. When he was age 15, Lee quit working at the bakery for $.40 per hour and got a job at B&B earning

$.65 per hour. Now he was rolling in the money. Eating all the restaurant food he could hold was also better than eating all the bakery goods he could hold, he had thought at the time he took the job.

"Go ahead, try it," his bosses urged him. "Try it," their 13 year old daughter said. Lee was a little sweet on her, and she was a little sweet on him, but she called another boy her boyfriend. She couldn't be seen by her friends hanging out with this poor boy from the wrong part of town. But they were in a Chinese restaurant outside of town, so she was safe here. Lee bit cautiously into the piece of sweet and sour chicken. What a strange flavor, he thought, but edible. "No more," he said. I could never eat Chinese food. It is too weird. Chinese people are weird.

Now the truth is that Lee had no basis for his opinion about Chinese people. He had never seen one. His family didn't have a television, so he had never even seen one on television. But he felt safe in declaring that they were weird. He had read a few things about China in a book. Coolies, he believed they were called. They worked like slaves on the railroad, and worked like slaves in laundries. Not the kind of people he wanted to be around, he decided with all the conviction and certainty of a teenager.

But here he was, on this big old bus, right smack in China. He had a different opinion about Chinese people these days. He remembered how he responded to Ping's letter.

Good morning beautiful Ping -

Your photos are so nice. They display your breathtaking beauty so wonderfully. I missed you while you were gone, but I am happy that you and Cici were able to enjoy some shopping together. Your letters are also very romantic, and they make me feel fortunate to have met you.

I must confess that I dream of you pretty much every night. I have read every one of your messages to me multiple times, and I feel like we have developed a warm and loving relationship. I know that it makes me very excited each time I receive a message from you. I can't wait to open it to see what you have said. When there is a photo attached I like it even better. I go back and look at all your photos over and over again as well.

I don't know exactly why, but you have earned not only my love and affection but my trust. You have a very honest face, and you have communicated with me very well. You have also impressed me as being a person with excellent character and morals. I firmly believe that when we meet, we will both feel a spark and will know that our feelings for each other are genuine.

It excites me to think of meeting you and Cici and the rest of your family. I know that my family will love you because your warm personality and your love of life are quite evident in your messages to me. I will be proud of you and will treat you with love and respect. If you wish, you can learn more about me by accessing my law firm website which you can find at this address on the Internet. You will know you are at the right place because you will find my photo there. There is also information about my educational background and my professional career. Many of our clients come to us because of what they see on our website. They find our website because we typically appear on the first page of search results on Google and Yahoo. They usually like what they see because our law firm is ranked in the top 5% of all law firms in the United States.

I know that I have already written to you two times today, but this evening in Houston as I read your message again and looked at all your lovely photos again, I felt compelled to write to you once more.

I come home every day to an empty home that is begging for you to be here with your beautiful face, your sexy body, and your smile that would cause the sun to rise and shine through the darkest clouds. Ping, you are such an exciting and personable person. I will never understand how you have remained single for so many years. I wish I had found you years ago when you were first single. We could have raised Cici together and you could have been my wife all these empty years.

My greatest wish is that you and I will be together for the rest of our lives. Not just together, but madly in love with each other, with a passionate relationship that other people will envy. Do you think we can do that Ping? I want to love you, admire you, respect you, and crave you every day. I want you to be my passionate lover, my best friend, my soul mate. I dream that you will be my loyal and faithful wife, if you are willing to do that with me. Come and cook for us, organize and clean our home, be my lover and my wife, keep us in good health, and be my forever life mate. You are too good to be true, my love. Please tell me that this is not a dream.

Your loving Lee

The bus braked suddenly, exiting the divided highway. Lee could see that they were coming into a more urban area. He looked, fascinated to see the clothes hanging from line after line, floor after floor, on the balconies of the high rise residential buildings that lined both sides of the streets. I wonder if I will recognize the Garden Hotel when we arrive, he thought. He knew that the bus was scheduled to make several stops, and was not a direct run from the airport to the Garden Hotel. Hmm, there is something called China Hotel, he saw. Written in English. Wait, we are stopping here. The other passengers were exiting the bus but Lee stayed seated. This was clearly not the Garden Hotel.

Soon Lee was the only one still on the bus. A young and pretty Chinese girl boarded the bus and motioned for him to follow her. She motioned for him to get his luggage from the belly of the bus. Puzzled, he didn't know what to do except follow her directions. Then through a combination of motions and pointing, with Lee saying Garden Hotel and the girl pointing at the round sticker on his chest, he figured out that he was supposed to get in a waiting taxi. His luggage was loaded in the trunk of the taxi. The girl handed the taxi driver some money, spoke to him in Chinese, pointed at Lee's sticker one last time and said in English, "Garden Hotel." Smiling now, Lee said "Thank You" to her in English, and she smiled in return.

The taxi took off at a tear. Weaving in and out of traffic, accelerating quickly, braking suddenly, the driver seemed to deliberately speed up and point the car at any pedestrian who dared to step into a crosswalk. Lee had always loved driving, and he appreciated the skill if not the daring of this driver. He couldn't wait until he had a license so he could start driving. When he was age 15 he had paid $5 down on a $60 worn out 1953 Chevy and had driven it to death. With blue smoke coming from what was left of its tailpipe, he paid a quarter for each gallon of gasoline and drove the car round and round the block where his family then lived. This house was just a few blocks from their earlier home, and just about as run down. This one cost his mother $40 dollars each month in rent.

They had to move from the first house when the landlord died, his lungs eaten up by cancer. Lee remembered when his father had descended the steep, almost never used, flight of steps from the ground floor of the old house to the basement. The door that separated the two floors was always locked, except on Thanksgiving and Christmas. On those days, Lee's mother would fix a plate of turkey and dressing and mashed potatoes and gravy and sundry other side items. The food came from members of the Junior Civic League, who would come at Thanksgiving and Christmas each year to make the holidays more enjoyable for the family. If it had not been for their kindness, Lee and his family would likely never have enjoyed the aroma and taste of those huge turkeys and all the fixings. His father would sit in his wheelchair, the plate in his lap, have Lee open the door, and he would call down the stairs. "Mr. Dobson," he would call loudly. "Mr. Dobson." This is one of the anecdotal stories that Lee had told Ping in response to her question.

Dobson Stone was once a magician, Lee learned after he died.

Whoa, look out for that car, Lee almost yelled. If there was a one foot opening, it seemed that the taxi driver believed he could fit the car into it. What was amazing to Lee is that in all this maze of traffic, with all the rules of the road thrown out the window, with all the rude behavior that was practiced by the drivers, there was no blaring of horns. No angry hand and arm gestures. Just do unto others as they do unto you, or maybe before they do unto you. Whatever it was, it worked. The only person who seemed to have a knot in his stomach was Lee, so he sat back in his seat and held on for the ride.

Lee had walked down the stairs behind his father, who was able to take one stair at a time by holding on to the wooden hand rail that was attached to the wall. It took a long time to get to the bottom of the stairs. Once his father fell, and Lee had to help him struggle to his feet. When he got to the bottom of the dusty stairs, Lee's father kept calling for Mr. Dobson, who hadn't been seen around the house for days. They knew he was sick, because they could often hear him coughing. Sometimes he coughed so hard and so long that he couldn't breathe. No answer, so Lee helped his father mount his crutches and they began walking through the basement of the house. It had a floor made of stone. The stone had become polished in areas where it was used a lot over the years. There was a human skull sitting on the mantle of the fireplace, and Lee wasn't so sure that it wasn't real.

The stench was overpowering. They found his body lying in his rumpled narrow bed. He had been dead for days. "Stay back, son," his father said. Lee had learned that Mr. Dobson had been a magician when they had to start moving out of the house a couple of months later when Mr. Dobson's kin sold the house to another man. What a strange man he was. He lived down in what was called Nigger Hollow back in those days. There were quite a few Negros, as they were more politely called back then, who lived down in the Hollow. The country road that lead out to Round Mountain where Lee's grandparents lived curved and headed up the steep hill to town, right at the edge of the Hollow. The farmers had another name for the place where the road turned and headed up the hill. Tin Cup, they called it. That is because there was a small spring flowing there, and someone had put an old tin cup there so that farmers coming to town could stop and have a drink of the clear cool water before attempting the last leg of their trip up that hill. I wonder if Ping will ever accompany me out that road to our annual family reunion, Lee mused, as the taxi sped ahead into the traffic.

Whitestone the Magician, the old trunk in the back of the attic said in big letters. It was Lee's job to go through everything in that big old attic and find everything that belonged to his family. He couldn't resist looking inside that old trunk. Everything was long unused and very dusty. Spiders scurried everywhere. Some of the things inside looked scary to Lee, so he closed the top and never explored what was inside. Mr. Dobson had once told a few tales about his days as a magician to Lee's father, but he didn't talk about it much.

Suddenly the taxi pulled into a semicircular driveway in front of a beautiful hotel. Garden Hotel. Lee saw the sign. And he was early because his plane had arrived early in Hong Kong. Only ten forty-five, so he took his bags and went inside to look around. The lobby was beautifully furnished. The bell boys wore little hats and pants with stripes down the sides and jackets with high collars and colored epaulets, sort of like the monkey grinders of old. There were expensive looking shops along a wide hallway that was at the back of the lobby. Walking along the hallway, Lee found the men's room. Inside he was surprised to see porcelain trench toilets in stalls along one wall, but was relieved to see that there were also a few Western style toilets in some of the stalls.

Back in the wide hallway with time to kill and thoughts to gather, Lee saw a little tea restaurant with no walls. He stepped up onto the raised floor and looked for a place to sit. He was the only person there, so he chose a place with a good vantage point to watch the lobby. I should be able to see Ping from here, he thought. He ordered some tea and settled back to wait, letting his mind remember again why he was here.

Dear Lee,

I was touched by your story about your Thanksgiving Day. I couldn't help tearing at reading your story. My love, only the hard past can make you cherish the nice life you have now. Anyway, we should hold a thanksgiving and a kind heart every day. Dear Lee, you are glittering in my eyes. I have come to adore you.

Thanksgiving is not a special festival here, so I don't know much about it. Now I know, and what is most important is that I know it means a lot to you. I won't forget the day. I hope I can cook turkey with you in the rest of our Thanksgiving Days, and we will remember the kind persons who helped your family have food to eat on those days when you were young. Your story is so touching. In our daily lives, there are many small things to be done. As long as we try our best to do it, we can make others happy so that we will be happy too. Then our lives will be more meaningful. I will try to do everything to help someone who needs help, just like those kind persons who helped your family.

Darling, you asked me about tea. I like tea. I drink green tea in summer, and I drink black tea in the winter. In fact, making tea and tasting tea is a kind of art itself in Chinese culture. If you want to know more about Chinese culture, let us start from tea. I am sending a picture for you, showing an old yard in which there is a table and chairs. This is a place where people can drink tea, and enjoy their leisure time. Maybe you will fall in love with such a nice atmosphere, and decide you want to marry only a Chinese woman. Hee!

Ok, so much for today now. Monday is a little busy. We shall talk again tomorrow.

Your good friend, Ping

Lee remembered that letter from Ping as he sat in the little open tea garden restaurant, sipping his tea. It was one of the very early letters that she wrote to him. He also remembered his response, as he glanced at his watch. Almost eleven thirty. He had butterflies in his stomach. She should be walking into the lobby at any moment.

Good morning Ping,

I love the photo of the little tea garden that you sent to me. That is a beautiful place and I would love to share a cup of tea with you there. We could talk about many things and grow close to each other. I have already decided that I want to marry a Chinese woman, and now I can dream of being with her in the tea garden in the photo.

I am glad you like tea. I agree that the ceremony is an important part of drinking tea. I did some research and purchased a clay tea set, but having tea alone just isn't as enjoyable as it would be if you were with me. The intimacy of sharing a cup of tea could be almost as good as foreplay, don't you think? The anticipation can build as the feelings grow, and the touching and kissing can follow the tea.

My day is also rather busy today as well so I will talk with again tomorrow.

Lee

"Pardon me, do you speak English"? Lee was getting concerned. The time was almost noon and there was still no sign of Ping. The young Chinese girl to whom he had spoken went to bring someone else to his table. "Is it possible for me to call this phone number from here?" he asked. The lady smiled graciously and led him to a telephone. "How do I use it?" he asked. He had no idea how many of the numbers he needed to press, or if he had to push 9 or 8 or some other number first.

"I am trying to call this number," he told the lady. "Can you please help me"? He watched her push in the numbers and heard the telephone ringing on the other end of the line. No answer. "Please try again," Lee asked. "This is a cell phone number, and she should answer it. She is expecting my call." Still no answer. The lady looked at him with growing skepticism, and Lee sat back down. As the time got later and still no sign of Ping, all those feelings of rejection from his childhood began to eat at him. He began to make contingency plans in his mind. All I have to do is take the bus back to Hong Kong and I can fly back to Houston. No, I will just take a taxi. I don't care what it costs. There is no reason to stay here when there is no Ping. I just want to get back to America.

He cursed his stupidity, paid the bill, took his bags, and headed back to the front of the hotel. Almost one o'clock now, but still no sign of Ping. "Can you call this number for me please?" he asked one of the men at the concierge desk. No answer. Fifteen more minutes. Then one thirty. Still no answer. "If it is too good to be true, it isn't true," his grandmother's words were ringing in his ears. Sad and disillusioned, sleepy and tired, and very upset with himself, he walked out the front door of the hotel and waved for a taxi to take him back to the airport.

Frustration

Chapter Three

"My God!" Ping slapped the wheel in frustration. Traffic could be so bad in Guangzhou, even on Sunday. She had been driving for years, and considered herself to be a good driver. But not even a good driver could overcome the problems with congestion caused by accidents, road construction, or just plain too many vehicles on the street at the same time. Why today, why now, she steamed. Normally calm under the most difficult conditions, she felt an extreme level of frustration and almost panic. There is no way I will make it in time, she thought. Will he wait for me?

Normally she would have felt better, but she had forgotten her cell phone in her haste to get to the hotel. What if he calls my cell phone, she fretted. Maybe his plane was late. Maybe he isn't at the hotel yet. I can't believe I left my phone at home. Now here I am stuck in traffic that isn't moving. I could be stuck here for hours. "Has the bus from Hong Kong arrived yet?" she had asked the concierge at the Garden Hotel when she called just before leaving her home. Assured that the bus had not yet arrived, she had left her home for what she thought would be a fifteen or twenty minute drive to the hotel. Only when she was stuck in traffic did she realize that she had forgotten her cell phone. Unknown to her at the time was the fact that the bus from Hong Kong would not be arriving at the Garden Hotel as scheduled. With only one passenger destined for that hotel, the bus company had paid for a taxi to take Lee to the Garden Hotel from the China Hotel.

Who is this man, she wondered, trying to take her mind off the problem. He seems so nice in his letters. I haven't even heard his voice, she realized. When they first started writing to each other, the friend who had introduced them was happily married to an American man. Since then, however, the man had disappeared, abandoning her friend and their small son. Her friend had learned that her husband was back in China with a new girlfriend. If this man, who has been to my home and seemed so wonderful, could not be trusted, then why am I going through with this, she thought.

She had read so many horror stories about how Chinese women had been used, abused, and taken advantage of physically, emotionally, and financially by Western men. Just a few weeks ago she had sat next to a Chinese man who lived in San Francisco, but who was in China for a business meeting with her company. He told her stories at the dinner meeting about how American men in San Francisco didn't respect their Chinese wives, and how they could not be trusted. She had told Lee about it, and told him that she had dismissed the man's comments as being just his one-sided opinion about things. She nevertheless had a level of concern about this, because her future and the future of her daughter were at stake. She remembered when she had first introduced the subject of her daughter to this Western man, worrying about whether or not he would still want to continue getting to know her.

Dear Lee,

First of all I would like to wish you a good weekend. How are you going to spend your weekend? Is the weather there very cold? It is fall here, the weather is nice and I might take a stroll on the streets with my daughter, go shopping or go to the suburbs as a getaway to smell the fresh air.

You asked about my daughter. My daughter's English name is Cici, and she is just so adorable and cute. And she is already as tall as me. I will send you a photo of my daughter. When we go out for shopping, we are considered to be sisters instead of mother and daughter. I have shown her your photo and she said that you look like the Santa Claus in our home. And my daughter said she likes you and you look like a kind person. I believe you will like her and get along with her in the future.

Lee, your words are so tempting. I could imagine the scenario on that beautiful beach with you. I will like to go on vacation with you. To tell you the truth, I am also not a good swimmer, but I like the feeling of staying in the water or lying on the floating board while the waves move it. I like to rest my hands behind my head and look up at the blue sky. Once in a while seagulls come into my sight and I listen to the sound of waves and I might listen to them until they put me to sleep.

Dear, do you like the feeling of staying in the water? Why were you not allowed to go swimming when you were a kid? Did they worry about you getting drowned? You know what, when I learned to swim as I was a child, I often drank sea water. Adults in China said that you could never swim if you don't drink sea water. I call the sea water seafood soup since there is so much seafood in the sea. Hee hee.

Lee, I like what you said about enjoying getting to know me. I feel that way too. My world has become more wonderful because of you.

Your Ping

Then she worried that she had insulted him when she received his reply to her letter. Western men are so different than Chinese men, she had thought. But then she liked the way Lee was different. She trusted him. She wanted to meet him and make him happy. I can learn, she thought. I can learn how to communicate with him. We could be so happy together.

Hi sweet Ping,

I wrote to you earlier today but I didn't answer all of your questions. I am also curious about how you learned to communicate so well in English. I wish I could communicate with you in Chinese as well as in English, but I cannot.

One question I didn't answer is why I was not allowed to go swimming when I was young. It is actually a silly reason that I didn't agree with then, and that wouldn't apply today. My parents were attending a church with very fundamentalist beliefs. One of those beliefs was that a person should not be seen in public wearing shorts, and certainly not wearing a bathing suit. We were even required to wear long pants in gym class when playing basketball and other sports. My mother is still a member of the same church, but its beliefs have loosened up considerably over the years.

I don't know whether to be flattered or insulted by Cici's comment that I look like the Santa Claus in your home. In America, Santa Claus is a very fat and jolly person. I know that I am in better shape than the American version of Santa Claus. Perhaps the Chinese version follows a more healthy lifestyle and isn't as fat. I am honored that you would show Cici my photo and that you have apparently discussed me with her. I look forward to meeting her one day.

Ping, you have been successful in business. Do you plan to continue with a business in the United States, or do you plan to focus only on your marriage and your home? There is no correct answer to this question, as I am open minded about the subject. You don't seem to fit the image of a traditional Chinese woman who would be happy if she were told that her place is in the home and nowhere else. You seem to be very outgoing and adventurous, which are great characteristics. I would never want you to feel "trapped" in the home. How do you feel about this?

Talk to you more soon.

Lee

If he only could see inside my heart, she thought. How she longed for a loving and devoted husband for herself, and a loving and devoted father for Cici. Our life could be so perfect if we just had a family like this, she thought. It took a lot of courage for her to answer his question, because she was afraid that he would not want her if he knew how she longed to stay at home and care for her family. But she told him. She told him all about her loneliness while raising her daughter alone. She told him about how disillusioned she became at one point.

She told him about her dreams of having the perfect family.

When we are together in person, she promised herself, she would tell Lee even more. She would tell him how Cici cried the few times she went on a date after she divorced her father. Not because she missed her father, but because she missed her mother. After a few such attempts, Ping had decided to just focus on her career and her daughter, and that is what she had done. I know he won't believe me, Ping told herself, but I know it is true. Perhaps when he gets to know me better he will believe me.

Things had gone well in her career, she thought, trying to ease the car forward into a narrow space that might give her an edge when the traffic started to move again. Working long days was possible only with the support of her family. Her older sister had also moved to Guangzhou with her husband and her son, and she was always there for Ping when meetings ran late, or when she had to work on weekends. As Cici grew older, Ping had placed her in a private school and she lived there during the week. This had also helped Ping with her career. At least a couple of evenings each week Ping would be at the school, though, taking some of Cici's favorite food to her and spending time with her. The other evenings Ping would go work out at the nearby fitness club, trying to keep her body in shape and her mind and heart focused on something other than loneliness. Holidays were especially difficult for her, as the loneliness would creep into her mind, absorbing her thoughts.

She remembered the night last year when she had walked the beach alone late at night on Hainan Island. It was on that night that she had looked up at the stars and promised them that she would find a man who would love her and grow old with her. She remembered how she felt when she wrote to Lee soon after she was introduced to him.

Dear Lee,

I am so glad that you haven't forgotten me. I feel like I am on the top of the world.

Thank you for your compliment, Lee. I bet when you get to know more about me you will learn that I am not only with beautiful appearance, but that I also have a beautiful soul.

I am a traditional Chinese woman. I am an understanding, tender, and humorous person. I have a decent job in Guangzhou and I work hard and play hard. And I am leading a kind of good life with my daughter.

What I am pursuing are not material things. Instead I would rather have a simple, natural and healthy life. I want to find my life partner so that we can depend on each other. As a woman, I need a good husband to love me. I am a monogamous and family oriented woman. I would like to totally devote myself to my family, my husband. With me taking care of the family, he can totally focus on his career.

There is an ancient Chinese saying that goes like, "If we lived in the sky we would like to be inseparable kind birds; if we lived under the earth we would like to be connecting roots." This saying describes the ancient outlook toward marriage. Which simply means a couple would like to be together under whatever circumstance. And this is also my outlook toward marriage.

Lee, I want to find my destiny and spend the rest of my life with him. I am very serious about it. I hope you have the same goal. I would be willing to relocate to anywhere in the world for love.

I hope that after reading this letter, you will have a better understanding of me.

Your sincere friend, Ping

It seemed like they had very quickly grown very close to each other. Ping and Cici often talked about Lee, and had secretly begun to call him Leelee. Cici was very anxious to meet him, so the plan was for Cici to have dinner with him and Ping that evening. Oh no, Ping thought, I am ruining all of our plans because I am stuck in this traffic. I don't have a way to contact Lee. Please, oh please, wait for me, she thought. She wasn't a religious person but she believed in a higher power. Please, she prayed silently, please help me. I want to meet this man. I think I love him already but I want to meet him and spend time with him and be sure. Her stomach in knots now, the traffic had barely moved.

Lee was so direct in the way he talked with her sometimes, while other times he was very careful in what he said. She remembered one of his early letters. He had later apologized to her for being so direct, and so indiscreet in it. She had accepted his apology, but secretly she didn't mind. She liked this side of him. It had been a lot of years since she had last been with a man, so the thought of it was particularly exciting for her.

Hello Ping,

What a great way the Chinese have of expressing the type of commitment that two people should have for each other when they are married. Thank you for sharing that with me. It is much more descriptive and meaningful than how we say it in the United States. The wedding vows here just say that the couple will remain together in good times and bad. Then 60% of the people break up at the first sign of bad times. They have no connected roots to hold them together, so they easily come apart.

It sounds like you enjoy cooking and cleaning and caring for the home. That is very important, and it helps a lot to have a woman who is willing to focus on that part of building a good marriage. It is difficult to find a western woman who has those traditional values, which of course is one reason that I am interested in a woman with traditional eastern values.

How do you feel about the physical relationship between a man and wife? Do you feel like it is a burden or a chore or an undesirable activity when a man wants to engage in sex with his wife (perhaps even on a daily basis), or do you enjoy that as well? This is just as important to me as having a loving wife who cares for our home and prepares our meals and is my lifelong companion and partner.

Mutual trust and respect between a husband and wife is also very important to me. I want to be with a woman who I can love and cherish, and who will do the same for me. All of this, combined with living a healthy lifestyle, is what I envision in a marriage. Am I being unrealistic in my wishes? Am I being too direct in my questions?

I look forward to hearing from you again soon.

Lee

She had sent a carefully controlled response to his letter, but inside she was thrilled. My kind of man, she had thought. I might get lucky here too!

Good morning my dear friend Lee.

First I would like to wish you a good weekend. How time flies and our friendship grows over time. You give me a nice feeling, and when I read your words it feels like you are an old friend to me.

You really understand me. As a matter of fact I feel that as a traditional Chinese woman, I have a responsibility to my family. I think it is my job to take care of my family and husband. If I were in a romance relationship, with marriage and family, I would be totally dedicated to it. But I also enjoy the simple pleasures in life. However, so far I haven't found someone who I appreciate and who appreciates me. I hope that you are the one with the best taste to choose me.

As for the sex aspect, although I do feel kind of embarrassed to talk about it as a woman with traditional values; I have a good impression of you and would like to talk about it with you when our relationship reaches a certain point. What do you say? I think sex is a big factor in a marriage. I don't think it is a burden or a job (it never crosses my mind). I think a good sex life can enhance a marriage, making it go from good to better, from better to best. Don't you agree?

Dear Lee, your vision for the marriage that the husband and wife should love and cherish one another is a positive one, and I totally go with it. I think a life without a real and happy marriage and a warm family is not complete. This is my two cents on the subject.

Before I end this letter, I wish that you will have a good mood. And I wish that you will think of me.

Your sweet friend, Ping

This isn't right, she thought. Am I being punished? Her watch was showing one o'clock and she was supposed to meet Lee at eleven thirty. The best she could do now was hope that his plane or his bus had been delayed. She knew he was concerned about coming to China to see her. He had been very open and direct on that issue. She could understand his concerns. She knew he was busy, and that he was risking a lot more than the cost of travel by coming to see her. She had looked at his law firm website. She believed he was a man of substance, an accomplished professional. This is the kind of man I need in my life, she believed. This is the kind of role model I want for my daughter. He seems to be tender and sweet. Just wait for me, she thought. Wait just a little longer.

She had tried to send new photos of herself to Lee with almost every letter she wrote to him. He seemed to be so appreciative of them, and he was always so complimentary of her appearance. She enjoyed that part of their relationship very much, and she remembered fondly one particular exchange of letters that left her unbelievably excited.

My dearest Lee,

I am glad to know that you are in a good mood. I am happy about it because I know that you are happy. Our hearts are connected. Now I can feel that I can share with your happiness and joy. We are like two in one.

It is nice to learn that you have bought a home gym system. You know what? I also like working out. I want to tell you something, Lee. I go to a health club around my place at 7:30 pm every Tuesday, Thursday and Sunday evening. I do aerobics and sometimes I even do folk dance. The aerobics I do is an exercise combining yoga and ballet. Every time I do about two hours and it helps me keep in shape physically and mentally. I will stick with doing it. In the future we can work out together. I hope both of us have a great shape and with the great shape we can make love for a long time. Hee!

I am sending you pictures from our company Christmas party. Let me tell you something about the party. The party is actually for celebrating our chairman of the board's 60th birthday. The party was held in my company's own hotel. Every year we hold six functions like this. Our hotel is full of Christmas atmosphere because it is just around the corner. The large cake-set in one of the pictures consists of 6 levels of cakes. A lot of wine glasses are around it and there is also a pumpkin-carved Shou Xing Gong. (That is an elderly person whose birthday is being celebrated, the god of longevity in Chinese fairy tales, and this figure represents longevity.)

I took many photos with my colleagues and I took them especially for showing you. I was not interested in doing this, but for you I wanted to do it because I wanted you to see more of my photos. I hope it makes you feel like I was just by your side. I hope that by seeing these photos you can know more about my life, my job and me. I hope that seeing these photos you will feel my sincerity, and it will make you love me more. I will show you these photos bit by bit. I think that you will like to see my smiling face from time to time. I hope they will have a big impact on you, and that you can't get them out of your mind.

Dear Lee, I miss you so much. I have been thinking of you all the time. When I go to bed at night I don't even want to lay in it. I feel so lonely. I often hug a big pillow and pretend it is you. I want to lie beside you and stroke every part of your body, kiss every inch of your skin. I crave for having you to hold me in your arms as I fall asleep, and waking up to your kiss and your smile.

That is the life I have been dreaming of. Lee, will you help me realize my dream. Do you want to make me the happiest woman on earth? Will you spoil your Ping all your life? Will you always love your Ping, never betray her, and be her only husband?

I love you Lee. I haven't been telling you that, but I think you know. I am looking forward to seeing you and jumping into your hug soon.

Love very deeply, Ping

It took all of her nerve to send that letter, Ping remembered. What will he think of me when he reads my words, she had thought. His response was something that she would never have envisioned, could not imagine in her wildest dreams that it would happen. She had replayed his letter in her mind a million times.

Ping my love -

I was so delighted to find your messages tonight. Your astounding beauty is so apparent from the photos that you so thoughtfully attached to your messages. Do you know what Ping? Your knees are very sexy! Your great taste in clothing is also wonderful. You are so elegant, so refined, yet so sultry and sexy. I love this about you.

We can work out together if you wish, Ping. I need and welcome your encouragement so we can both be in good shape and in good health. I want to spend the rest of my life with you. I want to feel your touch and I want to kiss and touch you everywhere. I want to spoil you and see your happy smile every day. Come to me, beautiful Ping. Be my bride. I also love you.

Your Lee

"Cici, Cici, Leelee asked me to marry him." She had actually awakened Cici so she could share her excitement and her good news with her. Oh my God, she thought. I love this man so much. And he loves me! She couldn't wait to write back to him, to give him her answer.

My Love Lee,

Today is the happiest day of my life! I am so surprised by your letter. I really couldn't believe my eyes. But it all comes to me so true. Thank you for your compliments, Lee.

The most important thing is that you would like me to be your bride. I would like to be, and I am happy to be, your bride. I even think of it in my dreams. I am craving for coming to your bed, and I am imagining what will happen next, how you are going to hug me, kiss me and make love with me. Lee, I am yearning for all these things to happen soon. I really can't wait for it. Could you come here to see me soon?

It has been raining all day today and I really don't like this weather. But because you have asked me to marry you, I am feeling good. There is sunshine full in my heart. I live happily every day since I met you, and when I think of you I can't help smiling. My colleagues wonder why I am so cheerful now, and they say that I am becoming more beautiful. Ha ha. I really wanted to tell them the woman in love looks especially attractive. What do you say dear?

My darling Lee, I haven't told my colleagues about us. I would love to tell them if you confirm that nothing will change. I would like to introduce you to them when you come here. I want all of them to share my happiness. Last night when I talked to my family over the phone I told my eldest sister and second eldest sister about us. At first they were kind of worried. But at last they gave me their blessing after I told them all about us, what you are like, how we met, how we communicate. And they hope to meet you when you come.

I haven't told my father about us yet. My mother and my father are very traditional, and she worries that he might not accept our exotic love. I am kind of worried also, Lee. I am the apple of my father's eyes. He was born in the year of the ox, like you, and we have a very close bond. He is tolerant of me and does not make me do anything I don't want to do. I grew up with my father and I have his favor. I love him and am filial to him. But I believe he will understand when I talk with him and when he meets you.

Dear Lee, I wish that you could come over and marry me tomorrow. I want to be your beautiful bride, and live happy ever after like the ending of fairy tales. I do believe in our future. I am glad to hear that you like the photo where I sit on the chair the best. It is also my favorite photo. And I also took two more photos of me sitting on the chair; I will show you today in the attachment to this letter. I want to share these pictures with you and I hope you will like them as well. Dear, can you also send me some photos? I want to see more.

Kiss your lips. All of them.

Your lovely bride, Ping

Finally, finally, the traffic is moving. I bet I am still ten minutes from the hotel, Ping thought. Well maybe less if the traffic keeps moving like this. It will be past one thirty before I get to the hotel, she calculated. She sped through the remaining distance to the hotel. Garden Hotel, she saw on the sign. A beautiful hotel, but the plan was to meet Lee here and take him to the Golden Bridge Hotel near her home. It was owned by the Garden Hotel company, so it was also very nice. It was only a block from her home, so with him staying there, it would make it very easy to walk back and forth to her home.

Ping whipped her Toyota Crown into the circular drive at the hotel. She loved the car. It went everywhere with her. She washed it and cleaned it every week. She had bought it new, and it had been her constant companion for nine years. The door man signaled for her to park along the curb of the circle drive. She told him she would just be a moment, and she raced into the lobby. Please be here, she thought. But her heart sank as her eyes scanned the almost empty lobby. There was no American man in the lobby. She could see the small tea restaurant near the lobby, and could see that he was also not there. With a heavy heart she walked back toward her car. Where could he be?

"Have you seen a lao wei?" she asked the doorman. A tall American man with a mustache? "Yes," he said, "he left in a taxi a few minutes ago. I think he was trying to tell the driver that he wanted to go to the Hong Kong airport, but the taxi could not take him there. I don't know where he went."

Okay Leelee, she thought, it is time for you to believe in your Pingping. Find me. Find a way to find me. I will look for you everywhere, she promised. I will find you. Don't leave me. I love you. She climbed back in her car and drove away, with no idea where to look. Her dreams for the future seemed to be blowing up in her face. How can I ever tell Cici?

Look at Your Wife

Chapter Four

Think, Ping, she told herself as she drove away. You know this man. What is he thinking? Where is he going? Should I go home and get my cell phone first, or look for Lee, she debated.

Traffic is so heavy in this part of town, Ping thought. Lee had originally booked a room at the Garden Hotel, but Ping had dissuaded him from staying there. "It will be much more convenient if you stay at the Golden Bridge Hotel near my home," she said. "I will make the reservations for you there, but I will still meet you at the Garden Hotel when you arrive because that is where the bus from the airport stops." "Sure, Ping, no problem," he said. Lee was so easy to get along with, she thought.

I should have met him at the airport in Hong Kong like I wanted to do, she thought. Why did I let him talk me into waiting for him at the hotel? "Ping, I want to see you as soon as possible too, but think about it. It makes no sense for you to travel to Hong Kong to meet me. It is at least a three hour trip in each direction," he said. "Not only that, but you would have to go the day before, since my flight arrives so early in the morning. You would have to spend the night, and then get up very early to get to the airport to meet my plane. The plane could be delayed, or I might miss my connection in San Francisco, and then you could be stuck in Hong Kong waiting for me for hours or even another day. Don't waste your weekend that way. Just wait for me in Guangzhou."

What a considerate man, she thought. When is the last time that happened to me? Her sisters were married to men who treated them well, but they expected her sisters to cater to their every need. They never helped around the house. They never cooked. From the way Lee talked, he knew his way around the kitchen and didn't mind spending time there. She was excited about the kind of life they could live together if she could go to America. Cici had told her that America was the country where she most wanted to live. She was also very excited about meeting Leelee, as they called him. That was actually the name that Cici had given him, but Ping liked it a lot, so she also used it. She had told Lee about it in an email so he wouldn't be surprised, and had asked him if it was okay if they called him Leelee. He didn't mind. He seemed to like it too.

As she drove back in the direction of her home, she became much calmer. The one place I know Lee is not going to go is to the airport, she thought. I know his life story. He even told me about his weaknesses, and about things that happened that did not make him proud. This is a man who accepts responsibility for things even when it hurts. He wouldn't change just because he is in China. He might go to my house, but more likely he will go to the Golden Bridge Hotel. He knows I made the reservations for him there. If I know anything at all about his character, I know that he will not just walk away. He will do the right thing.

"Listen to me, Lee. I am a Chinese woman. I know how Chinese women think. I don't know Ping, but I know Chinese women, and I can tell you that you cannot trust her. She doesn't love you except with a purpose. Love with a purpose is not love. Once she is here and has fulfilled her purpose, she will leave you. The age difference is a huge factor. It will only get worse as time goes by. Don't go to China, Lee. If you want to marry a Chinese woman it would be easy to marry one who already lives here. Then you can trust her love. Is she meeting you in Hong Kong? See, if she really loved you she would be there when you arrive. I would walk across China to meet you. If she loved you, she wouldn't care what you said about it, she would be there. Don't do it, Lee. Don't do it."

This fervent plea came from one of the Chinese women who Lee knew in Houston. The opinion of this one he could discount because she also had her purpose. He received the same kind of message from the other Chinese women he knew, however, and also from the Chinese men. If they had a purpose for their opinions it was unknown to Lee. None of them spoke highly of the motives of a woman who lived in China who wanted to move to a Western country. All of them said that it was foolish to even think about marrying a Chinese woman unless she already lived in America. Why would a man in your position even think about doing such a thing, they asked. The risk is simply too great.

The sound of those words had grown louder in Lee's head as the minutes passed with no word from Ping. Doubt began to creep into his mind as he waited at the hotel. They must be right, he thought. If meeting me was important to her, she would have been here an hour early. That is what I would have done.

No, that is a crazy way to think about it, he told himself. Very few people are as concerned about being on time as you are. Maybe her mother became sick and she had to go to the hospital right at the time she intended to meet me. Maybe Cici is sick. Maybe she isn't where she could call me at the hotel. Maybe she did call the hotel but whoever she spoke with didn't give the message to me. Why would she write all of those letters to me if she didn't want to meet me; if she didn't really love me? You aren't being rational.

"But remember, Lee, you can't trust her. She is a Chinese woman with a purpose."

"This woman loves me. I can feel it."

"All you have heard are her words, and you haven't even heard them. You have only read them. How can you trust someone you have never met"?

The arguments raged inside his head. The emotions surged through his body. In the end, he did exactly as Ping had predicted. He did the right thing. Recognizing that he wasn't thinking clearly because he was overtired and too emotional, Lee went to the Golden Bridge Hotel. I will check in and Ping will call me there, he decided. I know there must be a good reason that she wasn't able to meet me at our agreed time. If it turns out that she doesn't love me, or doesn't want to be with me, I am still in China. I will make an adventure out of this.

Feeling better now, he exited the taxi and entered the hotel. The desk clerk greeted him with a smile. "Hello," she said in English, looking a little surprised to see him. I bet there aren't many Americans who stay at this hotel, he thought. “Hello,” Lee said. He thought the appropriate greeting in Chinese was ni hao, but he wasn’t sure. “Can I leave my bags here while I go to the restroom, please?” By repeating and gesturing, he was able to communicate with her. ”Yes”, she said, pointing across the large lobby. This is really nice, he thought as he walked across the lobby. Ping made a good choice. I hope I get to see her today. Oh good, a Western style bathroom. Even urinals mounted on the wall. Clean too. Done with his business, Lee walked back across the lobby to the front desk.

“Will you be staying until the twelfth as scheduled,” the clerk asked. “Yes, yes I will.” “Do you have any messages for me”? She didn’t seem to understand him so he dropped it. I am so tired, he thought. I just need to sleep. About that time a flash of movement caught the corner of Lee’s eye, and he could hear the sound of running feet on the marble floor. He turned and saw a vision in white running across the lobby, high heels and all. With her long dark hair flowing behind her, Ping was coming to greet him. “Ping!” “Leelee!” Then she was in his arms. “I am so sorry, I am so sorry.” “Shh,” he said. “Just hold me.” “Leelee, I forgot my cell phone and there was too much traffic so I was very late. I am so happy to see you. Thank you for waiting for me. I knew you would come here.” The desk clerk was smiling at them, but the bell hop who was waiting with the luggage looked a little embarrassed. What was I thinking? Lee thought. What was I thinking?

“Look at your wife,” the photographer and his assistant kept saying in broken English. They would laugh, and Ping and Lee would smile lovingly at each other. She was dressed in a white wedding gown that flowed behind her as she moved. It was pinned up the back because the one she loved was too small for her body. That didn't matter, since the camera could not see behind her. Her long dark hair had been styled and put up by hairdressers, who placed a gleaming tiara in it. Matching dangling earrings, and a matching broad and long necklace, added to her elegant bridal look. Lee was dressed in the only tuxedo they could find that would fit his tall American frame. Ten hours they had been in the wedding photo studio. Ten hours they had smiled and posed for the camera.

They weren't actually married, but the studio crew didn't know the difference. The ten hours seemed like ten minutes to the bride and groom. The same song had played over and over again the entire day. They still loved the song. They were the only interracial couple at the three story studio. Before the end of the day they had attracted quite a following. Ping's beauty was so captivating that other bridal couples, and sometimes their families, were following them from one photo shoot location to another. The young brides in particular were enthralled with the way Ping looked. She carried herself with such grace, and smiled so beautifully, that she looked like a precious China doll.

Look at this Leelee, Ping had said one day as they drove past the studio on the way to the hospital. He had stepped off the curb wrong in the dark a few nights previously and had pulled the ligament in his ankle. By the next morning, he was unable to walk. He insisted he would be fine. Ping insisted that they go to the hospital. She drove him to the hospital, arranged for him to be examined by the head doctor, and took him upstairs for laser irradiation therapy. She personally held the wand and administered the treatment to his ankle. Every day for three days she brought him back to the hospital and treated him. Every night she changed the medicine filled bandage on his ankle. Every day his condition improved, and after three days he was able to walk again.

This wasn't much of a romantic beginning for the two of them, most anyone would think. In reality, though, it brought them closer together. He needed her. She wanted to help him. He saw a side of her that he was happy to see was there. Behind her beautiful face and smile was a tender heart. It seemed to beat only for him now. She took him to the wedding photo studio as soon as his ankle got better, and they inquired about having pictures taken. A time was scheduled, which had led them to the ten hour photo shoot.

They only had eight days to spend together. How is it possible to get to know anyone in just eight days? During the week Ping would go to the office in the morning, and then return a few hours later to spend her time with Lee. He had met her daughter and her two nephews. He had met her two sisters and her two brothers in law. He had met her mother. He had met her best friends. He had eaten in her favorite restaurants, sampled her favorite foods. They had discovered their mutual love of fresh fruit, and had stocked their hotel suite with it. Ping fed him fruits that he had never seen or tried before. But the days passed all too quickly.

They watched the bus pull in at the number five slot. Wrapped in each other's arms, they stood in the lower part of the terminal at Hong Kong International Airport.

Her head was pressed against his shoulder. They watched as people boarded the bus. "Go back with me, Leelee. Don't leave me."

"I must go back to Houston, Ping. I will be back to see you again. Let's focus on getting all of our documents ready so we can file our visa petition right away." "Look at your wife," she said fondly, looking up at him. "Look at your wife," he responded, and they laughed. It was all a blur now, their time together.

He remembered their first evening together. They had walked together to a restaurant near the hotel. It had a Western menu as well as a Chinese menu. Cici and her two cousins were waiting for them. He wanted to say hello to Cici first, but had read that the most senior person in the family should be greeted first, so he shook hands with the older nephew, then the second nephew. Then he turned to Cici, who had a big smile on her face. He refrained from hugging her, and also shook her hand.

He remembered how Cici had ordered a huge dessert; ice cream with whipped cream on top, with fresh fruit also on it. She had shared it with everyone at the table, offering the first bite to Lee. Ping had discreetly shown one of the nephews how to use the steak knife and fork to cut his steak. Lee fumbled with the chopsticks and Ping handed him a fork. Pictures were taken, as the process of collecting proof about their relationship to present to the Consulate started in earnest. They didn't know much about the visa process yet, but they knew that having plenty of pictures of them together, especially when they were with family members, was very important.

In their many letters, Ping and Lee had talked about walking the streets of Guangzhou hand in hand, arm in arm. He was therefore a little taken aback when they walked to the restaurant, because she kept a respectful distance between them. "It is because the people here don't like to see a Chinese woman holding hands with a Western man," she told him. In the restaurant, though, she was very affectionate with him. I have a lot to learn, Lee thought. None of the three cousins were confident enough in their English to speak it at the table, but they still managed to say a few words. Lee handed them the gifts he had brought for them, and Ping added to the gifts by handing each of them a little red envelope in which she had placed some money before they left the hotel. "This is a gift from Leelee," she told them.

Ping had scheduled a lunch meeting on their second day together. They met one of her close friends, who had a friend who owned a company that assisted Chinese women with the visa process. Lee and Ping had discussed this in advance and agreed it would be a good idea. The four of them met in a crowded restaurant, but they were escorted to a private room. How nice, Lee thought. "How convenient," his skeptical Chinese friend would say in Houston after he returned. "Don't you realize that she just didn't want to be seen in public with you, so she arranged for a private room?"

Hmm, Lee thought. So I guess you would tell me the same thing about the private room in which her family joined us for dinner the next night. But that had been a special dinner. Lots of pictures had been taken. Ping looked radiant in a yellow pantsuit. She couldn't stop smiling, and she was bubbly and talkative. Lee had been worried about what gifts to bring for the occasion, so he had asked for Ping's advice before he left Houston. What he had read about giving gifts in China was very confusing. Never give this number of gifts, never give this for a gift, and never wrap a gift in this color of paper. "Don't worry about gifts," she had replied. "I will help you and we will buy them together when you are here."

The previous night after they had dinner together, just the two of them, Ping had taken Lee to another restaurant. Sitting in one of its private rooms was a man who had brought several nice bracelets with him. Ping introduced Lee to him and told him that he owned several jewelry stores. The young Chinese girl sitting with the man excused herself and left the room. Cigarette smoke swirled around the man's head and filled the room. Ping inspected and then paid for the bracelets as she talked with the man rapidly in Chinese. The bracelets were presented at the family dinner to the two sisters and the best friend as gifts from Lee. At the dinner, Ping ordered many dishes of food, and spent much of her time peeling and feeding fresh shrimp to Lee. Two attentive Chinese girls kept the tea cups filled and brought dish after dish to the table. One brother in law was working, but the brother in law who was there designated himself the official photographer, and kept snapping photos. Lee learned that he wanted to go to America so he could visit Las Vegas.

In the days that followed they had met Mama, and gone to visit Cici at her school. Mama had a wary look in her eyes. Cici was in her room with five other Chinese girls, some of her classmates. They were in their bed clothes, since it was getting late in the evening. Lee was surprised when one of the girls spoke to him in perfect English. "Nice to meet you," she said. "Mama!" Cici had said excitedly when she saw them at the door to their room. They handed her one of her favorite snacks that they had bought on their way to the school. Later in the week they met more friends, ate a lot of fresh fruit, explored Ping's favorite restaurants, learned that they loved the same kind of music, and talked for hours. By the third day their hands were touching as they walked the streets together. Just an occasional touch, as though accidental. "Be careful," Lee would tease, "someone might see us." Ping would laugh. By day five Ping was reaching for Lee's hand as they walked along the streets, holding it ever so briefly but then releasing it. Teasing, tantalizing, and knowing the effect it had on him. She would walk close so that the sway of her hips would bump Lee as they walked along. Sometimes she would slip her arm around him for a few seconds. They were becoming good friends.

Always she talked with him. Tell me about Houston. Tell me about your family. Tell me about your home. "What are you thinking about Leelee," Ping asked, as she squeezed her arm tight around his waist, bringing his mind back to the airport? Her concerns about what other people might think if they saw public displays of affection between them had disappeared by day six. "Just remembering our time together," he said. "Do you promise not to forget me," she asked, looking into his face. "I will never forget you," he said. "Do you promise to send our wedding photos to me as soon as you have them," he asked? "Yes, and I will also send more photos to you before then. Cici and I will scan all of our pictures and I will send them to you a few at a time. Would you like that?"

"I would love that. Look Ping, they are about to close the door of the bus and this is the last one of the night."

Lee stood just inside the terminal looking out at the bus. It would be another two hours before his flight was scheduled to depart. The driver was closing the side doors that covered the luggage. It was dark outside the terminal, but the lights inside the bus allowed Lee to see Ping. She was sitting almost at the back of the bus, in a window seat, looking back at him. The driver walked around the front of the bus and started to climb aboard. Almost as though in a trance, Lee started walking toward the bus. He walked down beside it until he reached the window where Ping was sitting, looking at him. He could see the tears on her face. She was sitting high above him but he was able to place his hand flat against the window where she sat. She placed her hand flat on the other side of the glass and mouthed the words in English. "I love you." With tears blurring his eyes, Lee turned and walked away as the bus engine roared to life. Blinking his eyes rapidly, not knowing if he would ever see her again, he never looked back.

Goodbye Ping, he said to himself.

Separate Lives

Chapter Five

After they had their wedding photos taken, and had confirmed their love for each other in Guangzhou, they began calling themselves husband and wife. Just between the two of them. It felt good to hear it and see it. Lee returned to Houston and the long wait began. The process of obtaining a visa to bring a fiancée or wife to America from some countries is very long and arduous. China is one of those countries.

"How long will it take, Leelee?" Ping had asked.

"I don't know, but the average time from filing to interview has been about seven and a half to nine months," Lee told her. But the law changed shortly before they filed their application, and the fees that the United States charged for each step of the process from application to green card to citizenship were increased very significantly. There was a resulting huge surge in the filing of visa applications by people who wanted to beat the fee increase for the filing fee. It was almost thirty days before Lee and Ping even received an acknowledgment that they had filed an application.

Filing an application can be a daunting task. Mistakes can lead to requests for additional information, which causes delays in the process. Some people hire an attorney. Others do it themselves. Lee was a lawyer.

"Will you prepare our application for us Leelee," Ping asked him? "No Ping," he said. "If a prospective client came to my law firm seeking such help, we would decline to take the case because we are not competent to handle a visa application. Yes, I could read the forms and the instructions and file our application, but I don't think it is fair to you for me to handle our application when I would not agree to handle it for a stranger. Not only that, Ping, but even if we hire a law firm to represent us, it will be our responsibility to provide all the necessary information and copies of required documents, so we have a lot of work to do." They set about trying to accomplish this task, with hopes of filing their visa application before April 1, but it was May 8 before it was filed.

In the meantime, the loneliness crept into their lives. It ate at their very souls. The worst part was knowing that the passing days didn't even count toward being together until their visa application was actually on file. Some of their letters reflected those feelings.

"My darling husband Leelee,

Tomorrow night I will write a long letter to you. I am sorry I am so busy and worked all day. I am very tired and want to sleep very much. I am sorry. Love you and kiss you, my Leelee. I sent some pictures to you. Remember to send to me the pictures we took together. I want to see them.

Your beautiful wife, Ping"

This was not the kind of inspiring, uplifting letter that Ping had always sent. It came across to Lee more like a chore that she felt she had to accomplish before she went to bed at night. After nearly two weeks of letters this short or shorter, he reacted. He remembered something that she had said when they were together and blew it out of proportion. Oh how he wished that they were together so they could talk about things like they had in Guangzhou. If he could just see her, hold her, kiss her, everything would be fine, he thought. He went to bed, slept fitfully, and then lay there awake, letting it gnaw away at him.

"My beautiful wife Ping,

It is the middle of the night but I must talk with you. I am really struggling with my emotions, because I feel a deep sense of loss that is eating away at my heart. This sense of loss is because I can no longer read all the letters that I received from you and hold the words to my heart, knowing that they were your true feelings.

I have read your letters dozens of times, and each time I read them before coming to Guangzhou, they gave me confidence and strength and an unwavering belief in your love for me. Whether you intended to or not, you took all of that away from me when you told me in Guangzhou that what you said on the Internet was not real life - it was just you talking on the Internet.

Surely you could tell from my eyes that the statement you made, and the cavalier manner in which you said it, cut me like a knife. It shattered everything that I believed my life was about in an instant. It took every ounce of my willpower, but I love you so much that I suppressed my feelings about what you said so we could enjoy our time together. Now that moment in time has returned to haunt me. It eats away at me day and night.

While I was with you and could hold your hand and kiss you, it helped me manage the pain. Since my return from Guangzhou, I have tried to read your letters again. It hurts me very much when I read them, so I abandon the effort rather than torture myself. The words you wrote that once gave me great comfort and that caused me to believe that you and I will always be inseparable, now cause only pain and sorrow.

Somehow I must get past this feeling, because the foundation for any relationship is trust. In order for us to be married, we must both take a lot of risk. It is difficult if not impossible for me to evaluate the risk when the very foundation on which our relationship with each other was built has been removed. All you have left me as a foundation upon which to base my trust in you are the eight days that we spent together.

Before I came to Guangzhou, each letter that I received from you added a little more trust and a little more confidence to my feelings about you. No letter alone would have been sufficient to convince me that your love for me is true. You and I both know that love, especially in its infancy, is very fragile. Every letter that you wrote to me was critically important to holding together and strengthening the fabric of our love.

Removing your words in even one letter would have weakened that fabric. When you took away all of the words you ever said to me before I arrived in Guangzhou, I was cast adrift in the proverbial sea of love. I clung to you in that sea of love because it was our only opportunity to be together before we had to make life-changing decisions. I forced myself to ignore the sudden empty feeling that I had in my heart. I loved the time we spent together, but I was also hurting inside.

I want so much for the words in your letters to have been true, but instead I am aching inside and trying to convince myself that I am not being foolish by wanting to marry a woman who could write so convincingly about her love for me, and then tell me that it wasn't real life and she was just talking on the Internet.

I feel so lost, and so lonely. You have been very busy since I left Guangzhou, and that is quite understandable. You made many sacrifices while I was there so that you could be with me, and I will never forget that. Yet the only thing you have left me as a foundation for our love are the words we spoke to each other during the short time we were together, and a few short messages that you have sent to me after my departure.

Please help me Ping. Help me understand if and why you believe that your love for me is true, and tell me why I can trust you and believe in you. Tell me why you want to be with me, and tell me why you believe we will always be together.

Finally, and most important of all, please explain to me if you can, why you told me that when you sent your love letters to me and made so many promises and commitments to me that it wasn't real life, and that you were just talking on the Internet.

I love you Ping, and no matter what the future holds, I will always love you. Every word in my love letters to you was true. All of the feelings I expressed to you and all of the promises and commitments I made to you were real, and not just me talking on the Internet.

Your loving husband needs your help to heal the open wound that I have described in this letter. We aren't where you can hold me and kiss me and reassure me in that manner. I hope you can do it with words.

Your Leelee"

Ping was distraught to receive his letter, but she knew Lee quite well by now. She knew very well the conversation he was talking about, and she also knew why he had misunderstood what she had said. She had never clarified it for him, because she knew in her heart what she meant. She realized now that she had made a mistake in judgment. It wasn't part of her culture to provide explanations about such things, but she acted quickly now to correct the problem.

"My darling husband Leelee:

I love you so much and I will give up the trip this morning to go to Zhongshan City that our company has planned and promoted for the woman's celebration. This will give me time to write a letter to you. I will stay at home and read again your letters that you sent to me from the time you left Guangzhou to go back to Houston.

I love you Leelee, do not wobble and lose your belief with our reins. I will teach you a good way: when you are unhappy or lonely, think of the wonderful time that we had together. Our time together was the truth. We know it and we can touch it with our hand. I really loved you when we were together. There is something I have not told you. That night when I saw your form disappear at the door of the Hong Kong airport, my heart ached very much and tears fell from my eyes for a long time.

I felt very unhappy with our parting and did not want you to leave me. I just wanted you to come back to Guangzhou with me so that we could be together and make love after we came back. I want you to be here with me.

Yesterday night Cici came back to our home from school. I cooked some food that she likes to eat. After supper we went to the supermarket to buy many things that she needed. Now Cici is sleeping very well, and I like to kiss her face sometimes when she is asleep. I very much enjoy this time with her.

You know when you were in Guangzhou I consorted with you almost the whole day every day and didn't do any work during that time. But I was really very busy and needed to do plenty of work. I never told you about that. I just wanted you to feel happy during the time when you were with me, even though my boss became very angry with me. I think it was very worthy to do that so we could have a nice time when we were together. I will remember our time together forever because it was really nice and wonderful.

Although eight days is very short, I could see your heart. I could see that you really love me deeply, and I knew you were the man I want to marry. We will have a beautiful life, and you will have a beautiful wife. My words were truly not only words on the Internet. You can believe all of them. So please believe our feelings about our love.

I love the pictures you sent to me. We were so happy at that time, and I really want you to be here with me so you can kiss me sometimes. I love it when you kiss me, hold me, caress me, and make love with me.

By the way, Eric's mother is very beautiful. I love her wonderful smile. Best regards to her.

All my love to you, my darling Leelee.

Your beautiful wife, Ping"

You know you have a loving woman when she takes the time to compliment your ex-wife about her looks, Lee thought. Ping's words were just what Lee needed to hear. The emotional roller coaster that they each experienced in turn went back to the top for Lee.

"My beautiful wife Ping,

As it got later and later in the day in Houston and later in the night in Guangzhou, I lost all hope that I would hear from you today. Then your letter arrived, and it made me so happy.

Please don't get the wrong impression from the long letter that I wrote to you during the night last night. I am not unhappy with you or upset with you in any way, and I promise I am trying to understand you. I just wanted to know that I can read all of your letters to me and believe every word that you told me. You told me in this letter that I can believe what you said was true. That is all I wanted you to confirm for me. I want to be able to keep all of our love letters and put them in a book as you suggested so that we will always have our memories to cherish. Maybe we can even write a beautiful love story based on our letters and our love for each other.

My darling, you have written the most wonderful love letters in the world to me, and that is why I fell in love with you. Meeting you in person was important, and it certainly confirmed my love for you. Then during the eight days we were together, my love for you grew immensely. When I left you on the bus in Hong Kong, my heart was aching already because I knew that it was going to be very difficult to wait for your arrival in Houston. You looked so beautiful when our hands touched through the window of the bus. I walked away with tears in my eyes, but I knew that I had just spent eight days with the woman who I wanted to be my wife forever. I will never stop loving you.

On the plane from Los Angeles to Houston, there were several people who were constantly coughing. They spread their germs through the air recirculation system on the plane. Late yesterday I started having symptoms of a cold, and during the night it got worse. Today I clearly have a cold or something, but I am treating it with Vitamin C and Vitamin A and controlling the cough the best I can with cough drops and some over the counter medication. I think that is part of the reason that I was feeling so low during the night when I was writing the long letter.

I agree with you about the pictures. We look very happy together, and I was happily surprised by how many photos were taken of us. I like to refer to the dinner we had with your family as our "engagement party." I don't know if it is the custom in China, but in the U.S. an engagement party is usually held to celebrate when two people agree to be married. Your sisters looked happy about our engagement, which made me feel good.

My darling, I hope you are getting some rest. You have been up late many nights this week. I look forward to hearing from you again after you have rested. Thank you for being such a wonderful wife.

Your loving husband, Leelee"

They stood on the pedestrian bridge, high over the wide divided road that separated Ping's home from where she parked her car. The full moon over their heads was a bit hazy. They were out for a walk, trying to digest the food they had enjoyed with family and friends at a nearby restaurant. Their bodies could have been molded together, they were so close. "Look at the moon, Leelee," she said. "I am so happy you came to be with me and our family for the moon festival." Her family had become their family. His family had become their family. Ping and Lee and Cici felt like they were a family.

But they still weren't together. Not even close. It had been six long months, but they still had no idea how long it would be before Ping would be interviewed at the United States Consulate in Guangzhou, where the decision would be made that would determine their future. All visa interviews for the entire country of China are conducted at the Consulate in Guangzhou. Ping was more fortunate than most Chinese women, because she lived in Guangzhou. Some fiancée visas are approved, but some are denied. Some are denied for legitimate reasons, such as visa fraud. Women who pay men to file a visa application to help them move to America are a typical example of visa fraud. Some visas are denied for reasons unknown, however, with explanations either not given for long periods of time, sometimes years, or never given. Lee and Ping knew people to whom this had happened. It could be completely arbitrary. It was scary for everyone because they knew it could happen to them.

The Moon Festival. Ask what it is in China and you might well hear different stories, different legends, Lee had learned. In the six months since he had last seen Ping, he had read many books. Most of the books were about China or Chinese culture, or they were fiction written by Chinese authors who included cultural and historical events in their stories. The Moon Festival, or Mid-Autumn festival as it is also known, is a time for families to reunite and celebrate. In theory, it is a time for them to watch the moon together and eat moon cake. In practice, he was to learn, there doesn't seem to be much moon watching any more, and some Chinese people don't particularly enjoy eating moon cake. He and Ping had decided that they had been apart for too long, and had decided that this would be a good time for Lee to return to China.

Ping was concerned about Lee making the trip, but she missed him badly. When he had returned to Houston from China six months before, he ended up enduring a bout with kidney stones, and was unable to walk for weeks because of recurring gout attacks that would not go away. His blood pressure was very high. Food was sticking in his esophagus instead of working its way to his stomach. He had constant heartburn from acid reflux. What he originally thought was a cold or allergies turned out to be walking pneumonia. He didn't eat well, didn't sleep well, and didn't work well. In fact, for a two month stretch he didn't even lie in a bed. It was too painful. He slept sitting up in a chair with his feet on the ottoman. The pain from the gout was so intense that his legs would spasm uncontrollably, especially at night, drawing up near his chest. He missed Ping every day and night.

Like Ping, Lee was a believer in natural remedies, so they shared their home remedy ideas with each other. He forced down a two liter bottle of Coca Cola in an hour, and then ate asparagus that had been steamed and put in a blender. This relieved the pain and took away part of the kidney stones. He drank a mixture of olive oil and fresh squeezed lemon juice every few hours for a couple of days and that took care of the rest of the problem. But eating massive amounts of fresh cherries and taking the recommended herbal solutions wasn't working on the gout. Neither was the recommended medication. Not even for the pain. And the recommended pain medicine could be dangerous, so Lee and Ping looked for other solutions. Long term solutions.

Partly because of the pain, Lee ate less. Partly because of searching for a solution to his health problems, Lee ate less. After extensive research and discussions with Ping, Lee changed his diet. He stopped eating meat and dairy products and eggs and sugar in any form. He stopped drinking coffee. He stopped eating nightshade vegetables. He stopped eating any kind of refined foods. With a diet consisting almost entirely of fruit, vegetables, and whole grains, he lost thirty pounds. His health problems went away. No more heartburn or acid reflux. His esophagus healed and he had no more difficulty swallowing food. No more sleepless nights. He began to exercise again, riding his bicycle. Soon he could walk again without being in pain. When he arrived in China this time Ping told him he was too thin. Her family worried about him too, saying he was too thin. But they were happy with how healthy he was now. His blood pressure had also dropped almost down to a normal range, though it still spiked higher too often.

The arrangements were the same. "Just meet me at the Garden Hotel, Ping." This time Lee's flight into Hong Kong arrived in the late afternoon. It arrived a little early and Lee was whisked by a waiting van to the second of the two bus stations he had visited on his previous trip. There he boarded a bus with his luggage after clearing immigration and customs. I will be there a little early, he thought happily as the bus sped smoothly down the divided highway. Suddenly, about an hour from Guangzhou, there was a loud noise underneath and near the rear of the bus. The bus veered off the road and stopped alongside the highway. The driver got off the bus to inspect it, and saw that one of the rear tires had exploded. He called someone on his cell phone, then sat down in the driver's seat, and told no one anything. "Why doesn't he at least tell everyone what is happening and what to expect?" Lee asked a Chinese man near him who he learned had attended college in Chicago. "It wouldn't matter if he did," the man said. "It wouldn't be the truth, and no one would believe him."

An hour passed and the passengers were restless. Some of them were angry. Lee was the only non-Chinese person on the bus. Ping will be so worried, he thought, I wish I had a way to contact her. A bottle of water had been given to each passenger when they boarded the bus, so there was no problem with thirstiness. It was getting late in the evening, though, so people were hungry. On the flight to Hong Kong Lee had purchased some Tobler chocolate in long triangular tubes, intending to give them to people as gifts. He counted them mentally and realized he had enough for each person on the bus to have a tube, so he took them out of his bag. He was sitting at the front of the bus, so he started offering a tube of candy to each passenger as he walked from the front to the back of the bus.

With surprise in their eyes, some of the passengers accepted the proffered gift. The older passengers declined the candy at first, but accepted it when it was offered a second time. The mood on the bus improved considerably as everyone started to eat their candy. A middle aged lady motioned to Lee and asked him in English if someone was waiting for him in Guangzhou. He said yes, and told her about Ping. She handed him her cell phone, and told him that he could use it to call her. Very gratefully Lee called Ping. He told her what had happened, and handed the phone back to its owner. The lady spoke with Ping in Chinese and gave her details about the location of the bus. That problem solved, Lee said goodbye to Ping and sat back to wait some more. The driver still offered no explanation or reassurance to anyone about when or how they would be taken the rest of the way to Guangzhou.

The cell phone lady was talkative now, so she and Lee had a nice conversation. It turned out that she had friends who live in a town near where Lee lived, and had visited them there in the recent past. Another bus finally arrived after about two hours, and everyone boarded the second bus. The lady with the phone invited Lee to sit next to her. She pointed out things of interest when they arrived in Guangzhou. Lee had told Ping when he called her not to meet him at the Garden Hotel, because he would take a taxi from there to the Golden Bridge Hotel near her home. It was late at night now, so when the bus stopped at the China Hotel, Lee got off, took his luggage, and hailed a taxi. He told the cell phone lady that his plan was to go to the hotel, check in, take a shower, and then call Ping. He felt very dirty and smelly after traveling for so long.

As he had done on his first trip to Guangzhou, Lee left his bags at the front desk while he went to the restroom. The lobby was deserted because it was so late at night. It was almost déjà vu. Ping came running through the front door of the hotel, her small overnight case in her hand, just as Lee returned from the restroom. They hugged and kissed excitedly, with Lee apologizing for his appearance and his smelly body. Ping didn't care. She couldn't keep her hands off of him. "How did you know I would be here?" Lee asked. "The nice lady with the cell phone called me," Ping replied. I sure got a lot of mileage out of that candy, Lee thought. They were able to get the room right next to the one they had on Lee's previous trip. It felt so good to be together again. The surroundings felt so familiar. It was like coming home.

Every day for the three weeks Lee was there, they checked to see if their visa application had been approved in America. On the morning of October 1, Lee saw that it had been approved. It was very early in the morning, so he let Ping sleep a little longer while he went to eat breakfast downstairs. This was always an experience. He had learned that the staff would put the heat so high under the decanter of coffee that it would end up boiling, so he had jokingly told Ping that it was his responsibility each morning to turn down the heat on the coffee. Ping preferred to sleep and not get up for breakfast, so he almost always dined alone. When he returned to the room, he woke Ping with the good news. They celebrated all day. This was an important milestone for them, but the most difficult part still lay ahead. Almost all visa applications were approved in America, which is what had just happened for them. It was at the Consulate overseas where the dangers lurk. That was especially true in Guangzhou.

Before he headed back to China for his second visit, someone had a birthday. Lee had spent days writing and rewriting a birthday letter to Cici. She called him Papa Leelee now. He adored her and thought of her as his daughter. He sent the letter to Ping first, and then had second thoughts about sending it to Cici. He was afraid it might be inappropriate. Ping told him the letter was perfect, and urged him to send it to Cici because she would love it.

"Happy Birthday Cici!!

Dear Tianjiao,

I always call you Cici when I am talking with your Mom, but I am very happy that you will soon be known as Angela, and that you and your Mom will take my family name as yours. That is a beautiful name you have chosen for yourself, and very appropriate for a beautiful young lady. I am writing this letter to wish you a very happy birthday.

This year has been the best year of my life, because I met your Mom and you, and because you both agreed with me that we will become a family. I want you to know that I love your Mom very much and will always treat her with love and respect. That is my promise to you and my lifetime gift to her. She means more to me than anything else in the world, and I will treasure every moment that I spend with her. I also want you to know that I feel honored and humbled by your acceptance of my love for your Mom, and of her love for me. I feel like your acceptance of our love is your lifetime gift to us, as we could not be a real family without you.

Your Mom and I are so grateful that we found each other many miles apart in this great big world. We feel like fate must have had a hand in bringing us together, because the odds of us ever meeting were infinitesimal. We are very excited about our upcoming marriage, and about bringing our family together in Houston. It is a privilege for me to be able to share with your Mom the joy of raising you as our daughter in a real family. This is her lifetime gift to me. I hope you share our feeling about the importance of having a warm and loving home and family. We want to have the happiest and most loving family anywhere in the world.

My birthday gifts are small, but I hope they bring you much joy. I admire the courage that you and your Mom have shown by your willingness to move to a new country. You will both be completely conversant in English before you know it. One of your gifts is intended to help you make this transition to America. There is a saying that is often attributed to the great Chinese philosopher, Confucius, which is that a picture is worth a thousand words. I think the picture dictionary I got for you will help you a lot. If the authors had taken it just one additional step and included the Pinyin word with each picture, I could have used this same book to study Chinese.

Another gift I got for you is to help you have fun once you are here (I could only send a photo of this gift, because if I shipped it to you we would just have to ship it right back to Houston). I already purchased one just like it for your Mom so that you can float peacefully together in the swimming pool near our home in Houston.

This gift will be waiting for you when you arrive in Houston.

I also got a gift for you that is intended to provide a way for you to create a gift for your future descendants. You are one of the few people in the world who will have both a Chinese heritage and an American heritage. I am sure you know that these are two of the most important countries in the world. Your children and their children will want to know your story about how you were privileged to live in and be a part of these two great countries. I hope that this gift will help you keep a record of important events so that you will be able to tell that story to them.

There is a story that was written about a blue-eyed girl who was born in America long before Columbus arrived and "discovered" America in the year 1492. She was raised by an Indian tribe but her blue eyes marked her as a witch and she became an outcast. She was rescued from death by a powerful Toltec magician, and was taken to the Eagle Clan where she was treated as one who was "Chosen by the Gods". In this clan, one woman was trusted to learn and remember all of the ancient secrets that only women knew. This woman was called "She Who Remembers." After overcoming many struggles, the blue-eyed girl eventually became "She Who Remembers," and became the most powerful woman in the clan. Her life was changed forever, and she was responsible for teaching all the young girls the ancient secrets of life.

You have a similar opportunity to help your descendants if you choose to accept it. When you tell your story, please remember these words: Your life was changed and your descendants (at least the descendants to whom you will be speaking) exist only because of the love and the trust that your Mom and I have for each other. We chose not to allow language, culture, politics, government, ideology, religion, distance, or age come between us and our love. No matter what else happens, we know that our love is a love that will never die. Angela Tianjiao Solomon, the family that your Mom and I brought together because of our love for each other is our everlasting gift to you, and to all of our future descendants. We love you.

I wish you a very Happy Birthday, with lots of love. I look forward to celebrating your next birthday with all of us together as a family. I also am looking forward to seeing you in September and October this year when I return to Guangzhou for a visit.

Your Papa Leelee."

Little did Lee and Ping know, or even suspect, that their interview date was still nine months away when Lee sent this letter to Cici. The excitement of Lee's upcoming trip to Guangzhou had lifted their spirits and gave them something to look forward to each day. Again, however, their time together passed too quickly. Before they knew it they were boarding a train, taking their first family vacation together; an overnight stay in Hong Kong. They shopped, walked, talked, and played. The hotel was beautiful. The shopping was like being on Rodeo Drive in Beverly Hills. Designer store after designer store beckoned to them, but Cici said they shouldn't spend any money. "We have everything we need, Papa."

The next morning they made the dreaded trip from the hotel to the airport. Their spirits were very low as they ate breakfast together. There is no hug, no kiss, and no assurance that can be given at moments like this that will ease the pain of separation. Still with no assurance that they would ever see each other again, they said a long goodbye. Ping and Cici stood solemnly, silently, until Lee disappeared behind the security screen. This time he waved goodbye just before he disappeared. Then the girls broke into tears.

It Isn't Just Culture

Chapter Six

The feeling of rejection is a human emotion that can be debilitating. It can also spawn dogged determination. The boy knew nothing about psychology. He only knew what he felt. With parents who struggled with basic survival, with many mouths to feed, he never heard the words, "I love you." He never felt the comfort of a hug or a kiss. He never knew the feeling of safety and contentment that could come from being tucked into bed at night. His parents raised their children the only way they knew; the way their parents raised them. And their parents before them. And so it goes through time. Hard hands, harsh and demeaning words, a leather belt on the bare back. A circle unbroken, no way to escape.

"Lee, what are you doing?" No answer. "Lee, come here this minute." No answer. "Listen here young man," the teacher said, pulling him from his desk. "You will sit in the hallway until you learn to pay attention in class." The tiles in the wide hallway gleamed. They were polished every night by the custodian, the brother of the produce manager at the nearby supermarket. Barely forty years of age, he would die of cancer in just a couple of years. He didn't even know he was sick at the moment. His sudden death would be a traumatic event for the kids in the school. "Walter is dead," they would whisper to each other. "Walter is dead." It sounded so final. An end they did not understand.

No one walked in the hallway. All the classroom doors were closed. First through third grades downstairs, fourth through sixth grades upstairs. The boy sat in his penalty box outside the third grade classroom. He hadn't even heard the teacher when she called his name in the classroom. He was reading a good book. If he could sneak upstairs past the principal's office, he could slip into the library and get another book. Reading a book in the classroom is what had earned him this punishment, but he didn't care. He wanted to read more. He had learned that he could escape from the confines of his rundown house, the little town where he lived, the classroom, the church, wherever he might be, if he could just bury his nose in a book. He often dreamed that reading would help him escape from the little world in which he lived. There was so much more to see. He knew, he had read about it.

"What are you doing!" she thundered. Shaken by the anger in her voice, the boy heard her this time. But he hadn't heard her when she opened the classroom door to check on him, so there he sat, guilty as sin. "Where did you get that book?" she demanded to know, her hands on her wide hips. "I am taking you up to the principal's office right now!" The angry teacher marched the boy up to Mrs. Wilson's office.

The principal was a stern faced woman with blue tinted hair, dark lipstick, and big round lenses on her heavy framed glasses. A few years later she would take the boy with her and a bus load of teachers to see things that fascinated him. Monticello. Mt. Vernon. The

Smithsonian Institute. The Empire State Building. Niagara Falls. They visited almost all of the historical sites in the Northeastern part of the United States. The teachers and the principal paid the cost of his trip, using the excuse that he could help them with their bags. The truth is that they had discovered a young mind that was eager for food, and they dug into their own pockets to feed it.

At the moment, the principal listened to the teacher. "Okay Mrs. O'Mally," she said. "I will handle it from here." The teacher left in a huff to return to her classroom. The boy was scared. Mrs. Wilson was a powerful figure in his life.

"So you like to read, do you?" she asked. The boy shook his head yes, looking ashamed. "Look at me," the principal ordered. The boy looked up at her. "Reading is nothing to be ashamed about, Lee," she said. "In fact, reading is something that is very important. Reading is something that you can be proud of, something that will help you in life. But what we need to do is help you with your reading. And you need to help us by reading only when you are not in the classroom. If you will help us, I will help you. Will you do that with me?" Surprised by her words and the gentle tone of her voice, the boy nodded yes to her. "Tell me," she said. "Yes ma'am," the boy said.

"Then come with me," the principal told him. She led him into the school library. The boy loved the feel of the library, the smell of the books. He wished he could read every one of them. Most of them he couldn't reach. There were so many that he had no idea where to start looking the few times he had been in the library. During the summer he would run barefoot to the local city library and check out stacks of books to read. He would devour the books and return them, each time bringing more of the treasures he found there home with him. Mrs. Wilson knew where to look. She pulled a book from way up on one of the top shelves. "Now this book is a little advanced for a child your age, but I think you can understand it," she told the boy. "Take it home with you. Read it at home. Then bring it back to me in a few weeks after you finish reading it."

The boy looked at the book. "The Call of the Wild." By Jack London. Two days later a surprised Mrs. Wilson saw the boy standing at her door, the book in his hand. "It was too hard for you to read, wasn't it? I was afraid of that, but I wanted you to know that story if you could read it. Here, let's put that one back and we will find an easier book for you to read."

"I read the book," the boy said. "You what?" Mrs. Wilson raised her heavy eyebrows. "I just gave it to you day before yesterday, you couldn't have read the book yet." "I read the book," the boy said again. "Tell me about it," the disbelieving principal challenged him. Slowly, his confidence building as he talked, he told the principal the story about Buck, a dog that was able to rise above his pampered background to survive in a dog eat dog world. Not just survive, but become lead sled dog. To overcome human torture and neglect, to find love and contentment only to lose it when his owner was killed. To kill when he needed to kill, to become leader of a wolf pack, to be two devils and not one, to survive in an environment of fear. "I want to be Buck," the boy said simply.

First among equals is not an easy place to be in life, the boy learned. Later the man would learn it again. Not every dog in the pack supports the leader. Some of them are constantly looking for opportunities to attack the leader. But he became the equivalent of Buck the sled dog, the leader of the pack. In every role he played in life, the dogged determination to overcome the feelings of rejection drove him relentlessly to the top. In combat, in jobs as a teenager, in college, in law school, in large law firms, Buck was always there. If you have no role model in your life, find one, the boy learned. Find one and learn; study and remember. The boy learned; the man remembered.

The principal talked with the boy's parents. His parents learned that they had a child who was a little unusual. "He needs your support and your encouragement," the principal told them. They nodded in agreement, but they didn't know what they could do to help him. They did, however, begin to treat him as first among equals. They began to expect more of him, but he disappointed them. All he wanted to do was read and work. Studying was not important to him. He never brought books home except books that he wanted to read. His parents eventually gave up on him and just let him read. They had more important things to do.

Years later, on the other side of the world, Cici lay in bed every night of her young life, knowing the feeling of rejection that Lee had felt. She had a mother who loved her. She had the love of an extended family. She had friends and she lived a comfortable life. But she didn't have the love of a father. He had rejected her. She never knew him. This left a hole in her heart and in her life.

But who was this man who had written such a loving birthday letter to her? Papa Leelee was so loving with her and Mama. It was a strange feeling at first. He was a Western man, so different from the men she had known in her life. He was scary to her at first, but he was always nice to her. He also made her laugh. He made Mama laugh. She had never seen Mama so happy. They often talked about Papa Leelee late at night as they lay in bed. Mama loved him, she told Cici. "I want to marry him," she said. "I want to move to America to be with him," she told the wide eyed girl. "What do you think about living in America?"

Mrs. Bridenstein was a terror to eighth grade students. She was heavy and she was mean. She ruled her classroom with an iron fist. No talking, no gum, no bathroom breaks, no kidding. All the kids dreaded going into her classroom. Lee watched her write words and draw lines on the blackboard. She would write a sentence and then diagram it, as she called it. She talked about nouns and pronouns and verbs and adverbs. She taught them about adjectives and dangling participles and other parts of speech. This was fascinating to Lee. It was so structured, so logical to him. He could understand it. He could remember it. Where the other kids wilted and died of boredom, he was energized and thrived. This class, more than any other class he ever attended, turned out to be a determining factor in his life. This was where he learned the power of words. He also learned how to string them together. Is it better this way, or that? Change it, shorten the sentences. Don't use punctuation sometimes. Let the words do the work.

Just a few years later, the boy would sit hunched over a school desk in a crowded room, tense with fear and anxiety. It was the third day of boot camp in the Marine Corps. He sat there with the other recruits, the drill instructors pacing the room, handing out the IQ tests, timing the sections, terrorizing the test takers. In the past two days they had been issued clothing, exercised to death, and been given batteries of shots. The shots were usually given with air guns, a Navy Corpsman standing on each side, shooting into each arm at the same time. Most of the Marines had blood running down their arms as they were pushed and shoved to keep the line moving. "Drop and give me twenty," the drill instructors screamed in their ears as they exited the building. The blacktop was scorching hot in the midday sun as the recruits struggled with the push ups. It blistered their hands. Their arms ached. "Give me twenty more," the screams were louder now.

Sitting in the cooler environment of the Quonset hut now was a welcome relief. Lee was just as scared as the rest of the boys in the room, but he did as he had learned to do as a child. He read the passages in the test books, studied the diagrams and charts and unusual figures. He remembered his rather limited exposure to mathematics as best he could. He reasoned things out when he had no mathematical basis to find a solution. Trial and error. Logic and guesswork. A tenth grade education is not a great foundation for an IQ test for a boy who had just turned eighteen. Lee shut out the rest of the world and concentrated on the test. Just like reading a book. Immerse yourself in it. Become the character with whom you most identify. Live the story. Understand the questions. Guess where necessary, but make it an educated guess by eliminating the bad choices.

First among equals. When the test results came back a few weeks later, there was a different look in the eyes of the drill instructors now when they talked to Private Lee. Even when they screamed at Lee there was a different look. "Damn," the psycho drill instructor from Argentina said to him. "Damn, you are smart." Lee had never heard of MENSA. He didn't know it, but as an eighteen year old high school dropout he had just scored at the MENSA level on the IQ test. Those test scores helped propel Lee's short career in the military to the top in each of his assignments. They later gave him the confidence to go to college. They helped him believe in himself. Buck the sled dog. Buck wasn't just doggedly determined. Buck also had a brain.

Just give me a chance, Lee said to the college admissions counselor. I know I never finished high school, but just give me a chance. As a veteran of the Vietnam War, he was allowed to enroll in college without taking the SAT or the ACT admissions tests if a college would admit him as a student. To this day, Lee doesn't know if he could have made an acceptable score on the tests, but it doesn't matter now. He was given a chance. Buck took it from there. Getting a passing grade was not Lee's goal. Never get less than an "A." That is the standard Lee set for himself. That is what Buck achieved. Law school was much the same. He had an advantage over the other students. On the tough days when it was easy to get discouraged, Lee simply reminded himself of a few simple things. There is no one shooting at me. I have food to eat. I have survived tougher times.

Cici had read about America. It sounded like a place that she would like to live. She had secretly wished that she could live there one day. She told Mama about that wish. "Then you need to study English very hard," Mama told her. "Leelee also wants to marry me," she told Cici. "I trust him and believe he will be good to us. I love the way he treats you. It is as though you are his natural daughter. Let's dream of moving to America to be with him. We can have the warm and loving family that we always wanted." They fell asleep in each other's arms, their minds sharing the same dream. America.

If Ping and Cici were on a path that led to America, it was sometimes a rocky one. The historical average time from the time a visa application was approved in America until the interview in Guangzhou had been roughly two to three months. Even now, with all the historical time periods meaningless because of the surge in visa applications, Lee and Ping saw that other couples who filed after they filed were receiving the next item that was part of the visa process long before they received theirs. It was a packet of information that was mailed to a Chinese fiancée when the Consulate in Guangzhou had received their paperwork from America and was ready to obtain more information from them. Packet Three, or P-3 as everyone called it, was a much awaited item.

When the ninety day mark arrived, they thought the P-3 would arrive any day. "Why has it not arrived, Leelee," Ping asked almost every day? Lee began calling the Department of State every day to ask about the status. Four months went by, then five months, but still no sign of the P-3. Even the officers at the Department of State finally acknowledged that there was some problem. They eventually called the National Visa Center, and a trace on the documents was initiated. The waiting wore on both of them. It also wore on Cici, who was attending an English language school instead of her regular junior high school classes. It felt like they would never be together. They were all discouraged and it showed. Tomorrow would never come.

Sometimes even Buck needs an understanding hand, and Lee was a lucky man. Ping understood him so well, even when he seemed to lose faith in her. During their long wait, he wrote a long letter to her, and then immediately felt bad about it. They spoke on the telephone for a long time, and then Ping wrote back to him. It was one more step that strengthened their confidence in their ability to overcome cultural and language differences. Ping came from a culture where there were no hugs of hello or goodbye. Everyone just understood that the feelings were there. Lee didn't have hugs and kisses and expressions of affection in his childhood, which made it all the more important to him now. It took a while, but Ping learned the importance of expressing her love and affection to Lee. She no longer was content to believe that he already knew her feelings. This was a big change for her, but once she made it, she never stopped. She also came to look for and welcome Lee's hugs. Cici was the same.

"My darling Ping,

Don't read this letter today. Wait until this weekend and then read it and think about it. I won't call you on Saturday and you can use that time to read this letter. It is sort of a stream of consciousness letter, so if it appears a bit disjointed that is the reason.

I told you this story before but I want to tell you again so I can put things in perspective. Before you were born, I met and fell madly in love with a young Chinese girl in Hong Kong. We were the same age as each other - just 18 - so you must factor our young age in as well. We were able to spend less than a week together out of our entire lives. We got almost no sleep because every moment we were together was precious, and we didn't want to lose even one moment. Whether we were sitting in a movie theater or a restaurant or anywhere else, the rest of the world didn't matter to us. We just wanted to be together. We cried in each other's arms for hours before we said goodbye, and although we made all kinds of promises to each other, we knew that we would never see each other again. Don't do that to me Ping.

Until I fell in love with you, I never believed that I could ever replace the love that I felt for this Chinese girl. I don't remember her name, and she probably doesn't remember my name. I never forgot her, though, and I bet she never forgot me. We had no chance to stay together or to remain in contact with each other. I never wanted to love and lose like that again. It hurt too much.

It is too late to not love like that again, because I have gone too far with you. It is ironic that you are also Chinese, and that the two great loves of my life are from China. The difference is that I have offered more to you than I was ever able to offer to her. I had nothing to offer her except my heart, but that was enough for her. In return, she gave me her heart and every moment of her life that we could be together. I have offered you everything I have, including my heart, but I sometimes feel in my heart that this is not enough for you. You seem to have other priorities in life, and I do not intend to suffer again the loss that I already suffered once in my life.

There are many American men, and probably many other Western men as well, who would kill for an opportunity to be with you. I can't tell you who they are, but I guarantee you that they are there waiting for you. The problem that many, or maybe even most, of them have is that they have somewhat limited choices when it comes to women. I am sorry but I don't feel like I face that problem. The only problem I have is that I fell so deeply in love with you. This has been the source of more pain than pleasure for me lately it seems, and I don't want it to control my life.

Other than this problem, I am living a happy and comfortable life. I have my own business, I enjoy what I do, I am happy, and I can work in this business until I die. For this I feel very fortunate. I can focus on my business and it will never be unfaithful to me. It will be there every day, and it will return as much or more to me than I put in it, with no questions asked.

Ping, you can have your choice of men in the world. You are young, beautiful, sexy, smart, successful, funny, and fun to be around. Unfortunately I just don't feel like you are very affectionate, or at least you are not very affectionate toward me right now. I felt that way sometimes when we were together, and I feel that way even more when we are not together. I think you chose (settled for) the wrong man, because I don't feel like I give you the pleasure you are seeking. I love you too much for this. Don't settle for me - go with a man who you feel like you cannot live without. I crave affection and you should crave it as well. For me, love without affection is not really love because it leaves me feeling empty inside.

I read almost daily about how some American men and Chinese women who love each other spend a couple of hours every day talking to each other on the telephone and on the computer. On the one hand I think that they need to get a life, but on the other hand I think they must be deeply devoted to each other to spend that much time talking to each other every day. We don't have this between us. I wish we did, but we don't. Sometimes I think we wouldn't even be talking on the telephone once a week if I hadn't pushed for it. You gave me the impression that it isn't very important to you.

I am not telling you these things as a criticism, but just as an observation. Affection is almost as important as sex for me. I was crushed when I sometimes felt like you showed no affection for me when we were together in Guangzhou. I was crushed when I sometimes felt no affection from you after I returned to Houston. I have tried in every way I can to rationalize your lack of affection for me, but it hasn't gotten any better. I have to be honest with myself and recognize that something is missing from our relationship. At least it feels that way at the moment.

Be honest with yourself. I feel no affection from you when we talk on the telephone. Do you feel any affection? I feel like it is a burden for you to spend time on the telephone with me. It is also very obvious to me that it is a burden to you to spend time reading and writing letters to me. Out of the 24 hours we have each day, my impression is that I am your absolute lowest priority every day. I don't get it, because you are my absolute highest priority.

You have asked me to be understanding, and I have tried very hard to be understanding with something that I don't understand at all. No matter what else I have happening each day, my number one concern, and my number one priority, is to be sure I make time to communicate with you. I am sorry but I can't dismiss this as a cultural difference, because I have never felt more affection from a woman than I felt years ago in Hong Kong.

My concern is that if you don't show affection now, it isn't going to get any better later. I don't want to go through life feeling lonely and unloved. You shouldn't go through life feeling like you settled for a man who doesn't light your fire every day. I also don't want to go through a pretend marriage ceremony and end up being divorced a few years later. I don't want people laughing at me behind my back for my foolishness in loving you and believing in you.

These feelings have been building in me for a while. It is hard to say these words and admit these things, because I have told everyone about you. I have told everyone how much I love you and how we will be married and will always be together. I have been so proud of you and I cannot imagine life without you. What would be worse, though, is to have a few years of life with you and then lose you. I just can't go down that road again.

I can promise you this. It doesn't matter where you are or what you do, I will always love you. It is too late for me to change that fact. I just don't have an answer for anything else.

Leelee"

Ping knew just what to do. First she called, and then she wrote.

"My darling Leelee:

I can understand you from your letter and feel your deep love for me, even though I have disappointed you by my inability to express my affection and love for you. I do not have any querimony with you. I also will not be angry with you. I promise you I will forget this unhappy thing and never mention it. You know I also love you deeply, so I do not want you to feel any unhappiness or discomfort with this thing. In fact, when I heard your voice on the telephone this morning I said to myself in my heart that I love you and I understand you and I forgive you.

Darling I love you so much. I do not want you to be sad with me. I hope you will have a happy mood every day. I think we should both forget every unhappy thing in our life. All we need to do is love each other and use our hearts. From the time we were first together until now, I know I have been your life and you have been my life too. We cannot live without life. So do not worry about anything. I also love you like you love me. You can feel my love for you when I come to Houston to be with you. At that time you will see and know my love for you. It is only because of the difference in language that I am unable to express my love for you the way I feel it.

If I could talk with you in Chinese you would know how much you mean to me.

I want you to come to Guangzhou again to be with me. We can share and enjoy our life being together. I want you to cuddle me, caress me, kiss me, and make love with me. We will hold each other tightly without saying any words. We can feel our love from each other's eyes. I know I am your life. But I want you to know that you are also my life. We cannot be apart no matter what else happens in our lives. I want the happy warm family that you and I hold in our hearts, and I want to be your wife. I want to take care of you and Cici. You are the most important person in my life. I love you and Cici. I hope we can be together quickly so we can enjoy our wonderful life.

Do not doubt me, and please trust me. You should have a strong belief with our love, our marriage, our future. You will see, we will have our nice life in the future. We can snuggle and cuddle together to see the sun rise and see the sun go down. This is the life I want to get and that you can give me. I will be happy to be your beautiful wife in the future. I also think the future is very near us. So we just need to wait for our visa.

You cannot imagine how much I also love you. It is as deeply as you love me. Many kisses to you my darling. Remember, I will always be yours.

Your loving Ping"

Wait for Me

Chapter Seven

The P-3 was finally mailed to Ping on March 3. They had been waiting for it since their visa application had been approved on October 1 the previous year. The excuse given at the Consulate in Guangzhou for the long delays from the time that documents are sent from the National Visa Center is that they are hung up in Customs in China. The information that visa applicants believe to be reliable is that in fact the documents are just sitting in a warehouse in Guangzhou gathering dust until the Consulate decides to open another box.

Applications are supposed to be processed in order of their "Receipt Date." This isn't the day they were actually filed or received. It is the day that an applicant's visa package is eventually opened after it was filed. In Lee and Ping's case, that delay period was almost a month. Their "Receipt Date" was May 30. Their application was approved on October 1, and they received a letter from the National Visa Center dated October 18, telling them that within a week their documents would be sent to the Consulate in Guangzhou for further processing.

Lee and Ping tracked applications filed by others and watched as people who filed months after they filed were scheduled for interviews, completed their interviews, and started their lives together in America. While they were happy for the other couples, they wondered about their case. Was their file dropped in the warehouse? Did someone deliberately delay its processing? Was their file mishandled? Whatever the reason, it languished. Lee went back to China for another visit on January 31. They had thought for sure the P-3 would be mailed to Ping while he was in Guangzhou. It wasn't. They went to the Consulate for something called American Citizen's Hour while Lee was in Guangzhou. They went at the scheduled time and scheduled day that week. They even checked the website of the Consulate the evening before to see if there was any change in the schedule. There was no change.

When they arrived at the Consulate there was a small sign announcing that American Citizen's Hour would not be held that day. There were other disappointed couples there as well. One man had traveled all the way from Arizona to be there that day in reliance on the schedule that the Consulate had posted on its website. The Consulate celebrates both Chinese holidays and American holidays. They apparently take arbitrary holidays as well. It was neither a Chinese nor an American holiday, but they were not working that day, except for a skeletal crew. Lee spoke with one of the skeletal crew members, but she said she had no access to anything and could not check on the status of their P-3. Another couple there had filed their visa application six months before Lee and Ping had filed their application, and they were also still waiting for their P-3.

Visa applicants seem to be a hardy, resourceful, and resilient group. They tend to find ways to communicate with each other, sharing information and providing encouragement and support. For tracking visa timelines for many people, and for lots of general information about the visa process, Ping and Lee found a website called Visa Journey to be good. For information specific to fiancée visas for a Chinese beneficiary, they found a website called A Candle for Love to be the best. While not immune from the tendency to grouse a bit about some things, sometimes about everything, most everyone on these websites seemed to accept the fact that the process would take a long time. They understood that the Consulate in Guangzhou was responsible for processing applications for an entire country. What frustrated them the most seemed to be that they were not treated like human beings.

There often seemed to be no compassion, no sense of concern, let alone urgency, in processing their cases. Typically a visa would be available to be picked up within two to three days after approval in Guangzhou. Sometimes they just weren't ready on time. Sometimes days would go by, sometimes weeks, and still no visa in hand after it had been approved. Sometimes a visa would be approved at the Consulate, but when the couple would go to pick it up, the Consulate had changed its mind. No visa!

Another source of extreme frustration was that the rules seemed to change frequently without notice. New requirements would be sprung on unsuspecting Chinese women who appeared for their interview. We need a DNA test result to prove that is your child. We need to see pictures of you with your child since birth. We need your American fiancé's former spouse's social security number. We need to see your American fiancé's former spouse's current utility bills to prove that she no longer lives with him. Yes, tell your fiancé to go talk to that woman he divorced years ago who wouldn't give him a glass of water if he were dying and she had all the water in the world. Tell him. Okay, make the rules as arbitrary and as difficult as you wish. After all, you are in control and are not subject to any second guessing. But for God's sake, tell us the rules and stick with the rules. These are human lives you are playing with! This might be the sentiment of many waiting applicants. They would have a good point.

It was a beautiful ceremony. On Lee's second trip to Guangzhou, they had an official engagement party for family and close friends. It was in a relatively large private dining room in a beautiful hotel within walking distance of Ping's home and the Golden Bridge Hotel. The day before the ceremony, Ping and Lee went to a jewelry store and bought Ping's engagement ring. "I don't want a diamond ring, Leelee. A diamond ring won't bring me happiness. I want to select a ring that I will want to wear every day. I want to wear a ring that will remind me of you every day." She selected a beautiful ring with two leopards cuddled face to face, with tiny jewels set in their bodies to reflect the light. She wore it proudly to their engagement party. She arranged for a photographer and a videographer to be present. They received a music video of the event, with full audio, plus hundreds of photos.

The highlight of the evening was when Cici faced Ping and Lee, raised her glass, and made a simple toast to them. "Happy Every Day."

That toast became their mantra.

Now during Lee's third visit, they went as a family to the wedding photo studio. This time Cici was also in the wedding photos that were taken. Mama, Papa, Daughter. The happiness on their faces was preserved in photos, with another music video presentation that they could watch over and over again.

The love and passion between Ping and Lee was markedly stronger by this time. Lee could see in her eyes, feel in her touch, and sense in her words, that her love for him had reached a new level. There was also a deeper hunger in her kisses, and they didn't go anywhere unless they were hand in hand, arm in arm. Whatever concerns or discomfort that Ping had once felt when they walked the streets of Guangzhou together was gone. She did tell Lee, however, that sometimes Chinese people made rude comments to her because she was with a Western man. They cursed her and told her she was abusing the face of China by being with Lee. She held her head high anyway, proud to be seen with her husband and her daughter. This was her family.

It had been a difficult trip getting to Guangzhou this time. The flight out of Houston was delayed by weather problems, so Lee and twenty nine other passengers from Houston did not arrive at the departure gate in San Francisco for the connecting flight to Beijing until the scheduled departure time. The flight to Beijing was on the same airline that had brought them from Houston. The airline therefore knew they were coming. It knew they had arrived. It even knew they were there ready to board at the scheduled departure time. The airline personnel nevertheless pulled the ramp back from the plane and would not allow them to board. The Consulate in Guangzhou is missing some good employee candidates, Lee thought.

Because of the airline's callous attitude, all of the passengers from Houston had to be reticketed and rerouted. Lee ended up having to fly to Narita Airport, about two hours outside of Tokyo. Then he was reticketed again and routed to Beijing, but of course he was too late to make his original connecting flight to Guangzhou. He had to scramble to find a hotel room late at night in a strange city where he could not speak the language, and then scramble back to the airport at 5:00 a.m. the next day to try to book a flight to Guangzhou. This was during peak travel season for Chinese New Year. Not only that, but China was having its worst winter in fifty years. There was snow everywhere, even in places where it usually did not snow. Because of the bad weather, tens of thousands of travelers were stranded in train stations and at airports. Lee was lucky and was able to book a flight early the next morning, so he arrived in Guangzhou around mid-day. He had called ahead and Ping and Cici were there to meet him at the airport, along with Cici's two male cousins. The cousins greeted Lee with a hug, welcoming him like family.

This time it was cold in Guangzhou too. The cold and wet winter had reached way south. Ping insisted on buying long underwear for Lee. The buildings in Guangzhou typically do not have heat because the weather is usually not too cold. This year was different. They needed but did not have heat. Even the hotel had no heat. Stepping out of the hot shower into the cold room wasn't particularly fun. It also rained every day for the first two weeks Lee was there. Despite the cold and miserable weather, the little family was very happy together.

The parting this time was even more difficult than the previous times. Ping held onto Lee even as he walked into the screening booth at airport security when he was leaving. It had been almost exactly a year since Lee and Ping had first met in person. They still had no idea if or when they would actually be together.

"Wait for me," she pleaded. This was the third time she had said those words to him that morning. What was her intuition telling her? What did she sense that Lee didn't know? When Lee looked back at Ping and Cici after he cleared security, they were waving sadly, and Ping mouthed the words to Lee once again. "Wait for me." She later told Lee that she and Cici burst into tears again as he walked away.

Last Farewell

Chapter Eight

"Goodbye Ping.

Your silence has confirmed many things for me. My suspicions, my doubts, my fears, and finally my belief that we are not meant to be together.

I packed 35 boxes with all of your things and will ship them back to you. Maybe you can find a more suitable man for you. I really do want a warm and loving family, and I will find one, but it will be built on a foundation of trust that you and I didn't find with each other.

I will notify the Consulate that I no longer support your visa, so there is no need to prepare for or go to the interview.

Despite the way this has ended, I still love you. I will always love you.

Lee"

Blinking back the tears, Lee pushed the "send" button. The fateful message was torn apart, reconstructed, directed here, redirected there, blindly finding its way through cyberspace to her home in Guangzhou, coming back together just in time for it to appear in readable form wherever she was in the world.

Ping knew it was coming, but its finality struck her in the heart, taking her to her knees, leaving her reeling, bewildered, shocked. But she was high on Wu Tai Shan, able to access a computer only when surrounded by other Chinese people who were waiting to use the only computer within miles that had access to the Internet. Ping and Cici had traveled to the mountain as they did every four years. They wanted Lee to come with them every four years in the future. It was a spiritual experience for them, and very important in their lives. This was something they were doing in preparation for leaving their home in China to move to America in exactly three weeks. The long wait was over. Their dream was in sight. But everything had fallen apart. Ping knew it was over, but she hadn't told Cici about it yet. She would wait until they arrived in her home town in Zibo City.

Lee had spent the day buying and packing boxes. He wrapped all of the breakable items in bubble wrap to protect them. He placed all of Cici's beloved stuffed animals in boxes with tears falling on them. The little pink blanket with the bear on it that he hoped she would love when she came to America was used to tuck some of the little animals in a box. She would hate it now, and throw it away, but he still wanted to send it to her. It belonged to her, not him. She should be the one who destroyed it.

The twelve little Hello Kitty dolls in their festive clothes, six matched little kitty couples, found their place in one of the boxes. Was it his imagination, or did he see sadness in their little eyes? An ominous darkness surrounded them, clawing at them, gripping their little bodies, when the lid closed tightly on the box. They could hear the tape ripping from the spool, could almost feel its smothering grip, as it sealed the box tightly. Their short visit to America had come to an end.

Hours passed. The silence was deafening.

We Want to Come Home

Chapter Nine

Their journey took them to the edge of the abyss, a Chinese woman and an American man. They gazed into the darkness below. This was a darkness borne of fear, a fear that chilled them to the soul. Whether bravely or foolishly, they had decided they would never be together. Their passion and love for each other notwithstanding, they had made that decision. The decision made, with heavy hearts they had said a last goodbye.

And then silence. Forty eight hours of silence. Grief so overbearing that they could not sleep. Too hurt to cry. Too hurt to think. Too scared to think about the future, they suffered alone.

They had to tell the girl, and that is when the tears began to fall. The girl's tears would not stop. She cried all afternoon. Then late at night, still sobbing, she fell into a restless sleep. Her world fallen apart, her eyes so puffy she could no longer see. She lay there in the darkness with a broken spirit, wet tissues clenched in her hands.

The woman also cried now. Half a world away, the man shared their grief and their tears. Earlier, the girl had asked to talk to the man. The woman had said no. "He is hurting too," she said. "We are all hurting. We are so sorry. We don't want to hurt you. We don't want to hurt each other." "I never, ever want to go to America now," the girl had shouted at the woman, tears streaming down her face.

The woman sat in the darkness, deep into the night, mourning their loss. Her dark eyes had lost their sparkle. The long dark hair that spilled in curls from her head cast a shadow across her face as dim light from the moon crept into the room. She was a strikingly beautiful woman. Taller and shapelier than would be expected for a woman of her race, her appearance usually dominated when she entered a room. Tonight, however, she was overcome with emotion. Her shoulders were slumped. Her breathing was shallow. Time stood still in her heart, while the minutes ticked surely by in the silent room. Shortly before dawn, with strength from somewhere deep within, the woman stirred. "This is not how we want this to end," the woman whispered to the exhausted body of the little girl.

The woman reached through the darkness. Searching for their future, their very life, her hand closed around the telephone. She pulled it to her chest, and with the precision of a surgeon, she touched the buttons in the darkness. "Lao Po," he said in a soft voice. She heard the man, his every breath reaching for her, calling her to him. "We want to come home," she whispered.

Welcome Home

Chapter Ten

They arrived in America at the airport in Minneapolis/St Paul in the early afternoon on a day late in May. The sun was shining brightly through the windows of the airplane. They were too excited, happy, hungry, and exhausted to speak. They just waited and watched, with no idea what to expect next. The girls were so tired that once inside the airport, they would find a deserted section and lay on the seats to rest while Lee stood guard over his Chinese treasure.

They were sitting near the back of the plane, so about three hundred people preceded them into the large room where everyone would clear immigration. There were many lines of people, with many people in each line, so it looked like a long wait was ahead of them. Thanks to a tip from a considerate friend, however, they had received exact instructions about how to proceed through immigration at the airport. They ignored the crowd and went immediately to the far right side of the room to lane two, where they were first in line.

In less than ten minutes the immigration officer had greeted them, looked through the paperwork in the brown envelope that had the ominous warning from the Consulate in Guangzhou: DO NOT OPEN, and taken the required digital fingerprints and photos. The officer stamped their passports while Ping and Cici conversed with him in English. When he finished and handed their passports back to them, he looked at Ping and Cici with a smile and said,

"Welcome Home!"

They had flown from Guangzhou in China, to Narita airport, in Tokyo, to Minneapolis, in America. The trip was long, but they had a lot of fun. When they were still in Guangzhou, Lee had started saying "Bless you" to Ping and Cici if they sneezed. Neither of them responded, because they had no idea what he meant. After a few times, he told them that when they were in America, people would often say "Bless You" when they sneezed, and that they should respond by saying "Thank You", and that the other person might say "You are Welcome".

Well, just like Lee would get confused sometimes with xiexie and bu ke qi (the Chinese words for thank you and you are welcome), Ping and Cici were confused with "Thank You" and "You are Welcome". They kept saying "You are Welcome" when Lee said "Bless You", but they would all laugh at the mistake, and it soon became a running joke. They would deliberately say "You are Welcome", to prevent Lee from being able to say it after they said "Thank You".

What started as a joke soon became second nature for the girls, and by analogy they learned a valuable lesson. Soon when Lee or someone else said "Thank You" to them, they immediately responded by saying "You are Welcome". Lee saw it in action many times on the airplanes and at the airports on their trip home. If anyone ever saw them, Lee thought, they may get a laugh. Some of the people on the flight from Narita had figured out their little joke, and laughed along with them. By the time they landed, they would even skip the "Bless You" part, and just say "You are Welcome" when someone sneezed. Then they would laugh and enjoy their little private joke.

After all, it was just an expression, and they knew what it meant.

Lee had arrived in Guangzhou eight days before the girls were to appear at the Consulate for their interview. He had flown through this very same airport in Minneapolis en route to Narita, where he would connect on a flight to Guangzhou. In shades of how life repeats itself, the weather in Houston again delayed his departure. This time Lee sat in the plane on the runway in Houston with the rain pouring down, feeling helpless. There were dozens of airplanes in the long line that were in front of his plane. He knew they would never arrive in Minneapolis in time to catch the flight to Narita. He knew that there would not be another flight to Narita until late the next day. He dreaded another long, long trip.

On his third trip to see the girls, he had flown out of Guangzhou a day early so he could meet with a client in Beijing. The client had driven him to the airport in Beijing the next morning, arriving in plenty of time before the flight was scheduled to depart. The line of people waiting to check in for the flight to San Francisco was staggering in size, and it was barely moving. It didn't matter, there was already a sign that said the flight had been delayed for several hours. When Lee finally reached one of the check-in counters, he was told that he would be reticketed because he would miss his connection in San Francisco. The only thing he could do, he was told, was spend the night in San Francisco and fly out the next morning.

"Just put me on a non-stop," Lee asked, "and whatever you do, don't send me through Denver. Every time I fly to Denver there are delays," he said. "Okay, now you are sure this is a nonstop from San Francisco to Houston, right?" he asked the lady. She assured him it was. She lied. He had to spend the night in San Francisco when the airline finally got him there. When he arrived at the airport to check in at four o'clock the next morning, he learned that he was on a flight to Denver, connecting to a flight to Houston. Same airline, same story. Sure enough, when he was standing in line in Denver waiting for the Houston-bound plane to board, the passengers were told that there would be a delay of unknown length while they tried to locate another aircraft. When he arrived in Houston a full day and many hours later than he was supposed to arrive, only one of his two bags arrived with him. He wasn't even surprised.

What a difference an airline made. When his plane from Houston finally took off en route to Minneapolis, they made excellent time and the plane landed in Minneapolis about fifteen minutes before the flight to Narita was scheduled to depart. There were eighteen passengers from Houston who wanted to make the connecting flight to Narita. The airline had enough of the oversized golf carts waiting at the arrival gate to take those eighteen passengers to the departure gate, where they boarded the plane exactly at the scheduled departure time. The waiting passengers were not grumbling. The new passengers were welcomed on board, the plane departed a little later than scheduled, but still arrived at its destination on time. Thank you Northwest Airlines.

The flights from Guangzhou to Narita to Minneapolis also ran smoothly for the little family. The flight from Minneapolis to Houston also left as scheduled. While on the plane, a woman about Ping's age was walking a baby in the aisle of the plane, trying to help it go to sleep. She was getting a bit frustrated so Ping got up and went to her and struck up a conversation with her about the baby. As Ping admired the baby, the mother because less frustrated, and as she became less frustrated she must have relaxed and the baby could sense it, because the baby was soon fast asleep.

Lee was so proud of her. He told Ping that she had been in America only a few hours and she was already touching people's lives.

The girls were great travel companions.

Probably everyone knows how to play rock, paper, and scissors with their hands, where paper covers rock, rock crushes scissors, and scissors cut paper, thereby determining the winner. The competing hands are usually displayed on the count of three.

On the airplane, Lee learned a variation of that game from his girls, which is set to rhythmic motion and the singing of a little ditty interspersed with words that sounded to him like fay yah and chop-chop.

The game began with each competitor holding up the first two fingers on each hand to simulate two bees in flight. As the song began and the bees flew away to the right, the arms and fingers of the girls went in that direction, and the same was true when the bees flew to the left. Their bodies swayed to enhance this feeling of flight. This part occurred only at the beginning of a new game, not between each display of the hands, Lee observed.

Lee didn't understand the rest of the lyrics or their meaning, but from the motions it looked like the bees landed on flowers (simulated by each competitor displaying rock paper or scissors with their hands) when the words fay yah were spoken, and the words that sounded like chop-chop were immediately spoken when the winner was determined.

As the words chop-chop were spoken, the winner would swing her hand through the air toward the face of the loser as though to strike her, and the loser's head would pull back and to the side as though she had been struck by the blow. If it was a draw, the hands of the competitors would sweep over the flowers in unison as the words chop-chop were spoken.

When Ping and Cici played this game, their bodies would move and sway in rhythmic motion as they sang the little ditty and showed their hands and faked blows to the head and the receipt of the blow. Listening and watching, the words fay yah chop-chop, fay yah chop-chop and the movement of the hands and bodies had a hypnotic effect.

Their games moved so quickly that it was sometimes difficult to see how the winner was determined in each display of the hands. When one of them mistakenly declared herself the winner, there were howls of infectious laughter, and Lee was caught up in the action. Laughing along with the girls was about all he felt qualified to do in their game.

Because of their enjoyment of the little game, they began to tease each other at odd moments by faking a blow to the head with an open hand and saying chop-chop, which always caused the three of them to laugh. This little game became part of their bonding experience.

While in Guangzhou, Ping and Lee had become minor celebrities quite by accident. Ping had signed them up to walk in the fifth annual run/walk hosted by the Italian Consulate for the benefit of the mentally disabled. They joined hundreds of other people at a local park on a gorgeous Saturday morning. Because of the earthquake in Sichuan Province about a week earlier, a catastrophe that would claim more than eighty thousand lives, the proceeds from the walk/run had been redirected to help the earthquake victims. They met people from England and Italy and Finland and Spain and of course China. While talking with some of them, Lee was tapped on the shoulder by a young Chinese lady. “Excuse me, could I interview you?”

Surprised, Lee looked at Ping, who seemed to think it would be okay. The lady turned him to face a waiting camera, held her microphone between them, and started asking questions. At first she asked for his name, and where he was from. “America!” Her eyes widened. In response to her questions, Lee explained how he and Ping came to be there that morning. He praised the Chinese government for welcoming aid from America and other countries, saying it was a catastrophe of International proportion. Not said, but clearly understandable by anyone who was knowledgeable of world events at the time, his comments were also a slap at the military junta in Myanmar that had rebuffed efforts by the International community to help its people who were suffering from lack of food and shelter and water because of another natural disaster that had occurred around the same time.

The day after the interview was the first of three National days of mourning in China. There was nothing broadcast on television on those three days except news. The interview was played on television, especially on the Guangzhou English channel, and Ping started receiving telephone calls from family and friends who had seen it. Lee was approached by people in restaurants who recognized him from the interview. The unexpected excitement helped divert their attention from the upcoming interview at the Consulate. "Maybe they saw us on television and will give you extra points," Lee joked with Ping.

Their interview was scheduled at 7:15 a.m. on Monday morning. Ping and Lee spent the previous afternoon with Cici in their hotel suite doing a final organization of all the documents and pictures. Ping had purchased many clear plastic folders that were large enough to hold groups of documents. Each folder had a snap so that the documents would not spill out of it. She had removed the plastic "guts" from the two photo albums they had assembled so that they could easily be slipped under the window the next morning for viewing by the officer who would conduct the interview.

Photos are an important part of the proof that a couple has a bona fide relationship, so Lee and Ping had hundreds of photos of them with family and friends during Lee's four trips to Guangzhou. They had selected what they thought were the best and put them in the two photo albums. Ping had gone through them and put descriptive labels on each picture. Not the usual description, mind you. Done in Ping's creative way, each picture told a story. Lee and Ping cuddle together with happy smile. Lee and Ping cuddle and kiss together with delightful emotion. Ping sits on Lee's leg with a smile. Lee and Ping sit on the Chinese Chair with hand in hand and smile. Lee and Ping with daughter, warm, happy, wonderful family.

The visa officer the next morning was a beautiful Caucasian woman. When she looked at the photos, she looked up at Ping and mouthed to her one word, "Wow!"

Now you can arrive at the Consulate as early as you wish, but it is not first come, first served. Lee and Ping still arrived at 6:45 a.m., but they were near the back of a huge mass of people who stood loosely in multiple lines. It was raining and everyone had an umbrella. You might think it would be an advantage to be the tallest people in the crowd, since your umbrella would be above all the others. Not true. Lee and Ping's umbrella drained on the umbrellas that surrounded them, which in turn drained on Lee and Ping and Cici. They didn't care. They would have stood in the pouring rain. They savored every second of the time they stood in line.

At 7:40 a.m. the Consulate personnel started looking at documents and allowing people to go inside. Americans were required to leave the lines, but Ping and Cici were allowed to go into the Consulate a little after eight o'clock, where they were taken initially to the fourth floor, and then on up to the fifth floor. They had their hands full of documents and photographs. Tax returns for the previous three years for Lee, government forms like the required Affidavit of Support, copies of their respective divorce decrees, birth certificates , a marriage eligibility certificate and a police certificate for Ping, a letter from Lee's law firm and his banker, all three of their passports. Any document written in Chinese had to be accompanied by an official English translation. Lee went to the coffee shop on the fourth floor to await news of their future. He didn't even complain about the $5.00 cups of coffee. He was just happy that their day had finally arrived.

How did you meet your fiancé, how many times has he visited you, let me see your photos, and now the Affidavit of Support. Congratulations, your visa is approved. These are words that Ping heard. This came after she had been asked by another officer if she had ever been a member of the Communist Party of China.

All the waiting, the agony, the fears, the tears, the sleepless nights, the frustration, the feelings of helplessness, and the emotional highs and lows were forgotten when the girls came running excitedly into the coffee shop to hug Lee and tell him the good news. Two days later, after a whirlwind of activity, their passports were back in their hands, this time with United States of America Visa's in each of the girl's passports.

They packed and shipped the final ten boxes of clothing and other items to Houston. They had one last dinner at a restaurant with Ping's older sister and her husband and son. They dropped Lee off back at the hotel after dinner. "We will talk in Chinese with Mama," Ping told Lee, "you won't have any interest. You should rest." Ping and Cici did not return to the hotel until well after midnight. They didn't go to bed until about 2:30 a.m., and they all got up at 4:00 a.m. to go to the airport.

Ping's older sister and her husband and son also got up at four in the morning to accompany Lee and Ping and Cici to the airport to say goodbye. They traveled in two taxis to the airport, nearly an hour away. Traffic was light at that hour, and the airport was still almost empty of people when they arrived.

They sat and talked quietly until it was time to go through security. When they said goodbye to each other, Ping's older sister sobbed uncontrollably as she clung to Cici. They were like mother and daughter all of Cici's life. The pain of parting was almost unbearable. Cici couldn't hold back the tears for too long, but she controlled them well. Ping was touched also, but she held on to Lee and her eyes only glistened. There were no hugs between Ping and her sister, even though they are very close. Chinese culture. They each knew how the other felt. The hugs were invisible.

The three of them walked down a very long and wide passageway as they left those who were staying behind. The passageway was empty except for the three of them. None of them looked back to wave a final farewell. They held each other close and walked away with sadness, but also full of hope and excitement, walking toward their new life together without saying a word.

Merging Cultures

Chapter Eleven

After they arrived at their home in Houston, Lee began to chronicle their first days together. Many changes were happening in their lives, just in the remaining days in May. Realizing that he was witnessing the merging of two cultures, and would soon be numb to the significance of the little every day events that were unfolding before him, Lee began posting the story of life in America on the forum "A Candle for Love". He was inspired by a dedicated group of readers on the forum, where he found people who understood what he and Ping and Cici had lived through. Some of them had done it years before, some of them were just beginning their journey. If there was a common bond, it was probably fear of the unknown. Some admitted it. Some did not. Some only talked about it with each other in private messages or emails or telephone calls. Some were vocal, some were forever silent. Some made their first post when their visa was approved at the Consulate in Guangzhou; a post to thank the knowledgeable veterans on the forum.

Even some of the hardened veterans seemed to be appreciative of Lee's stories. What members of the forum had to say in response to Lee's posts was not his to include in this book, but he appreciated every word of thanks, every word of encouragement. It wasn't easy to expose the innermost thoughts and feelings of him and his family, their sometimes raw emotions, their wishes, their hopes and dreams, but he did it, day after day.

"You are working too hard, Leelee," Ping would say. She saw the hours he was putting into his little project, but it consumed him. She would take him by the hand, take him outside for a walk, bring fresh fruit for him to eat, cook healthy and delicious foods, rub his shoulders, drape her arms around him and hug him. When she saw that he had started writing this book, she devoted even more time to helping him. They had painters inside their home for two weeks while Lee was writing this book, so their home office which Ping usually kept organized and neat was full of clutter. Furniture from other rooms, paintings from the walls, lamps and screens and other things, all added to the clutter. His desk became covered with papers, then deep in papers.

But the words flowed. There was a guiding force that Lee called a muse. When the muse was with him, Lee's fingers never stopped on the keyboard. He didn't have to think about what to write. The muse guided his hands. Lee posted the Prologue of this book on the forum and received a few positive and encouraging comments, so he posted the first chapter, and received more encouragement. As he wrote and posted chapter after chapter, the comments became fewer and fewer. Sometimes it felt like no one was reading what he wrote. A few times there would be no comments at all. Those days were hard, because he felt like he had lost his way. The muse would desert him. His fingers wandered aimlessly on the keyboard. But then he would receive an encouraging post or a private message or an email or a phone call, and the muse would return. It turned out that there were many more people reading his stories and his book than he realized.

The comments that stunned him, that mattered the most to him, were the ones where he was told that some women in China were also reading his stories about life in America, even reading his book. Some members would cut and paste the stories in emails to their fiancée in China, who in turn would share them with her friends in China. Some members would read the stories and even chapters from the book aloud to their fiancée in China when they talked with them on the telephone from America. Some were even man enough to admit, sometimes publicly, that the stories would often choke them up, sometimes even bring tears falling from their eyes. That is what drove Lee relentlessly on with the writing of the book.

One night Lee skipped ahead and wrote the final chapter in the book. That effort is one that he was proud of at the time, but a couple of days later, here is what he posted on the forum.

"What a day.

I thought I had written the final chapter of the book a few nights ago. I was proud of myself. The perfect little ending, tying everything neatly together.

Boy was I ever wrong. When the muse came back today he was so angry with me. He literally took control of my mind. It was like an out of body experience. That has never happened to me before. It may never happen again.

It was so intense that I had to leave the office. I couldn't very well sit there with tears running down my face. I looked down and averted my face until I got to the car. Then I didn't worry so much about what the emotions were doing to me.

When I walked in the door of our home, Ping knew. She took one look at my face and knew what was happening. She held me close and kissed me. Then held me some more before she led me to the home office.

I had emailed the first few paragraphs that I had written at the office to me, so I was able to download and save the document, then literally pick up in mid sentence.

In a span of 5 hours I wrote the final three chapters of the book. I promise you they were never in my head before the muse seized me and took complete control. I know my fingers typed the words, but I can't even proofread them. Every time I try, the tears start falling. My eyes are burning from all the tears.

It may not be worth a damn, but you have just witnessed, or had the opportunity to witness, the writing of a 300 plus page book in what I would consider to be a relatively short period of time, but I am no expert when it comes to writing books.

I suspect the muse is gone now, leaving me to do the cleanup work. I owe the little bastard. He surprised the hell out of me.

And that is how this book came to be written."

****

May 25, 11:44 a.m.

When we arrived in Houston just after ten o'clock last night, we were surprised at the airport by Boris and Ella. Ella is a Chinese woman who Ping met in Guangzhou. She and Ping have become best friends, so the smiles and excitement on their faces was something to behold. Ella even had a beautiful flower for Ping.

We arrived at our home around eleven o'clock, after driving ever so briefly through Chinatown so the girls could see how close it is to our home. You would have thought it was Christmas when we walked into our home. I have never seen such excitement in my life. The girls were so appreciative and so expressive about everything. When Cici walked into her Hello Kitty bathroom (pink is her favorite color), she just stood there with her hands over her face saying over and over again, "this is so beautiful."

The girls were hungry but they also wanted a shower. I told them I would fix something for them to eat while they showered. I took out a frozen pizza and showed them how to operate the oven. They had never seen an oven. As soon as they smelled the pizza cooking, they forgot all about the shower. They marveled at the pizza cutter wheel, and then devoured the pizza. They made me feel like I had just done something wonderful, all because of a frozen pizza.

Now I know that the girls were dog tired when we arrived, because we had been traveling for just over 30 hours. I also know that they didn't go to bed the night before we left Guangzhou until 2:30 a.m. I know that we got up just 1.5 hours later at four o'clock to go to the airport. I know that neither of them slept more than a couple of hours on the airplanes. But they were so excited and so happy to be exploring their new home that we didn't go to bed until two o'clock this morning.

I knew they would sleep forever, so I told them not to be concerned if I wasn't here when they got up this morning, because I would just be at Starbucks or the grocery store.

I woke up with a start at seven o'clock this morning with the sunlight strong in our bedroom. Ping wasn't in our bed so I assumed she had gone to comfort Cici in her room, since it was her first night in a strange place. When I walked out of our bedroom I was greeted by Ping. She had a big smile on her face and she told me that she had been working since early this morning because she was so excited that she couldn't sleep.

Then Cici walked in, looking for the entire world like a young housewife taking care of her home. She told me that her Mama came to her room at four o'clock this morning to ask if she was sleeping. She also was too excited to sleep, so she got up and they began to work. They had explored the kitchen and found the cups of noodles that I had bought at Costco, but they didn't know how to heat the water, so they were waiting for me to wake up so they could eat something for breakfast. I felt like such a slacker!

By nine fifteen we were at the local Chinese food market, where they filled up a large grocery cart with their favorite Chinese spices and fresh fruits and vegetables and many other things. There was not a single complaint about not being able to find something. It was all there, just like shopping in Guangzhou.

Now they have been putting the food away in the two refrigerators and have started washing and cooking the fresh vegetables. They have mastered the rice cooker and it is busy doing its job. They work like a team in the kitchen, and told me I should go to our home office to play or work. After lunch we will go furniture shopping so they can select the dressers and chests and so forth for their bedrooms.

All I can say guys, is that it is well worth the long wait. As we lay in bed last night, Ping put her head on my chest and told me that she just loves our home, and that it is so comfortable for her and Cici. Hearing their laughter in the kitchen as they work together is the best sound in the world to me. It validates all of my dreams for the happy life that I envisioned we would have together.

I couldn't understand the words they have said when they called our family and friends in Guangzhou to tell them that we arrived safely, but I could see the happiness in their faces. I could also hear the excitement in their voices, so I believe that their dreams have also come true. I am a happy man.

May 25, 06:12 PM

The girls finally crashed for a nap, but said they want to be back up in an hour.

They are excited now because the bedroom furniture is on its way. "Unbelievable", said the girls when they learned it would be delivered the same day we bought it. This could never happen in Guangzhou.

They had no problem selecting the bedroom furniture that they want, but Cici can't believe this is really happening for her. The people at the furniture store even brought her some ice cream while we shopped, and her smile made everyone's day.

Our next stop was at Costco, where they said they now understand why we have so many of each thing like soap and toothpaste and so forth in our home. Ping made me smile when she asked me under her breath if they would have paper in the restroom as she headed in that direction. That was just one lesson about paper that we learned today.

The other lesson is that we always have something that we use for napkins in our home, and they aren't like little facial tissues like we had to buy in the restaurants in Guangzhou if we wanted any kind of napkin to use. You can actually wipe your mouth and hands on what we use. I am talking about paper towels. Use them at the dining table, and then use them again to pick up spills or wipe the stove. The girls learned this system immediately, and never complained that we were wasting paper.

"What's this?"

"Well darling, if you use two of them, you can put one on each end of an ear of corn on the cob, and then you won't burn or dirty your hands while you eat it." Guess who grabbed a package of fresh ears of corn on the cob at Costco? She will apply that lesson immediately.

"What's this?"

"Well darling, you put them on the table before you place hot dishes there so the dishes won't burn the table."

"What's this in the refrigerator ladies? Dried soup mix? No, it doesn't need to go in the refrigerator. We put things like this in the pantry."

They learn so fast, and it is amazing at how they are able to expand their respective English vocabularies by helping each other with a missing word when the need arises.

It is also impressive to me because these girls are not shrinking violets.

At Costco an Asian lady approached Cici and asked her in English where she found the fresh strawberries. Instead of ducking the question or pointing to me to handle it, she responded to the lady in English, and even walked her to the door of the refrigerated room so she could show her the strawberries.

Ping is the same. I know she was worried at first, but she has handled every conversation in English with no apparent difficulty. Certainly the people to whom she spoke would have no reason to guess that she just arrived in America.

I have been spoiled by the great Chinese food that is available here in Chinatown, but Ping has the touch that puts the restaurants all to shame. Not only that, but she was singing in the kitchen as she worked. She has always told me that she loves to cook, but now for the first time she has time to cook, and she is really enjoying it.

Now guess who is yawning and thinking he should also be catching a short nap while the opportunity is here? We still have a lot of work to do before this day is over, but I am not complaining.

May 26, 12:43 AM

We are pushing midnight now as I begin to write, and there is no slowdown in sight. Where do they get this energy? All they had today was a two hour nap. We had a great dinner (Did you ever eat fried rice that was so light that it felt like it was melting in your mouth?), but I am thinking they have about burned through that meal and I should surprise them with a midnight snack.

The bedroom furniture has been positioned and repositioned, sort of like discussing and debating the menu selection at a Chinese restaurant, though a bit more difficult to implement the decisions. Now the blending of our families in a material sense has also begun. All the things that Ping shipped to our home from China are showing up in unexpected places, and things that were there before have moved to a new place in our home. The effect of this transformation is startling, and very tasteful and beautiful, at least to me.

What I have learned, however, is that there is more to the decor than meets the eye. On one wall of our home office Ping has placed a beautiful circular tapestry with dangling wooden beads on strings and tassels at the ends. Inside the circle are two colorful birds that are swimming on the equally colorful layers of water.

Below that decoration, on the Chinese table (circular with the four wooden stools that fit beneath the table so it is all self-enclosed when it is not being used) that I found and bought in Chinatown months ago, sits the delicate tea set that Ping and I selected and purchased together in Guangzhou. There is a fish portrayed on each side of each little cup, and also on the teapot and the other pieces of the tea set.

Ping tells me that the water under the birds symbolizes money for my business, and that the fish symbolize that we will always have plenty of food to eat.

Then she told me that the beautiful, heavy globe that is about the size and weight of a small bowling ball, and which sits on a wooden stand, is intended to bless and protect me. She placed it on one of the built-in shelves in our home office. It has a picture of a robed Chinese woman on each of the four quadrants on the globe.

Next to the globe sits the limited edition crystal piece of art that commemorates the Beijing 2008 Olympic Games. This was given to us by a close friend in Guangzhou as a wedding gift.

The Chinese language that floats through our home now, mixed with the English, is like music to my ears. Our home office is right in the middle of our home, and we keep the doors on both sides of the office open, so they can traipse through it at will. One or the other of the girls will often stop to visit, and will sometimes rest for a few minutes in the soft leather chair that sits with its ottoman near my desk.

Boy did I hit the jackpot without knowing it when I selected the Hello Kitty decor for Cici's bathroom. She just showed me what she has lined up on top of her dresser. There are 12 little Hello Kitty dolls (6 little couples), dressed in festive clothing, sitting on the dresser and leaning against the wall. They look a lot happier here than they did when I closed the lid on them in that dark old box on our darkest day. While I was in the bedroom with Cici and Ping I asked them if they would like to have another Pizza. They looked at each other, smiled really big, looked back at me and said in unison: "Yes, no problem."

Uncle Adrian, one of our friends, once said something to me about why I have collected so many things that were pretty much randomly placed in our home. When he comes to our home now, he will have the answer to his question. I didn't know just where each of these things would fit, but I just felt they would fit somewhere. Now I know where they fit, because Ping has shown me. Wow! It doesn't even look like the same house.

One of the things I bought was a statuette of a fat little Chinese boy who is pulling on one ear with his hand. It reminded me of one of the photos of me when I was about 3-4 years old that I sent to Ping. She also recognized the resemblance immediately. We call this little guy LeePing. She loves him so much that she put him prominently on display in our bedroom on top of a small circular chest of drawers that I also bought as a collector's item a few years ago. He is so large that he fills the entire top of the chest of drawers.

And tell me this. How does someone select a marble topped dresser that has black marble that is a perfect match with an existing piece of furniture in the bedroom? This is one of the minor miracles that Ping has pulled off in a matter of hours. Even the carving and shape of the wood on the two pieces of furniture make it look like they were intended to be together.

I can smell that pizza, so I better feed these hard-working girls of mine. They have earned it in spades.

May 26, 02:53 AM

Yes, I am back again.

As we sat together talking in our living room at two o'clock this morning, what was happening suddenly struck me like a bolt of lightning. Ping and Cici were talking and laughing with me and showing no interest in going to bed to catch up on all the sleep they have missed.

What I sensed was that for them, these are the moments in time that they have craved. This is what Ping has been telling me for the past year and a half. They have yearned to be part of a warm and loving family with a father and a husband who cares about them.

In all the time I have spent with Ping and Cici, there has never been a moment of tension or anger or disagreement between them. They are very much like sisters who are very close. They trust and respect each other, and they enjoy being together. They rely on each other for friendship and caring. They have allowed me to come into their special relationship, and they have made me feel like I am the only man who could ever be this close to them.

In fact, yesterday I saw the English book that Cici has used in her English school. In the front of the book, in beautiful penmanship, she practiced writing her new name over and over again. Seeing how she wrote my family name as her family name was one of the most touching things I could imagine. What a great feeling my girls have given to me!

May 26, 09:20 AM

Ahhhhh!!

That is my muscles screaming at me for engaging them in some unusually vigorous activity. No, not that. Well, ok, some of that, but you know I am not one to brag.

At the hotel in Guangzhou, Ping saw them prepare an omelet for me one morning. This morning she greeted me with an omelet that she prepared, and it was perfect. She always told me that when she eats something that she likes in a restaurant, she asks them how they prepare it, and then she prepares it at home. I can see that she is very good at this.

So Ping was up at five o'clock, she tells me, and Cici got up at eight o'clock. Ping didn't tell me exactly what she was doing, but she didn't have to. The kitchen floor was back in pristine condition, and I could see other touches by her practiced eye in the way things have been organized.

Ping and Cici gave me another moment of pride when they each talked in turn with Uncle Adrian on my cell phone when he called me this morning. Somehow they were able to pick up and understand a new accent, as he spoke to them very quickly, and they were able to carry on a conversation with him. I know that this must have been a confidence builder for them as well. I heard Ping tell Adrian that they will spoil me, and they have already done that.

I noticed that Ping used the microwave to heat something for Cici this morning, and she didn't need any additional help to know how to use it. In fact, with each new thing, I have only shown her one time how to use it, and then she has been comfortable using it on her own. This transition has been much easier than I expected.

A big sneeze by me just now and I said "excuse me" loudly (a new term for them in this situation). From the next room Cici called to me, "Bless You." "Thank you," I said. "You are welcome," she said. "Don't mention it," I said (another phrase that we added to our little joke yesterday). Another big sneeze and Ping called out from the next room with a laugh, "You are Welcome." Then she came to me with a tissue so I could blow my nose. Family time in Houston.

May 26, 02:31 PM

Well, the kitchen no longer belongs to me. After our second trip (just completed) to buy more Chinese groceries, which Ping has put away, I doubt that I could find anything in our kitchen anymore.

This time we shopped in the larger and newer Asian Supermarket, and Ping fell in love with it. We ended up with another shopping cart full of food, but I know she will use all of it and we will eat very well. Our two formerly empty refrigerators are suddenly very full of fresh foods, and the cabinets and the pantry are also full of new items.

This has been a food learning experience for me, even though I regularly shop in Chinatown, eat Chinese food all the time, and have even learned to cook a good number of Chinese (real Chinese) dishes. I have never even dreamed of buying one of those 3-4 foot long, skinny fish like we just purchased. Ping told me that it is called a Bell Fish (although I think a more appropriate name, given its appearance, would be Belt Fish). That is just one example, but I look forward to experiencing each of the new items that came home with us yesterday and today.

I found that I can still contribute a few things to our culinary experience. Ping and Cici looked longingly at some pork chops, and Ping said that she doesn't know how to cook them. She asked me if I can cook them, and when I said yes, she told me in English that Cici had just told her in Chinese that her mouth was watering just thinking about eating the pork chops. I think I could have guessed that from the smile that had spread across her face.

Speaking of Cici, the child is taking a nap now, which she richly deserves. Ping should also take a nap, but she is working away in the kitchen.

I will offer a thought that others may disagree with, but I have come to the conclusion that we don't really know these ladies until we see them on our home turf. This is admittedly a rather unscientific conclusion, as I have attempted to extrapolate my experience across a broad range of people, but I would be surprised if it isn't true in most cases.

To continue with my unscientific views, I would suggest that we tend to be on sensory overload when we are in China visiting our ladies, so we don't really appreciate and perhaps don't even notice many things about them. Ping is such a happy person, very unselfish, and very easy to get along with no matter what we are doing. That much I have noticed in China as well.

But now that she is here with me, I notice so much more. She is very adaptable, she learns very quickly, she seems comfortable in any setting, and she had no problem accepting this house as our home, and then taking the steps necessary to actually make it our home. She told me before she arrived that she would redecorate our home using things that we already own, and that we would not need to buy anything. She has done exactly what she said she could do, and in my mind, that takes some real talent.

But there is something even deeper that I have in mind. What she has given to me in just the short time we have been here is the unspoken assurance that she is here with me for the duration, and not just for her own purposes. She proves this with everything she says and does, and a lot of it comes from her constant attention to what she believes is in my best interest from a health perspective. She even told me quietly, with no sense of drama that she will take care of me because she wants me to be with her forever. I believe her.

I believe I also need a Guangzhou nap. My body still thinks it is 3:00 a.m. Maybe I can talk Ping into taking a break so she can rest as well. Then I think it is time to show her how to operate the dishwasher.

Oh yes, that reminds me. I learned something quite by accident that I will share with those of you who are preparing the house for your lady's arrival.

One of the things that Ping and Cici asked if I had available for them after they arrived was a pair of gloves to wear when they are washing dishes and cleaning things in the kitchen. I had purchased a pair of gloves with the intention of using them when I cleaned the grout on the tile floors. I gave them to the girls and it made them very happy.

Time to rescue my Pingping from the kitchen and rest for a bit.

May 26, 07:48 PM

Well a friend confirmed my belief about the likely name for the beltfish. The name at the store was also written in Chinese so I asked Ping what it said. She told me the Chinese word, so I asked her to translate it for me. She said bellfish. I used motions with my hands and told her it looks like it would be called beltfish, not bellfish. She said no, it said bellfish in both Chinese and English. Sounds like a good example of garbage in garbage out.

I told Uncle Adrian that Ping has already given me the green light to buy the Pacair range hood vent system. She had asked me to wait until she arrived, but she immediately recognized the need to have a better venting system when she started cooking.

The girls hit the wall this afternoon and finally slept for several hours. Now they are up and I will take them out and keep them busy so they will stay awake. This is a good time of day to take a walk to the pool to check it out. They also like to play tennis, and the tennis courts are next to the pool area, so we can check that out as well.

I need to have Ping practice getting into and out of our home with the extra set of keys that I made for her. Fortunately we also have the ability to get into our home through the garage using an electronic key pad, so they should have no problems while I am at the office.

Cell phones are another decision we haven't made yet. I know how important a cell phone is to a teenage girl, so I am being very considerate in that regard. Cici has her heart set on a particular brand of cell phone, but apparently the easiest way to help her use that phone would be to change our cell phone company. I don't mind doing that, since Ping also has a rule for Cici, which is no text messaging (just like no TV in her bedroom). Ping and I share the view that kids need to have clearly defined boundaries, and this is one of them.

What I am hoping though is to find a good way to accommodate Cici with the cell phone that she wants without having to change carriers.

Well, off to see the wizard. It is a beautiful evening outside, so we need to go outside and enjoy it.

May 26, 11:20 PM

I guess one way for us to know we have reached a certain level of comfort with our ladies is when they engage us in the process of selecting their feminine napkins, and they show not a trace of embarrassment. We went through this experience today, and I learned that some of the terminology that is used on the American packages is unclear to the girls. I hope I gave helpful (and also accurate) answers to their questions.

We took pictures by the pool this evening. My girls love to swim, and I am sure they will be in the pool this week while I am at the office. Last summer, before we knew it would be forever before they would arrive, I bought each of them an over-sized beach towel and floats for them to lie on in the pool. I sent pictures to them, and now they are excited to be able to actually use them.

Ping always snuggles up next to me when our photo is taken, and now Cici has reached that level of comfort with me where she does the same. It is a good feeling. She wanted photos to post on her website and to send to her friends in China.

Our home office has become a favorite gathering place for us. Both Ping and Cici like to use what was once my desk, but what is now a family desk. When I am at the desk, Cici loves to sit near me on the two drawer cherry wood lateral filing cabinet and dangle her feet off the side. Ping likes to relax in the leather recliner or sit on my lap at the desk.

We make important decisions in this office - like whether we want to eat something at this late hour of the night. Ping asked the question after Cici snacked on one of the cups of noodles (she told Ping that she loves these noodles, and could eat them every day). They are easy to find if you have a Costco nearby. I suggested that Ping and I could also eat some of the noodles, but Cici whispered in my ear that "Mama is hoping that we can eat pizza again tonight".

Armed with that knowledge, I asked them if they wanted to eat pizza, and got a big smile from Ping. They immediately headed to the freezer in the garage to choose which of the frozen pizzas that we bought at Wal-Mart today would be their choice for the evening. They know the drill now, so they turned on the oven, sprayed some Pam on the pizza pan so it wouldn't stick to the pan, checked the cooking temperature and time on the package, set the oven, removed the pizza while saving the round cardboard bottom to be used when we cut the pizza after it has cooked, and placed the pizza on the pan.

Sure this is routine for us, but we have had a little experience. For the girls, it is still part of this great new world in which they are living. Tonight I asked them if they would like to add some mushrooms to the pizza, and they said yes. I had some mushrooms in a can and took out the can opener for them to open the can. They just looked at me with puzzled expressions on their faces. Well, now they know how to operate a can opener, and I have to say that I had never thought about the necessity for that particular bit of training.

Five minutes to pizza everyone.

May 27, 07:42 AM

I have been reminded several times in the past couple of days of something important. We all know this to be true, but we sometimes forget it. What I am talking about is that it is often the little things that make a difference in relationships with people. I am talking about the little things that show you care, the little things that you never expected would have such an impact.

As an example, I saw a small, very soft, pink blanket with a big bear on it in a shop in Chinatown some months ago. I couldn't resist buying it for Cici, and I put it on her bed with some of her many stuffed animals before I left our home to go get my girls. She fell in love with that little blanket for some reason when she arrived here. It has accompanied her wherever she goes in our home, but also in our car, even with the weather as hot as it has been in Houston.

I will probably never understand the significance of that blanket to Cici, but one thing she has made sure of is that I know she loves it. Ping even told me that Cici loves that blanket, and doesn't want to be without it. I never made a better $10 investment.

Well, maybe I came close yesterday, also without knowing it. We were shopping at Target and I saw some Hello Kitty peel and stick appliqués. I put a couple of packages of them in the cart without saying anything. I heard a squeal of delight from Cici last night when she saw them, and the next thing I knew, she and Ping were sticking them all over Cici's bathroom.

There is Hello Kitty on everything from the shower walls to the bathroom walls themselves to the mirror and the medicine chest. They even saved one for Cici's bedroom door. Then they proudly displayed their handiwork for me. It was another inexpensive investment that brought far greater rewards than I would ever have expected.

This goes both ways. The most recent example is this morning. I haven't shown Ping how to operate the coffee grinder and coffee maker yet, though she has been asking me to do that. This means I made the several block trip to Starbucks this morning.

When I got back to our home, Ping was out in our small atrium patio which is fully visible from inside our home. She was still in her housecoat, with scissors in her hand, lovingly trimming the half dozen large plants/small trees that we have on our patio. As I read the newspaper, she used the spray bottle that she bought yesterday at Target to spray water on the leaves of the plants.

I don't know exactly what button she pushed, but just seeing her like that told me that in her mind, this home is her home, right down to the plants outside, and she will take care of it for us. That gives me a very comfortable and satisfying feeling inside. This is her home. This is her family. This is the life for which she traded everything she knew so she could live it with Cici and me. The smile and happiness that I see on her face is worth every agonizing minute that we waited so we could be together.

May 27, 04:32 PM

We have had a productive day today.

I went to the office early to take care of pressing matters, and then returned to take Ping and Cici to the County Clerk's office to get a marriage license. We went to one of the Branch Offices because I expected it would be less crowded. That turned out to be a good call, as we walked in and were immediately helped.

Ten minutes in and out, with a little humor as a bonus. We were assisted by a matronly, middle aged, African American woman. We gave her my driver's license and Ping's passport. She asked us the questions that are required by Texas law, but had to smile as she asked one of them.

Are you related to each other by blood?

It went so quickly that I told the lady that we really appreciated the way she made it so easy for us. She gave us the knowing look of a woman who has learned that sustaining the marriage is the part that requires a lot of work and said with a little smile, "well, this is the easy part."

Cici took our photos with the Clerk's office in the background. She seems to have fully recovered from the jet lag and lack of sleep. She heard the garage door opening when I got home this afternoon and she opened the door to greet me with the happiest face and waving her hand, calling "Papa, Papa".

Our Chinese neighbor who Ping and Cici met in Guangzhou when she was there helping her mother and father with their visas called a few minutes ago to see if she could come to say hello. She just arrived at our door, and I could see from the excitement and the hugs that these ladies really like each other a lot. She reminds me of Ping's older sister, who dotes on Cici like her own daughter. This lady seems to have the same affection for Cici. She left work early today just so she could come to visit with Ping and Cici.

So what am I doing here? Well, after the welcome and hellos and hugs at the door, they headed into the living room and Ping turned with a smile and said, "Okay, you are finished now, you can go back to your work." That is such a nice way of letting me off the hook, plus it gives them a chance to converse in Chinese.

I am becoming a stranger in my own home, but it is a good thing. My girls have been washing my clothes and rearranging my closet and my chests of drawers. At first,

Ping asked me to tell them where to put things, but then she decided it would be better if they just did what they thought best, and then showed me where to find things. Works for me. I appreciate so much how they have made me feel like a priority in their lives.

We also got the cell phones this afternoon. After being given essentially free rein in selecting a phone, the girls talked it over and told me that because cell phones are frequently lost or stolen or broken, or technology changes and we want to buy a new one, that they thought it was best to get something that was inexpensive but still state of the art.

With that in mind, they took advantage of a promotion at our cell phone company and each of them got a $200 phone for $20, and I upgraded the same phone that I have been using for $35, and with a two year contract we walked out the door with working cell phones and everyone happy with their choices. Getting cell phones for them was a high priority for me, as I don't want them to be in a strange city without the ability to contact me any time. Even now, they left with our neighbor to visit her home just a couple of blocks away, but I feel much better knowing that they have their cell phones with them.

I guess I am also fortunate in other ways. I showed Ping how to work the washer and dryer and she seemed very savvy about it. She even asked if the Clorox for colors bottle contained the kind of bleach that could only be used on white clothing, or if it was okay to use it on other clothing as well. She understood the importance of not over drying things because they will shrink. I have seen the results of her work and I am very impressed.

I also took them to lunch in Chinatown and they agreed it was just like we were eating in Guangzhou. The food was great. The server even had a Guangdong accent when speaking Mandarin, and with many of the customers she spoke Cantonese. Cici lived in Guangzhou all of her life, so speaking Cantonese comes as naturally to her as speaking Mandarin. She jokes with Ping about not speaking Cantonese as well as she does, but then for Ping it is a second language.

For both of them, their ability to converse with anyone in English seems to be proceeding in quantum leaps on a daily basis. They devour the words on signs, pronouncing them, debating their meaning, and locking them away in their vocabulary banks after they confirm them with me.

May 27, 09:54 PM

Tonight we went to dinner to meet one of my closest friends. He is also one of the top partners in one of the large international accounting firms, and he runs their alliance program worldwide. He travels a lot, both domestically and internationally, and meets a lot of people. His company is a client of my law firm, so we had business as well as personal matters to discuss.

Ping's experience in business really shined at the dinner. Her graciousness as a hostess was also fantastic. She had my friend laughing and enjoying himself immensely the entire evening. She participated in discussions about world events, economic issues, strategic thinking at a global level, and traveling to other countries. There is no way that anyone would have believed that this is only her 4th day in America.

Something else that showed me her character also happened. We ate at a Malaysian restaurant. The young Chinese lady who took care of our table spoke very good English. When I asked Ping to help us select things from the menu, which was written in both Chinese and English, she politely asked the young lady in English if she spoke Chinese. When the young lady responded in Chinese, both of them looked at each other in amazement. She spoke in the dialect of Ping's home town in China, and it turned out that they are originally from the same place.

For a few minutes they spoke with each other with growing excitement, and my friend and I could tell that they had really made a connection with each other. As we left the restaurant, Ping called the young lady aside and obtained her name and telephone number. She told me in the car that she senses that this is a kind lady with a lot of substance, and she wants to remain in contact with her.

I was impressed because Ping didn't judge this lady by the job that she is currently doing in America. She looked beyond the labels and found someone who she believes could become a good friend in the future. I am very happy to learn this about Ping, because there was a time in my life when people had to look beyond the labels and believe in me before I could believe in myself.

May 28, 08:12 AM

Cici finally slept for a long time, from about five o'clock yesterday afternoon until four thirty this morning. She just bounced into our home office fresh from the shower, a big smile on her face, and ready to talk. It turns out that she and Mama were up at three o'clock yesterday morning working, and they started again at four thirty this morning. But she couldn't be happier. They even went outside and watered the magnolia tree this morning before daybreak.

Now you can believe this or not, but I think having my girls here has impacted my blood pressure in a significant way. I have no other explanation for the low readings that began after we arrived at our home. First it was 114/76, but it has trended down since then, and this morning it is 99/71. Trust me when I say that my blood pressure has never been this low.

Our home environment is so relaxing. These girls laugh and sing while they work. They walk through our home with a skip and a bounce in their step. When I am here they always stop and talk with me about things. I have to say that there is not a hint of the type of behavior that some have warned about, and certainly none of this mop slapping stuff that some American men talk about with their Chinese wives. They are very easy going and helpful. They ask questions and then handle things on their own, but in fact there have been very few questions.

So what about those clothes that they rearranged for me? Well, I didn't ask to be shown where anything is located. I just opened the drawers that would have been the logical place for me to find something if I had put them away, and there they were. I can't say yet whether this will be true of everything that was put away for me, but it is a good beginning.

When our neighbor came to visit yesterday I wondered where all of the slippers that had been on the floor near the door were located. I had bought a small trunk looking box with a long tassel in front some years ago just to use for decoration. It has been on the floor near the front door, with a couple of smaller "boxes" on top for decorative effect. This arrangement has survived the redecoration of our home, but the trunk is now serving a useful purpose, I learned. Ping found it to be the perfect place to store the shoes that visitors to our home will wear.

I have also learned a few things along the way. Socks should not be washed with other clothing, for example. In fact, dirty socks should not be put in the same hamper with other clothing. It turns out that there is a small pocket on the side of these web hampers that is the best place to put dirty socks. Hmmm, I wonder if they were made in China?

We plan to be married in three weeks in a small open air chapel that is located at the edge of a cliff in the hill country part of Texas. So that we can meet the "requirement" that we marry on a day that is good for us (China time), we will marry between 9:00 a.m. and 9:30 a.m. on our wedding day (local time). We will be at the wedding site early enough to have some wedding photos taken with the sun coming up over the horizon. This will just be a small private ceremony, and then we will invite others to wedding receptions in different locations on later dates.

Since we have already had many, many wedding photos taken with Ping wearing the white wedding gown of her dreams, for our wedding ceremony she will wear a Chinese cheongsam (qipao) that she had made for her in Guangzhou. The colors are so beautiful, and I love the way she looks in it. It should make for some great wedding photos.

May 28, 04:26 PM

You may not think this is much of a story, but I think I found another way to bond with Cici. In the process, I found Papa's little helper.

Ping asked me if I could put something on the back wall of Cici's closet so that she could hang her large carrying bags. I bought one of the wall mounted boards with half a dozen double hooks on the front for hanging things. I asked Cici to show me where and how high she wanted it mounted. I used a level to make it straight, and marked the holes with a pencil. She was fascinated by the level, so I explained to her what we were doing.

I brought in the drill and drill bits, the hammer and screwdriver, three plastic screw anchors, and three screws, plus an extension cord. She was right beside me asking questions. She had difficulty plugging in the extension cord to the wall socket, so I explained how one prong is wider than the other prong, and you must check to be sure you are putting each prong into the correct sized hole in the socket.

I put in the drill bit and tightened it in the drill, and then tried to plug the drill cord into the extension cord. It wouldn't go all the way in, so I was pushing as hard as I could. Now I swear I had put it in correctly, but Cici said, "Papa, you have it in wrong, that is why it won't go in". I said "No dear, I think I have it right", but she insisted. I checked and she was right. I reversed it and it fit right in. I think that might have made her day.

She had initially handed me the screws to put directly into the wall after I marked the spots, so I explained to her that they would rip right out of the wall if we did that. I explained the purpose of the anchors and showed her how they worked. She watched me drill the holes and hammer the anchors into the wall. She held the board while I placed the screws in the anchors and tightened them. Then she disassembled everything and helped me put it all away before skipping into our bedroom to tell Mama about our success.

Well, she also told Mama that she had to correct Papa when he couldn't plug in the drill. That's okay, I had it coming.

May 28, 04:48 PM

I started looking at what we will need to take with us to get a social security number for Ping. I realized then that I wasn't very diligent when we cleared immigration. We were having such a good time with the immigration officer that I didn't notice that he didn't attach or give us the I-94's with our passports. That is a critically important document that must be in their passports at all times. It also has a number on it that must be used when applying to adjust their status and obtain a green card to remain in America.

I called Customs and Immigration at the airport yesterday and then again today and finally got an answer from the Chief Immigration Officer at the airport. She gave me the telephone number and extension in Houston, and the title of the person who could help us. I spoke with that person today and she said no problem, just come by her office next Thursday and she will give us the I-94's, but that in the meantime there is no reason to be concerned because they are in the country legally as long as their passports reflect the entry, which they do. That much I did check before we left the immigration officer at the airport.

As soon as we have the I-94's in hand, we will go to the social security office to take care of the Social Security Number. There is an office within walking distance from my office, so this should be relatively easy. I have already printed and will take with me the internal rules about the issuance of Social Security Numbers to K-1 Visa holders.

May 28, 07:16 PM

Well, the two who have been working since well before dawn today had to succumb to the sleep monster for a little bit. Cici is in love with her bed and her bedroom. Ping was teasing her when she saw her climb into bed, but she lay down beside her. They are both still in their house coats. They never stopped working long enough to change.

They giggled and talked like two school girls in the bed. Ping called me in to sit next to her on the bed so we could all talk. They sometimes are so funny that they keep me in stitches. This was one of those occasions. I slipped away when they fell fast asleep.

There are some scattered but large drops of rain falling on the roof, and they are making even more noise on the skylights in our home office and kitchen. The sun has dropped behind the clouds near the horizon. The squirrels that are usually playing around our home are hiding from the rain, which just increased to a steady downpour.

It is peaceful and quiet in our home as I gaze out our window and think about these past few days. I never imagined that my life would be changed in such a dramatic, positive way when my girls arrived. The best I could tell, they never had a moment of doubt once we got to know each other.

May 29, 09:54 AM

This morning when I returned from Starbucks I heard laughter coming from our bedroom. Cici was in our bed with Ping and they were savoring the feeling of knowing that their hard work the past four days gives them the leisure of taking a day of rest. They looked so comfortable and happy under the white feather comforter. Cici said that she had come looking for Papa, and when she didn't find me in the house, she joined Mama in bed. Such close friends, these two are, that everyone thinks they must be sisters rather than mother and daughter.

Breakfast and dinner are family time for us at the dining table. The table is next to a floor to ceiling window that spans the entire wall, with the atrium patio on the other side of the glass. The potted trees and plants on the patio looked quite happy this morning after the rain last night. Bowls of congee, fresh strawberries, and Vietnamese barbeque pork sandwiches were our breakfast this morning. The girls like to have cups of fresh milk, to which they add some of my Starbucks coffee.

We were talking at the table after we finished eating, but I needed to shower and shave and come to the office so I said "excuse me," as I got up to leave the table. Then I explained that in America, when we leave the table at a restaurant or even in our home, it is the polite thing to say to others at the table. Ping asked what they should say in response, and I said that they don't have to respond.

So we practiced, as we do with everything that is new to them. I gave another example, "Excuse me, I will go to the restroom." Ping said "Bless You," and we immediately started laughing together. I knew she understood the humor in her response when she added with a laugh, "Enjoy your toilet." What a great sense of humor.

Well this is working just the way I had hoped it would work. Before I left for the office Ping said that next time I should take her and Cici with me. I told her I would come back today and take them to lunch if they would enjoy doing that. They agreed, but as I was driving to the office Ping called me on my cell phone to say that our neighbor, Lily, had called. She had arranged to take a long lunch hour from work today, and she invited Ping and Cici to go to lunch with her. Ping asked if she and Cici could change our lunch plans. I said of course, because this is a chance to spend some more time with Lily, so Ping said she would call Lily back and accept the invitation.

Little did I know, on that morning about a year ago when I stopped my bicycle to introduce myself to Lily when I saw her walking in our neighborhood, that it would actually lead to a friendship like this between her and Ping, and that Cici would have another surrogate mother much like Ping's older sister. We are so very lucky.

Last night as we lay in bed with Ping's head on my shoulder, we talked quietly about our life together. She told me that she and Cici love everything about our home and our family, and that they are both very happy in America. She has begun to walk up behind me when I am at the desk in our home office, or at the dining table, put her arms around my neck, squeeze me tightly and kiss my face. Then she just holds me for a while with our cheeks together. She doesn't have to say a word. I know exactly what she means.

May 29, 01:53 PM

If you saw us together, you would likely think we have always been together as a family. At the cell phone store, Cici put her arm through mine just the way Ping does it, and walked through the store that way with me. Sometimes she puts her arm on my shoulders and around my neck. Sometimes she just holds my arm or my hand. Always she reaches for her Papa to be sure I am with them, and always the smile is on her face and excitement is in her eyes. She has become my daughter at her own pace and by her own choice. I know how lucky I am.

May 29, 02:54 PM

One item that I didn't have on hand for Ping to use was a pressure cooker. Bad Leelee! She prefers to use one when she makes congee with whole grains because she can cook them much more quickly.

Cici and Ping also love congee, so we will likely eat some variation of it every day. Since we all like whole grains, and they are so good for our health, we will eat a lot of it prepared with them. I will therefore make sure Ping has a pressure cooker today. Maybe I should present it with a few flowers?

May 29, 06:41 PM

I just ate one of Ping's great meals. It was unbelievably good, and as healthy as they come. Mostly vegetables, with some tofu mixed in one of the vegetable dishes, and a primarily broth soup with just trace amounts of some black chicken in it. Now Cici is doing her self-designated job of washing the dishes, though Ping and I always help.

Ping just informed me that the three of us will go play tennis in about half an hour so we can work off the calories. There is a new sheriff in town, and she lives in our house....

May 29, 09:26 PM

When I arrived home today, Ping greeted me at the door with that big smile of hers and a kiss. She was wearing her apron and preparing our dinner. I began to unload the things I brought home with me, and Cici came running into the kitchen to join us.

I had a couple of colorful kickboards for them to use in the pool and the ocean, some picture frames for a few of our many pictures, and a round hour glass shaped (with the middle still pretty thick) small table or stool with irregular shaped tile pieces inset in the top. It has beautiful hand painted flowers on the top and on the sides.

I also had the pressure cooker for Ping, a new flat pizza cooking pan with holes in it, and a new apron that says, "Born to shop. Forced to cook."

They both loved what I brought home, but Cici chastised me for spending so much money. She began to tally it in her head by estimating the cost of each item. I told her I would make it easy for her and handed her the receipts. "What? Papa, you can't spend that much money!" "But Cici, I only spent money for you and Mama, not for me." To which she replied with a smile, "You are welcome, Papa."

Ping told me we should go look at Cici's room. She had been working on it all day, lovingly removing all of her stuffed animals from 4 banker's boxes and placing them in her room. She has a tall ladder bookshelf that was just perfect as a place for her to put many of the stuffed animals. These are her treasures. Many of them were given to her by her friends and classmates after they knew she would be moving to America. I have learned that each one of them has a story behind it, and she loves to tell me about them.

Two of Cici's stuffed animals ended up hanging on strings attached to suction cups on the glass portion of our double front doors. She was proud of her efforts, and they actually look very nice there.

After I got home, she asked to borrow my car keys. I didn't ask why, but after a few minutes she came and got me. She had put a large, more or less round, but rather flat shaped stuffed animal that looks like the head of a bear in the driver's seat as a lower back support for me. She then asked me if she could hang a stuffed Eeyore donkey from the rear view mirror. Can you guess my answer?

Well, after dinner we played 45 minutes of tennis and spent an hour walking through the neighborhood, so I feel like I had a suitable workout. We have talked about walking hand in hand through the neighborhood almost since the day we met, so this was another part of our dream coming true.

Ping is quite athletic. She has better technique than I have on the tennis court, and she can definitely keep the ball in play. I feel bad because she broke her 3 day a week exercise regimen just for me for the past 6-8 months so we could talk on MSN every morning and night. Now she is anxious to return to her accustomed level of fitness, and she intends to take me along with her.

It is Friday morning in Guangzhou so Ping is laughing as she sits in the recliner and talks with family and friends back in China. Cici and I are recovering from the workout. We are all in our home office while a last load of laundry that Cici started before we went to work out is spinning around in the dryer. Cici just brought in a plate of cut up watermelon to share with me.

This is the American dream, and we are living it together.

May 29, 11:11 PM

Except for the one event, I don't regret for a moment the second guessing that I put myself through before Ping came to America, and my admiration for Ping grew every day because she was as solid as a rock about our love. She told me from the very beginning that once she made up her mind, it would never waver, never change. She has proved over and over again to me that she meant what she said.

Frankly, a large part of the comfort I feel with Ping came from the passage of time, and seeing how our relationship grew stronger the longer we waited. There was a marked difference in our relationship on each of my four trips to see her. She could feel it and I could feel it.

Our relationship was severely tested at one point, but not by something either of us said or did. We held together despite everything that happened, and like steel that is put into the flame, our relationship only grew stronger. That is when I knew for sure that Ping would not lie to me or use me. That is when I knew for sure that she would always love me.

This evening as we walked through the neighborhood, Ping showed me some things that she wants to do to our home. Things that will take many years before it will accomplish what she envisions for our home. She is making long range plans for us here and in China.

The girls just called me into the kitchen to help prepare and eat another pizza. As Ping stood beside me taking bites off the slice of pizza I was holding, she held me close to her. We talked with Cici and enjoyed being together. There is no pretense in Ping. What she says and does is genuine.

I am at peace because I know we will always be together.

May 30, 07:55 AM

Well we did it. These hard working girls slept through the night and they are still sleeping this morning. No naps yesterday. Their bodies are on Houston time. Now I can be the first one up in the morning and not feel like a slacker all the time.

Our enterprising daughter noticed that our car needs to be washed, and after asking how I normally get it washed, she proposed to take over the responsibility for washing it, but with a more beneficial economic arrangement for me. I hate going to the car wash, so I like her proposal.

Now I won't take advantage of her of course, so she will do quite well in this arrangement, and I won't have to waste time at the car wash. I bought everything she needs to handle this job, which she and Ping tell me will start this evening. Somehow I suspect that Mama intends to make this a family project because it is another way for us to get some exercise.

One of the many benefits of having my girls here is that they help me decide what to wear each day. Only those of you who are color challenged like I am will truly appreciate what their help means to me. I do fine if you stay with primary colors, but when you start blending and mixing and calling the results funny names, it is very difficult for me to know what goes with what. I therefore memorize certain combinations of shirts and ties and coats and slacks and suits, and just go with what I have memorized.

No longer. Just like they debate selections on the menu, they debate the selection of just the right tie. They have come up with some combinations this week that I really like, and they must know what they are doing because I have received a lot of compliments. At first Cici was dumbfounded that I would wear a coat and tie or a suit and tie on these hot, humid days in Houston. I told her that sometimes I just wear a short sleeved shirt, but on days when I have important client meetings or go to court, a suit or a sport coat and tie are like a uniform.

That new lumbar support that Cici put in my car seat yesterday evening sure felt good this morning when I drove to Starbucks. How did she know? The fact that she would volunteer one of her beloved stuffed animals to help me means a lot. I think we may have some affection running in both directions here.

Ping is up now and is sitting with me in our home office. I handed her the Chinese telephone directory, which is more than 2 inches think, and she is going through it with great interest. I know she wants to find a place where she can go when she wants to get her hair trimmed and so forth, which is why I gave her the directory.

I know that Ping held an important position in her company, and I know that they tried right up until the end to convince her to stay for a few more months. I know that they are at the critical stage on an important project. Some of the phone calls she made last night were business related, as she has continued to help her company on a few important issues. She is helping them even though she is no longer eligible to receive the rather substantial bonus (more than a year's pay) she would have received if she had agreed to stay a few more months. She said that our family, not the money, is more important. I agree. I also believe that if you help others unselfishly like she is doing, it is the right thing to do, and it usually comes back around.

So, sounds from the kitchen now as my beautiful bride to be starts her day. Last night in bed she told me about some of the many phone calls that she made to family and friends and colleagues last night. I couldn't understand her words on the telephone, but I could see her animated expressions and her happy face. I could also hear the excitement and enthusiasm in her voice. It made me feel so good when she told me that she told all of her family and friends and colleagues that she is so happy here because she has the best lao gong (husband) in the world. Then we went to sleep in each other's arms.

May 30, 02:08 PM

Well I picked up the girls and took them to lunch at my favorite little dim sum restaurant in Chinatown. They devoured the food and said it tasted like we were eating in Guangzhou. In fact, they were asked by our Chinese neighbor yesterday at lunch how they feel about Houston, and they told her that they feel very comfortable here because they feel like they are still living in Guangzhou, except better. My strategy of inundating them with trips to Chinatown seems to have worked.

The lady who runs the dim sum place knows me because I go there at least once a week. She has seen our photos and has been waiting for Ping and Cici to arrive for the past 9 months or so. She made them feel very welcome. This will also happen when we go to see our family doctor and our dentist in Chinatown. Their entire office staffs are looking forward to meeting my girls. I feel like I have laid the foundation of a good network in the Chinese community for them here in Houston.

I am not the only one who understands how to build relationships. That is something that Ping understands exceptionally well. Our Chinese neighbor brought another Chinese lady to the lunch with Ping and Cici yesterday. By yesterday afternoon, I had received a telephone call from the second Chinese lady's husband regarding some business matters where I can help him. This certainly fits with my vision of Ping serving as our law firm marketing director if that will make her feel fulfilled and happy. We will be able to spend more time together this way, and Ping won't have a chance to feel lonely.

May 30, 07:19 PM

Safety issues

We decided to buy another piece of bedroom furniture, so I handled it by telephone. They delivered it this afternoon when I wasn't at home, so Ping had to handle the matter.

Before we ever left China I spent time teaching Ping and Cici about 911, and we reviewed it again yesterday and today to be sure it was fresh on their minds.

I told them to instruct the delivery men to place the item inside our front door, but not to allow them to take it into our bedroom, and to call 911 instantly if there was a problem. I also asked Ping to call me when they arrived and tell them she was talking with her husband on the telephone when she opened the door.

With those precautions in place, she handled everything beautifully. They needed a signature, so she asked if she should sign her name or her husband's name. They said to sign her husband's name, so she did. Cici asked her later how she was able to sign my name, and she said that she signed it her way, not my way. A little confidence. That was enough to take care of the issue.

"What is this?" she asked. "Those are shotgun shells" I replied.

"What are they for?" she asked. "See this? This is a shotgun. If someone breaks into our home, or tries to break into our home while we are here, I will use this shotgun and these shells to protect our family"

With wide eyes she uttered "Really?"

"Yes darling, this is Texas. We are allowed to protect our homes and our families here."

"What is this?"

"These are bullets for this rifle here. This is what I will use to protect our family if the shotgun fails me"

"Okay. Good Leelee."

May 30, 09:31 PM

Well, "we" finished washing the car. This was a new experience for us, but we brought a willing attitude and enthusiasm to the job. I am told that this will be a weekly family project. Good exercise and good chance to work together as a team.

Hmmm. Okay, now let's agree not to be like Linus picking daisies in the outfield during the baseball game. That means that the hose is for spraying water on the car, not up into the trees. If you want to know why you got bit by so many mosquitoes and I didn't, it is because they were dive bombing you from the trees. But hey, you looked a heck of a lot better picking daisies than I did washing the car, so I am not complaining.

Even the garage floor got a good scrubbing. Because we worked so hard, Cici and I were given a "pass" from walking this evening, with the warning that we will be back on the path tomorrow evening.

Zibo Soup for dinner, along with several kinds of vegetables. No meat allowed, because we had some chicken feet and small steamed pork ribs and vegetables for lunch. I named it Zibo Soup because Ping said it is her home town soup. That would be Zibo City in Shandong Province. A nice light tomato broth with little chunks of tofu, eggs swirled in it like egg drop soup, and vegetables. Cilantro helped give it a distinctive flavor, which I liked very much.

I was sentenced to the shower immediately after we came inside because I was dirty and sweaty and the air conditioning was bad for me. Now the girls are having their turn. It takes them just a "little" longer to shower than it takes me. The two hair dryers that I bought for them before they arrived have been a big hit in their bathrooms, so they don't have to take turns after they shower.

If they finish quickly enough maybe they will want to run to Baskin Robbins for a quick treat. I haven't tried that one on them yet.

May 31, 07:29 AM

Saturday morning in my new world. What a difference!

It felt "delicious" to lay there in bed with Ping this morning, and it was tempting to not get up, but Starbucks called. She understands this is something that I do because I was too lazy to make coffee here before she arrived, and I don't expect her to get up to make coffee for me now. I know she would do it anyway if I showed her how to operate the coffee maker, but this is something small that I can give back to her. A little extra time in bed each morning after all her years of hard work in her career.

Our home is kept in immaculate condition now. These girls are very organized and clean. All the clutter that is typically found in a home has found a place out of sight. So far the wall rack in our home office that holds my two cowboy hats and some of my many baseball caps, as well as the bridle for my horse, has survived the redecorating. Maybe it will be gone tomorrow, or maybe this is my man space that won't be disturbed. While I wasn't here one day Cici put on a pair of my cowboy boots and one of my hats and told me she loved the way she looked. Next time I need to be here so I can take pictures of her.

Stepping into the garage this morning to be greeted by a car that was clean inside and out, and a garage floor that was clean and tidy, felt good. My tools are cluttered, though. I have many tools, and many of each tool in some cases, and I should organize them better to reduce the clutter. Cici stood there last night picking up one screwdriver after another, every size and shape and purpose, and laughed.

But because for every task they have assigned to me I have had the tool to handle the job, they have quickly understood and accepted that there might be a reason for all those tools. Need a screw or nail of any size? Got it. Need a bolt and washer and nut, or wire to mount pictures, or picture hanging devices, or light bulbs of all types and sizes? Got it.

These two girls haven't had a man in their lives, but they have welcomed me like a duck welcomes water. Sometimes I teach them things, and sometimes they teach me things. Always we fit together like peas in a pod. In all the time we have spent together in China, and in the week we have been together here, there has never been a moment of tension. We haven't had problems communicating with each other. We all enjoy eating the same things. We enjoy our time together but we give each other space.

Last evening I sat in our living room for a few minutes. From where I was sitting I could see all the way through the adjoining sitting room, and through its floor to ceiling glass wall on the far side, and across the small patio atrium, through the floor to ceiling glass wall on its other side, across the breakfast area and the counter that separates it from the kitchen, into the kitchen itself.

There I could see Ping working, like poetry in motion. She wears that new apron I bought her, and she almost seems to float around the kitchen as she works. This is a woman who has inner peace and beauty, with outer beauty and a happy, radiant personality.

I no longer wonder why Ping chose me. I know why she chose me. We fit together in every way. She was smart enough to know this long before I was willing to accept it, and she was so right. We have the kind of relationship that one can only dream about and hope for, never expecting to find it. But here we are. Here we will stay. We love our little family, and we love each other. It is Saturday morning in Houston.

May 31, 07:49 AM

I have to add a post script to my Saturday morning post.

I went to the kitchen to heat my coffee in the microwave and I could hear my girls talking and giggling in the master bedroom. I went to the door and saw them snuggled under the comforter.

They saw me and called me into the room, then told me to join them under the comforter. Fully clothed, I lay beside Ping and she pulled me close. I had my left arm across her, above the comforter. Cici loves to play with the hair on my arms, so she started playing with it around my elbow. We all laughed and talked for a few minutes, and then I went to get the camera. Cici jumped out of bed laughing so I couldn't take the picture, and they came to our home office with me.

Now Ping has discovered for the first time, with my help, how our recliner really works. She has it fully reclined with her eyes closed. Now there is Cici beside her, in the recliner. I think this might be their new favorite spot in our home.

May 31, 12:12 PM

This morning as we drove out of our neighborhood we saw an elderly lady down on the street, like a turtle on its back, struggling but unable to get up. As we got closer we could see blood on her shirt and on her face. We stopped the car and got out to help her. She was bleeding quite a bit from a cut on her chin. Her walking cane was off to one side of her on the street.

We live in a quiet neighborhood with no thru streets, so there isn't much vehicular traffic. Because of the relatively early hour on a Saturday morning, there was no one out walking either, so she had bled a good bit in the street. We had facial tissues in the car and the girls used it to stop the bleeding. The lady said she takes chromium so she bleeds more than would be usual.

We helped her to her feet and she said that this has happened before. She looks to be at least 80 years old and lives alone, though she has a neighbor who looks in on her regularly. The neighbor wasn't at home this morning, but the lady insisted that she was fine once we got her back inside her home.

When we left, the girls were impressed that in America, we would stop and help this lady. They said that in China no one would want to get involved. The girls wanted to drive the lady to the hospital for stitches, but the lady insisted that she would be fine and didn't want to go to the hospital. She asked if we lived in the neighborhood, and was very grateful for our help.

I have seen my girls give money to elderly and disabled people in Guangzhou, and I was happy to see once again that my girls have tender, caring hearts.

May 31, 05:38 PM

These girls have sure made this house their home.

Ping is out on the little patio atrium pampering the little trees and plants. Cici is doing the laundry. We just had a family strategy session in our home office to discuss where Cici will attend school this fall. Cici is wrapped in her favorite little pink blanket that I got for her. Ping fixed some fresh fruit for all of us to share. They gave me a couple of things that need to be glued back together. It feels so good just to do ordinary things like this together.

I try to follow the same route each time we go to Chinatown, and the girls are beginning to recognize how everything fits together. We stopped for lunch at the little hole in the wall Vietnamese noodle place that is my favorite. Uncle Adrian ate there with me once but I don't think he was very impressed with the food. But then he didn't order the noodle soup either, and this place specializes in noodle soup.

Ping and Cici ate noodle soup like I always eat, and they both said it was delicious and they want to return for more. The owner, who has been waiting for almost a year to meet them, came over to say hello to them. He was very gracious, and very pleased to learn that they also love his soup.

Next I took them deeper into Chinatown than they have been before so I could show them Hong Kong City Mall. We visited the stores in the mall, which are primarily Vietnamese, but also some Korean, and to a more limited extent some Chinese. Cici ordered a tapioca flavored milk tea, which didn't sound particularly good to me, but it was very good. The three of us have no problem sharing the same straw or the same chopsticks or spoon or cup or bottle.

As we walked down the center of the mall, Ping was on one side with her arm intertwined with mine. At first Cici just touched my arm as we walked along, gently rubbing the hair almost as though she was asking permission, but then she slipped her arm through mine, just like Mama. I am glad that she feels comfortable doing that.

I am comfortable touching her shoulders or arm lightly now, and I can tell that my touch is welcome, but I am still careful. I want to treat her like my biological daughter, and I can tell that she wants to be treated that way, but I don't want to rush it. With time, I am sure I will also feel comfortable putting my arm through her arm as we walk along.

Cici also talks with me just as a daughter would talk with her father. She just came in a few minutes ago to discuss a telephone conversation she had with Aunt Ella's son about how school in America compares to school in China. He told her that the math he is doing in 8th grade here is the math they did in the 4th grade in China. Now she is sitting here with me eating a cup of yogurt and looking through one of my financial magazines.

This time a week ago we were still in Minneapolis, waiting for the airplane to bring us to Houston. Less than a week later, here we are, feeling perfectly at home together. There has not been one moment of homesickness or regret. All the girls have done is tell me and show me how happy they are to be here in our home.

May 31, 06:52 PM

What Ping has given to me in just the short time we have been here is the unspoken assurance that she is here with me for the duration, and not just for her own purposes. She proves this with everything she says and does.

It is peaceful and quiet in our home as I gaze out our window and think about the past week. I never imagined that my life would be changed in such a dramatic, positive way when my girls arrived. The best I could tell, they never had a moment of doubt once we got to know each other.

May 31, 09:46 PM

I told you that Ping was very athletic, and she certainly showed it tonight. We did our one hour walk, except that for roughly half of the time Ping was jogging backwards beside me as I walked fast with long strides. The other half of the time she was jogging forwards. We also did about 15 minutes off road, going up and down a couple of steep hills near the bayou.

Cici made an appearance, but she moved a little slower and took a break for a while to wait for Ping and me. When we went off road Ping spotted our neighbor Lily through her sliding glass door at the back of her house, so she had to run up close to the door and call to her and wave hello. The word bashful or shy isn't in this girl. They chatted for a few minutes and then we continued on our way.

The magnolia tree at the back of our house got another shower when we returned to the house. Then the wind blowing past the tree felt nice and cool as we stood there talking and enjoying the evening. Ping started singing a little song as she often does, borne of happiness and contentment, and then we came inside. Cici and I headed for our home office and Ping is preparing some fresh mango for us to eat before we shower.

Another world class dinner tonight (according to my taste buds) before we went out to walk. I like the way Ping thinks. No meat, just vegetables of different kinds and rice, plus a bowl of congee with some sweet potatoes in it. There were bits of meat in the noodle soup that we had for lunch, and that is all we need for the day.

Our bathroom has been attacked by Winnie the Pooh and friends. This is the fun part of Ping at play. I gave her a book of Winnie the Pooh appliqués for her birthday last November and she saved them for our home. This afternoon she applied them to the mirrors, shower door, toilet tank, medicine cabinets, and anything else that volunteered itself.

They just called me to the sliding glass door that opens onto the little patio atrium, very excited. They wanted me to see how much the tiny little mushrooms that had sprung up overnight in one of the potted trees had grown, just since we went out for a walk. We are laughing because at this rate of growth, they will take over the patio before morning.

In about half an hour it will be exactly one week since we landed in Houston. We have packed a lot of living into one week, and we have taken a house and turned it into a home. We have taken three people and brought them from different cultures and countries and blended them together into one very happy family. I have not spent even one minute of this time babysitting them. They have taken to America like they were born here, and we are living our dream.

Putting Down Roots

Chapter Twelve

Jun 1, 07:44 AM

Shhhh. The girls are sleeping on this quiet Sunday morning as we begin our second week together in Houston. Ping treasures these extra moments in bed, though she would be up in a second if there was something that needed to be done.

I love the calm way that Ping assesses information, defines the options, and makes decisions. I have been gathering information for months about schools for Cici. Yesterday a final bit of information arrived that eliminated what had seemed to be a good choice if she attends public schools. This particular high school was one of the highest rated public high schools in the area but it had slipped to second tier status and I was trying to find out what happened. Now we know.

Houston engaged in a great humanitarian effort when New Orleans was destroyed by hurricane Katrina a couple of years ago. It provided food and shelter for many thousands of evacuees, many of whom decided to make Houston their home. Not to speak ill of the evacuees, and not to say that they all share the same characteristics, but some of them were not very desirable neighbors. In the part of town where they settled, crime skyrocketed, especially violent crimes.

Well, this formerly high scoring and well regarded high school became a school that is attended by children of many evacuee families. Now the school has gangs and drug problems, and has been described to me as being almost like a combat zone at times. One thing I know for sure is that Cici will not attend that school. A second option, which was never on our list of possible choices, is a perennially low scoring high school with a student population that is roughly 90% Hispanic.

I suggested to Ping and Cici yesterday afternoon that we either pay the roughly $20 K in tuition each year for private school, or buy a house in a location where the high school is highly rated. There is one high school within 10 miles of here that has a 43% Asian student population and the average SAT and other test scores are eye popping. "First tell us more about the other public school option," Ping asked.

It is rare in Houston, as most homeowners only have one choice for a school, but (in theory at least, as we were to soon learn) our neighborhood has three choices.

Our third option is located across the street from the wealthiest neighborhood in Houston, and next to several other of the wealthiest neighborhoods. In fact, the country club sits prominently at one end of a beautifully landscaped boulevard with mansions on either side, and the high school sits prominently at the opposite end of the same boulevard. The joke is that it is the only street that has a country club at both ends. The students come almost exclusively from homes of middle and upper class professionals.

One thing that I like about the school is that uniforms are required. Another thing is that this school offers an

International Baccalaureate diploma, it does have high test scores, and it is highly rated. It is a little less conveniently located for us, and I have some concerns just because of the make up of the student population, but I know many people whose children attend this school. Cici looked at and read everything I found out about the school and she likes it a lot. She especially likes the uniforms because they are not drab colors like she wore at her private school in Guangzhou.

So Ping made a very logical decision. Let's go meet with the school and see if we like it. If we do, this is where Cici will attend school for the coming school year. If during the year we decide to change schools, we will have time to make the next decision about private school or buying another house and moving. Cici nodded her head excitedly in agreement. They really don't want to move from this house.

So this morning we will go meet Uncle Adrian and Aunt Maria and little cousin Alex. Ping wants to see the Pacair range hood that Adrian installed before I order one for us.

We discovered while we were at the airport in Minneapolis that we all like similar kinds of comedy. Quite by accident Cici mentioned the Mr. Bean movie that was released late last year. I bought it as a Christmas gift for my son, because we have watched all of the Mr. Bean skits. Ping and Cici and I laughed so hard that we had tears in our eyes as we reminded each other of some of the funnier scenes from Mr. Bean: the turkey on the head, the blind man on the beach, the three wheeled car, and so forth.

We have hardly had the TV on since they arrived here, but last night I put Seinfeld on while the girls showered. Cici came running into the living room with me and told me excitedly that she watched Seinfeld in China. She sat down on the soft leather sofa, pulled her feet up under her, covered herself with the little pink blanket, and settled in to watch Seinfeld with me. Who would have guessed?

Jun 1, 02:57 PM

Uncle Adrian solved in 30 seconds the lap top power connection issue I haven't been able to solve for Ping and Cici in a week. He had the connector they needed right at his house, so he gave it to them while we were there.

We had lunch in Chinatown with Adrian and Maria and lil' Alex, and as soon as we got back to our home, Cici got on line to check her email messages for the first time since we left Guangzhou.

Now I know we must live under a lucky star. Cici received an email from a Chinese girl her age who became her close friend over the past year when they attended English school together. Her friend told her that she is moving from Guangzhou to America. Cici was so excited that she was bouncing in her chair.

Ping's social network is already working. Her new Chinese friend Shirley, who she met through our friend Lily, also lives very close to our home. She has invited Ping and Cici to her home for lunch and mahjong tomorrow. Another Chinese friend of hers will also be there. The network continues to build.

Jun 1, 04:48 PM

Is this little girl special like her Mama or what?

Now that my girls are using their laptop in our home office, Cici has been sitting just a few feet from me talking with her friends. Ping was in the kitchen cooking so I sat in the recliner for a quick power nap. Within thirty seconds after I lay back in the recliner, Cici was at my side. She spread her pink blanket over me so the air conditioner would not be too cool on me.

I dozed and then woke to a delicious smell that was wafting through our home. I went to the kitchen to investigate and found that Ping has several things queued up to cook for dinner. That smell comes from a soup broth that she has made. Ahh, but where was Ping? There she was, grabbing a little nap of her own on our bed. But now she is back in the kitchen working away. She tells me that the soup broth will take the heat away from our bodies.

Cici is at her computer and just told me that she is talking with a friend of hers who lives in Canada, another one who lives in San Francisco, and another one who will come to New Jersey with her family in December. Oops, here comes Mama to check on my work.

"That is so nice, you have a great Papa," Cici. All I did was use some super glue to repair a couple of things for Ping, and that is the praise I received. Oh, and she was so pleased that the praise was accompanied by the assignment of another little project. This project required the use of a magnifying glass and some tweezers, but I was able to glue one of the tiny little jewels back in its place on one of Ping's earrings.

They aren't accustomed to having a man around the house, let alone a man who will help them with things. Without trying to be derogatory, Ping said that her sister's husbands never do anything to help in the home. She and Cici have seen how I always help with the dishes and take care of any problems in our home, and it gives them a very special feeling, she tells me. Good, I must be doing something right.

Jun 1, 09:43 PM

Ping has a great collection of songs on her laptop. We always listened to them in the hotel in Guangzhou. Now we are listening to them in our home office. She has been working for a couple of hours putting more appliqués of Pooh and friends, dolphins and fish, Mickey and Minnie, and so forth on appliances, floor to ceiling windows and doors around the patio/atrium, and places in the bathroom.

While Ping decorated for us, Cici and I worked together in our home office. We downloaded a lot of information about the school that Cici might attend and went through it together. She is inquisitive about everything, and she seems to absorb the information that she obtains. We were surprised to see that the school offers Mandarin Chinese courses at levels 1-5. It also has ESL (English as a Second Language) classes.

Our life must sound boring to anyone reading about it now, because we aren't doing anything out of the ordinary. Well, we did eat eel for dinner. Ping bought it in a vacuum sealed frozen package. She thawed it in the refrigerator and cooked it in the microwave for two minutes. No smell, and very tender and tasty.

But perhaps that is what is most important about our life now. We don't have any problems or difficulties to report. All that is happening in our lives is that we are enjoying doing things together as a family.

The sounds of Simon & Garfunkel are drifting through our home. Every time one of Cici's friends comes on line there is a "knock, knock, knock" on her computer. We have assembled another large stack of things that we are giving away to a charity when they come to pick them up tomorrow. When we finish a meal everyone works as a team to clean and put everything away. If I sneeze, either Ping or Cici or both say "Bless You," to show they know what to say, or "You are Welcome," to make our little joke. Ping proudly shows the results of her decorating efforts to Cici and me. Cici shows me the puzzle on the computer that she is trying to solve.

Now be honest with me. Don't you wish you could have such an "ordinary" family evening like we are having? I know that we wouldn't trade it for anything.

Jun 2, 06:27 AM

Ping and I always dreamed of living a simple, natural and healthy life, with family as the centerpiece. This shared dream is one of the things we found in each other. That is why we feel such a glow from the life I have described to you.

I got out of bed early to take care of some client matters, since I had too much fun this weekend and didn't get them done. I think best during the wee hours of the morning anyway. I closed the door to the hallway that leads to Cici's bedroom so the light from our home office won't disturb her. I did the same thing with our bedroom door so I won't disturb Ping.

To the outside world, it might look like I am all alone in our home office. What others can not see, however, is how the spirit and presence of these two girls is everywhere in our home. They have placed evidence of their love for me and our family and our home everywhere. The happy frogs, fish blowing love bubbles at each other, and playful dolphins, all portray happy, loving families.

The sounds of fay yah chop-chop, fay yah chop-chop, still ring in my ears. They keep everything clean and tidy, but I can still see the shoes on the little double rack by the front door, all the fresh fruit in the bowl on the dining table, our tea set on the round Chinese table, and their laptop computer in our home office. I can even see Ping's cell phone where she keeps it snuggled next to mine. Most important, I can feel their love as strongly as if they were here beside me, so I am not alone.

Jun 2, 06:20 PM

Mmmmm. The smell coming from that kitchen!! I see winter melon and lotus root and tree ears and mushrooms, among other things.

Ping loves to cook and it shows. She prepares and serves up gourmet quality meals and makes it look easy. The cleaver that I bought probably 20 years ago and never used has come out of its box and its protective wrapping, and has earned a prominent spot next to the knives in the chopping block. I have learned that a knife that is used to cut meat should never be used on vegetables or fruit no matter how clean you think it might be from washing it.

I am filling out an application for Cici to go to private school, because the public school that seemed to be a viable option has a waiting list of several thousand. I talked with Ping and Cici about private school and Cici said "no Papa, it costs too much money." I told her that it is my job to earn money to take care of her and Mama, and it is her job to study hard and get a good education.

She thought about it for a minute, and then held her hand out to me with the pinky finger extended and slightly curled. Her face looked very solemn. I extended my hand the same way and we hooked our pinky fingers together. Our eyes met but we didn't say a word. She smiled and squeezed her pinky finger on mine. With that unspoken promise, she pledged to do her best in school, which is all any parent can ask of a child. Ping put her head against my chest and hugged me really hard. I also received her message.

We have two new matching shiny red bicycles in our garage now. The girls are so anxious to ride them that they were riding them inside the bicycle store. It is a little warm in Houston right now, so we won't ride until later in the evening when the sun goes down. In the meantime, Cici is working on her ability to understand English by watching the Disney channel. Sometimes she laughs really loud, so I know she understands at least the gist of what is happening on the show.

In the meantime, we received an email from my son. He is studying abroad this summer in Argentina. Unfortunately he had to leave three days before we got here, so he and the girls won't meet until he gets back in late August. Even then, he will only be in Houston for two days before he must go back to Austin for the fall semester at UT. Then he will be off to study abroad in Spain for the spring semester next year.

With his travel schedule, they won't have a chance to spend much time together, and that is a shame, especially since Chinese food is his favorite. But he is capitalizing on his bilingual skills in order to position himself for a job with McKinsey & Co. I told him if he adds Chinese to his English and Spanish and Portuguese, he can write his own ticket in business or as a lawyer. Cici has volunteered to help him with Chinese, and she wants him to help her with calculus. They are both wholesome, All-American kids, and they will get along with each other very well.

I hear that Cici has Mash on the TV. Time to spend some more time with my daughter.

Jun 2, 09:52 PM

If you get a chance, do it. These girls had so much fun on their bikes. They had never ridden a bicycle in a place where they could really ride it, so at first they were a little tentative. It didn't take long though before the wind was blowing their hair out behind them and they were doing circles in our big wide streets in the neighborhood. We laughed and joked as we explored the neighborhood together. Every time they saw a cat or a squirrel or a bird, they wanted to go see it.

We rode for an hour and saw maybe three or four moving cars in the neighborhood. So peaceful and quiet, it was almost like there was no one in the world except the three of us. It was almost dark when we decided to come back to our home.

As we rode down the street for the last time, Ping rode beside me and put out her hand for me to hold. We rode that way the rest of the way home.

We got off our bikes and walked with our arms around each other to cool down. I looked at her and said, "Pingping, I think I could live with you forever." She looked at me and smiled, put out her pinky finger, and extracted a pinky promise from me. Then we came inside for a shower.

Jun 3, 09:15 AM

There is nothing quite like lifting the toilet seat and being surprised by a large sticker of Mickey chasing Goofy.

Yesterday I signed a contract with a painter who will paint all the walls inside our home. I got this guy because he has been doing it for 25 years and he does the work himself with just a couple of long time helpers, and they do it all with rollers and brushes, no spraying. He said it will take them about 10 days to do it, but they will move everything themselves, and will take everything down off the walls and replace it when the paint is dry. Just like the two brothers who put Hardie board siding on the outside of our home, this guy doesn't collect a dime until the work has been completed to our satisfaction. I like that kind of confidence in a contractor.

That is no small chore when it comes to the huge tapestry that came from Ping's home in Guangzhou. She calls it our home now, which is nice. The tapestry is the focal point of our rather large living room. It also has special memories for us. Ping sent a picture of it to me very soon after we met, and offered to have another one made for me. That was never necessary, because we soon knew deep inside that one day that tapestry would be hanging in OUR home.

It turns out, rather unexpectedly for me, that the words "our home" are easy to understand, but if we change them to "our house," they might become ambiguous. For anyone who might read my words about private school for Cici, and conclude that I am just being taken advantage of by a smart woman, I would offer a different picture.

In addition to the way she has made me the center of her universe, and the love that she shows me every day, and the way she shuns the needless acquisition of material things, Ping brought to our marriage a great hedge, security, and immediate diversification in our asset base. Long before it became evident that the Chinese real estate market would rise and rise in value, she began to purchase houses.

All those bonuses, which she typically received upon completion of each phase of a commercial real estate project, were invested in real estate, and not stuck in a savings account. Now if we so chose, we could live in China without working, just from the monthly rental income that she receives from these houses.

This is an astute business woman. She told me months ago that she wanted to help pay off the mortgage on this house in which we live, even though she understands that in America people usually carry a mortgage because of the tax benefits. She doesn't like debt of any kind. I wondered at the time how she intended to help, and now I know.

Our little family project this morning has been to complete all the forms that must accompany the application for Cici's private school. She is writing the required essays about what event in her life has been significant and why (rather easy for her - moving to America), and about her favorite book and why (reckon they will have anyone who has read the Chinese book she listed and discussed?).

I have learned some things as we have worked on this project. It turns out that this little girl has won a number of awards in school. We even have the school newspaper with color photos where Cici and some of her classmates took first place in Guangzhou with their musical group. There she sits with ribbons in her hair, playing the zither! She also plays the flute. The zither is rather large, so it is coming to America by itself.

Enough for now. Ping has breakfast ready for us. What a wonderful way to start the day.

Well, just one more thing. In the words of a child. Her essay about the significant event in her life:

"This year I move to America. I think this is the most important thing to me. It decides where I study. Where I work. Where I live. It changed my life."

And now there are tears in my eyes from reading these words.

Jun 3, 12:28 PM

Well the paperwork has been dropped off at the school. It is a very nice school, so clean and uplifting inside. The lady who handles the front office was very nice, and was impressed with how we had assembled all the paperwork for her. Little does she know - this was far easier than preparing to satisfy the Consulate in Guangzhou.

The Headmaster and the Director of Admissions were in a faculty/staff meeting, so I didn't meet them this morning. The school is only 2.5 miles from my office, though, so it will be easy to return. This short distance also gives me a comfort factor with Cici. If she ever needs me, I can be there in minutes.

Now we wait, just like for approval for our visa. One open item is the required recommendation from her math and English teachers at her previous school. We scanned and emailed the forms last night, and our sister in Guangzhou will have the forms completed, scanned, and emailed back to the school here in Houston. It helps that she and her husband both work at the school in Guangzhou.

I was accustomed to going to lunch around eleven thirty each day, but now I go later in the day. Ping prepares a good breakfast, and then sends me out the door with a freshly polished apple and a paper towel so I can eat the apple in the car. The apple is always accompanied by a big hug and a kiss, and then she grabs the broom as I back out of the garage so she can sweep the garage clean again.

Ping once promised me that if I will just focus on my career, she will take care of everything else for our family. She has delivered on that promise in a far better way than I ever expected. Every little thing is in its place. Our home sparkles with cleanliness. My clothes are always clean and neat in the closet, or neatly folded and put away in the chest of drawers.

But it is what happens when I walk back into our home that impresses me most. Ping and Cici both treat me so well, and it isn't because they were lonely or bored while I was gone. They always stay busy doing things and planning things. Their happiness is always very obvious, and they make my life essentially stress free. We owe a huge debt of gratitude to the two people who introduced us to each other. Little did they know....?

Jun 3, 07:28 PM

Yesterday and today Cici and I made the final moves to a comfortable way of walking together. Ping and I always walk hand in hand, or her arm in mine, or our arms around each other. We are very aware that before I was in the picture, she and Cici always walked that way together. We don't want Cici to feel pushed aside or excluded, so at first Ping insisted that Cici stop walking alone behind us, and walk on her other side.

But Cici began to walk beside me, and as I said previously, she slipped her arm through mine as the three of us walked together on Sunday. Yesterday I put my arm lightly through her arm as we walked, but only for a few seconds. Today as we walked together I put my arm firmly through hers and drew her forward with Ping and me. She responded just as firmly by locking her arm in my arm, and we walked that way until we reached our destination. It felt perfectly natural, and it felt good to walk along that way with them because everyone could see that we are one happy family.

Today we stopped in a water store in Chinatown, of all places, and bought the Pacair range hood that we needed in our kitchen. Uncle Adrian told us that we could find one there. We didn't have to wait for one to be shipped to us, and this one will be installed tomorrow.

I also introduced Ping and Cici to one more Asian food market in Houston today. This one is very large and has many international foods. Its fresh vegetable selection and fresh fish selection are especially impressive. The girls were repulsed a little by the rather large live frogs that were for sale.

When we first went in the store, Ping and Cici told me that we didn't need any more food. That was probably true, but it was fun watching their excitement build as they found one treasure after another that they hadn't found yet in the other Asian food markets. We walked out an hour and a half later pushing not one, but two, grocery carts.

Ping is in the kitchen doing what she loves to do. Last night she teased me by saying that maybe I can't really cook, since I haven't cooked for them yet. I will wait for my moment and surprise them. I know what they like to eat, and I am confident they will like what I prepare for them.

Cici and I are on our computers, sitting about four feet apart in our home office. She had a few "knock, knock, knocks" on her computer as a few of her early rising friends in China came on line to write to her. At the food market she spotted the long aisle with all kinds of ice cream. She has slimmed down a lot since I first met her more than a year ago, and now she would be described as tall and slender. She still enjoys good food, though, so she wanted to look at the ice cream.

They were eying the *Häagen*-Dazs, and asked for my advice, so I told them about the little creamery in Brenham, Texas. This is just a hop, skip and a jump from Houston, and they make Blue Bell ice cream, which I think is very good. They asked which one they should try, and before I could answer, Cici spotted the cookies and cream and grabbed it. Good choice! This is one of their very popular ice creams.

Ajax to the rescue! I went to the kitchen to see if Ping needed any help and she was trying to clean the remnants of one of her appliqués from the middle of the range top. It was too hot for it there, so it melted some and she peeled it off. She was trying to clean the discoloration from the stainless steel top with a brush. I introduced her to the power of Ajax powder with bleach and a Dobie scouring pad. It was clean as a whistle in a few minutes. Good Leelee, that is beautiful.

Speaking of beautiful, Cici was teasing Ping because she dressed and looked so beautiful when we went shopping. Ping said she dressed for Papa, and off we went. Most beautiful women crave the attention. Ping doesn't even notice when she turns heads. She was the same way in Guangzhou, which is something I have always appreciated about her.

In the kitchen, because our Pacair has not yet been installed, Ping wraps her hair in a towel Aunt Jamima style to keep the smoke out of her hair. You can't hide beauty and happiness like that, so it still shines through. Cici is helping her now, and I know that another delicious meal will be on the table very soon.

Oh yes, they received their first mail today at our home. The letters (actually just empty envelopes) that I mailed to them from the office were delivered today with the postal service's cancellation mark and date on them. Now let the Social Security Administration try to give us a hard time about whether or not this is their home address when we apply for Ping's card!

The dinner bell is ringing - "Papa, dinner"! "You are welcome, Cici."

Jun 4, 08:29 AM

And just like that it was gone.

But I don't miss it. It was just hanging there collecting dust. "What's this?"

"It is a bridle and bit."

"What is it for?"

"I use it when I ride my horse."

"Do you use it often?"

"No, my horse is 212 miles away."

"Can you show me how you use it?"

Sure, this part goes around the nose, this part goes over the ears, this part goes under the chin, this part goes in the mouth, and you use this part to control the horse."

"Does it hurt?"

"Only if you pull too hard."

"Oh. Can I find a special place to keep it for you?"

"Sure, our home looks a lot better when you decorate it."

"I will keep it for you right here."

"You're welcome."

We have learned the hard way that Cici and I share something in common. Ping tells us that we are just alike, and it seems we are in this way. I bumped my head on the corner of the range hood. Cici bumped her head on the corner of the cabinets.

One evening Ping and Cici were laughing as they described to me how Cici somehow managed to stump her toes on a piece of furniture that was sitting a couple of feet out of the "path" where everyone walks through our home. Cici and I both seem to always bump our heads on the wide Venetian blind that we lower to block the sun from coming into the wet bar area of our home so strongly. We do this when we slide the patio/atrium door open to step outside. It would be so easy to pull the cord to raise the blind a bit, but our minds don't seem to click on that fact, so this happens over and over again. Oh well, we do get a good laugh out of it, and in a funny way it does make it seem like we must be a biological father and daughter.

A small moment of panic last night. The girls were beside me at our desk and Cici picked up a birthday card that had come in the mail. She opened it and looked at it and handed it to Ping, admiring the bright colors. Then they looked at each other with a startled look in their eyes and asked me who it was for. I just looked at them, saying nothing. The card was from our insurance agent, who sends them out to all clients each year, with a reminder that their driver's license might be expiring.

"This isn't your birthday! Cici, what month is this?" Counting the months aloud together in Chinese, they recognized that this is June in America. They talking together rapidly in English.

"We thought this was still May. Oh no Cici, we have to get Papa's birthday present for next week."

"Let's get a cake for him Mama."

"Let's get him to make the cake Cici, he knows how to do that, and it will be more delicious. What do you want for your birthday, Leelee? Do you want Pingping?" Hmmm, that works for me.

Breakfast sounds in the kitchen. We eat like kings, but Ping cooks healthy meals. A lot of what she calls Guangzhou cooking, so mostly Cantonese. But she will also fire up some tasty Sichuan dishes or some home town Shandong surprises. They fell in love with the Vietnamese sandwiches I introduced them to, but when they are served a sandwich it is split three ways. When I asked if we should stop and get more, Cici said no, because we all love them too much and if we buy them all the time we will eat them all the time and we shouldn't do that. She is also quite health conscious. We didn't even break into that Blue Bell ice cream last night.

One of the breakfast sounds is the voice of Ping singing. But we hear that happy sound more often than just breakfast. Even when we walk in the evening she often hums or sings. Sometimes she also exerts a lot of energy when we walk, like last night. She jogged, sometimes in little circles around me, as we walked along. Then she was twisting her upper body side to side as we walked along. She tried to show me how to do it but the laws of physics were against it. Then she was kicking each leg in turn up nearly over her head as she goose stepped along with her head thrown back.

"Leelee, we need to use that medicine that we have in the living room."

I have learned that "medicine" sometimes means machine or equipment, so she was referring to the home gym system that is set up in one portion of the large living room. It seems to be done in a tasteful way, using a screen and plants as a partial divider, and even Ping has not complained about the arrangement. My guess is that the medicine will soon start earning its keep in our home.

Yesterday at the Asian market Ping saw some Buddha figurines, each dressed differently in colorful clothing, and each laughing and carrying different things with Chinese writing on them. She selected three of them, which are now sitting on one of the built-in shelves in our home office. "This is fat Leelee," she says jokingly. "I love them, and I would love you even if you were fat, Leelee." Now try to reconcile those remarks with the preceding paragraph. This is my woman, and I love her just the way she is.

Jun 4, 05:58 PM

It hardly seems fair. I think I am doing my best to make Ping and Cici feel special, but I am just not accustomed to the level of caring that they have brought to our home.

At first, they helped me select a tie, then a shirt and tie. This morning after my shower I saw that the girls had laid out on our bed my entire outfit for the day. The perfect combination of shirt and tie and slacks and coat. Even the socks.

This is something I would never ask Ping or Cici to do for me. Ping added the piece de resistance by pronouncing me to be very handsome when they saw me wearing their selection of clothing. Sure it wasn't objectively true, but it was enough that she would say it and look like she meant it.

Morning and night, Ping also puts the toothpaste on my toothbrush and fills the cup with water for me. I never bothered with the cup before, but now I feel compelled to use it. All I know to do in response is try to do little things that I think are special for them. I took Ping several places today so she could look at different kinds of facial creams and make up, since some of her things didn't make it through airport security. Well they made it through in Guangzhou, and twice in Tokyo, but I think the security lady in Minneapolis just wanted to have something for herself, so she claimed that it couldn't go through security.

I sat down in the cosmetics store in Chinatown so Ping would feel no pressure and could browse at will. As she conversed in Chinese with one of the ladies there, the other lady came over and started talking with me in English. She is from Beijing, and has been in Houston for more than five years. I would say that her ability to speak and understand English is about the same as Ping's and Cici's. I think more than anything she just wanted an opportunity to practice it with me while we were there.

Small world. Our neighbor Lily invited Ping to her home for lunch today. While they were there, Ping told her about our purchase of the Pacair range hood, and where we bought it. Lily said that she is good friends with the lady who we bought it from at the water store. We spoke with the lady earlier this afternoon, and she said that the man will be here to install it around 6 or 7 p.m. today. We wanted to get it done today because tomorrow we need to go get the I-94's for the girl's passports.

Ping tells me that we have been invited as a family to go to her new friend Shirley's home to meet her husband and son and have dinner with them on Saturday. Lily and her son have also been invited. Lily has been divorced for many years, so their family is just two people. Ping asked me to please not plan anything that would conflict with this dinner, because she is excited about going and getting to know everyone better.

I am very happy with this arrangement because I believe that the network of friends with which Ping started, and to which she has added, has kept her from having even a moment of loneliness. Neither she nor Cici has had a down moment since they arrived.

Jun 4, 11:36 PM

This little girl who has come into my life with the woman of my dreams is quite special, and I wouldn't trade her for a plug nickel, as my grandmother used to say. I think my feelings about our daughter have made a good impression with Ping. She showed me an email that she wrote to one of her best friends in Guangzhou, who we spent a lot of time with when I was there. Ping told her friend rather proudly that I treat Cici even better than she treats her, and that Cici and I have become very close.

Now about that Blue Bell ice cream. I had a hankering for some this evening and went to check it out. Some little mouse from somewhere had already been in it, so I carried it into our home office and asked for someone to fess up. Cici raised her hand and laughed, saying that she just had to try it. I asked her if it was good and she vigorously shook her head yes with a great big smile. So I served up just a couple of spoonfuls for each of us in some rice bowls, and I never saw such happy faces.

Our Pacair range hood was installed late this evening. It looks great and works great. The man who installed it is Chinese, and it turns out that he also remodels kitchens. We (Ping) talked with him and he said he can install Corian counter tops and a tile back splash for us with no problem. He certainly knew what he was doing when he took out the old range hood and installed the new one.

Ping was right there chatting him up and getting him to do some things for us that were outside the scope of his installation work, but she wanted to be sure we had an airtight seal on the exhaust pipe, even on the parts that he didn't install. The extra aluminum tape didn't cost him that much, and the good will he generated will probably lead to a larger project for him. It was $60 well spent for his hour of work. It would have taken me two days plus three trips to Lowes and some busted knuckles and plenty of frustration, I am sure.

The girls are getting their showers. Cici has her own shower in her bathroom, but it is in the tub. It is a good strong shower, with a new and very effective adjustable shower head. She used it at first, but has slowly worked her way into using the walk in shower in our bathroom. I noticed that her toothbrush is also in our bathroom. I don't mind, as she works hard to help keep our home looking great.

Cici told me yesterday not to bring the Mexican cleaning lady back any more because she didn't do a good enough job. I think as much as anything she just doesn't want me to spend the money for outside help. This lady cleans the homes of a number of people who I know, and she has done it for years. Everyone raves about the great work that she does, but now she is being held to a higher standard. I will do what the girls want me to do on this issue.

Ping and Cici talked to older sister in Guangzhou this evening, but there were no tears or sadness when they talked. They talked excitedly about everything, and made arrangements for completion of the teacher evaluation forms that we need for Cici's school. Then there was Ping, still working the phone for her old company, helping them through the critical phase of the project.

We don't spend time watching television. Instead we spend most of our time in our home office. Our neighbor Lily showed the Great Wall television package that Dish offers to Ping, but Ping told me we don't need it. She said that when she and Cici watch television, it will be in English, at least for the foreseeable future.

And one last thing for the evening. I spoke with the minister who will handle our wedding. He isn't one of the many fly by night "ministers" that we have in Texas. He actually has a pedigree that includes years of education and study, plus years of experience as the pastor in a large church. Earlier today I spoke with our photographer. I think these guys will do a good job for us. If you have the slightest curiosity and want to see where we will be married, you can find it at www.chapeldulcinea.org. Pretty romantic place, don't you think?

Jun 5, 08:05 AM

Well, sometimes we have to hurt them.

Oh no, here comes the negative stuff, a few of you are thinking. Not what I mean.

With our propensity for incurring little bumps and bruises, Cici picked up a few the other night when she was on her bike. She was riding while Ping and I walked. At one point, she rode up very close to us and was so interested in talking that she literally forgot to pedal, and forgot that a bicycle requires forward motion to stay upright. Over she went. I was standing just far enough from her that I couldn't break her fall.

We got her back on the horse, but she told us she couldn't pedal. She hadn't fallen hard enough to break anything, it seemed. It was dark outside by then, so Ping walked on one side holding the handlebars and I walked on the other side holding them. Cici sat on the bike and we propelled it along until we got back to our home.

Once inside we could see a couple of small scrapes like you would expect to see. Once her shoe came off, though, there was a nasty looking scrape down the back of her heel, apparently caused by the pedal when the bike fell on her with some of her weight on the bike. It was bleeding some, so we cleaned it and stopped the bleeding. Then I got the tincture of iodine and told Cici and Ping what it is, and told Cici that it would sting a lot but we should put it on to prevent infection. She just had her tetanus shot before we left Guangzhou, so no concerns there.

Well, little Cici released the pain from the stinging through her mouth as Ping applied the medicine, but we got it done. Then we bandaged it up for her and put her to bed. She walked a little gingerly yesterday, and after her shower last night we could see that the scrape needed more medication.

This time I got the Neosporin, and again explained what it was and why we should use it. I told Cici that it would not sting. She looked at me with trusting eyes even as Ping was a little skeptical, put some on her finger, and began to apply it lightly to the scrape.

"Papa, you have everything."

"No little one, not everything, but sometimes I have the right things."

"You are welcome."

Papa's little girl always dreamed of having a daddy. I think she found one.

Jun 5, 04:38 PM

We just came back from the local (if you can call something that is 35 miles away local) Customs and Border Patrol Office where we obtained the I-94's that were not put in the girls' passports or given to us when we cleared Immigration in Minneapolis. It wasn't much of a hassle, and I can only blame myself for not paying attention when we cleared Immigration. We were traveling on adrenaline by then, and flying high from being welcomed home, but that is no excuse. I should have caught the error.

I still didn't appreciate the attitude of the local customs officer who acted like he was doing us a favor by not charging us for "replacement" I-94's. There was no point in getting into a head butting contest with him, but I still corrected him each time he called them replacement I-94's. I even made sure I used his name when I said it. Officer.

I don't like it when someone is condescending to my girls. He was warning them that if they lost them again, they would have to pay to replace them. Maybe it was because they are both about six inches taller than him and he was wearing a uniform, so he needed to strut his "power."

There was also an incident at Costco the day after we arrived in Houston. A woman with an attitude told them that they could not stand on the side of the counter where the cart was being pushed through. I was on the proper side because I was paying for things, and the girls were just following our cart. There was plenty of room for them right where they were standing, and I didn't like the way she told them that they couldn't stand there. I just stared at her and told her that they weren't doing anything wrong, just leave them alone. The girls were nonplussed because they couldn't understand a word of what she mumbled.

As we sat there in the lobby waiting for the officer to return with the I-94's, Ping told me more details about the interview in Guangzhou. She said that the Chinese man who called them up to check their papers was saying inappropriate things to her, and asking inappropriate questions. You are so beautiful. Where do you live? Where do you work? What do you do? This was not the Visa officer, so she was guarded with her responses.

After she and Cici sat down, the man asked her to come back up by herself. He said that he had forgotten to ask her if she was a member of the Communist Party. She looked him squarely in the face and told him no, she had never been a member of the Communist Party, and ended the discussion by turning around and going back to sit beside Cici.

Before we went to the Customs office I took Ping and Cici to my office for the first time. The receptionist welcomed them and said that we make a beautiful family. Once we were in my office Cici started looking through the thick law directories and found that we are listed as one of the preeminent law firms in the United States. That word wasn't in her vocabulary yet, so I told her that it just means we do a good job for our clients and have been recognized by our peers as being one of the top law firms.

Well, that pretty little girl started calling me by my last name preceded by mister to show that she was suitably impressed. Then she saw that my son's names are also listed in the law directory as employees of the law firm. I told her that her name can also be listed there if that is her goal and desire. Now she is talking about law school with Ping, and Ping is telling her that she should aspire to do well in school and then pursue law school if that is her field of interest.

I took the girls to the deli in the bottom of the building to introduce them to one of the people who was instrumental in introducing Ping and me to begin with. She came to the U.S. twenty years ago on a K-1 Fiancée Visa, so she knows what we have been through. She counted down the days with me for more than a year. She is about forty-five years old, but could pass for thirty. Ping looked at her and told her that she is a very beautiful woman, which is true. She calls me her brother, and was very happy to welcome Ping and Cici to Houston.

Next stop was for lunch. Another welcoming party there. Uncle Adrian knows this place, since we have eaten lunch there. When Ping saw the name, she said, "This is from Guangzhou." They have a fairly typical buffet, but I try to stick mainly with the vegetables. The Chinese ladies who work there were happy to meet Ping and Cici. They have been waiting for them to arrive ever since Adrian and I showed them pictures of our respective families.

Wow did these girls enjoy eating there. They sampled many things, and then finished it off with a huge plate of fresh fruit. That gave us enough energy to drive to what we hope will be Cici's school, where we went inside and asked permission to look around. The ladies in the front office were very gracious, and Ping and Cici were quite impressed with the school. We even got to watch the girl's basketball team practicing in the gymnasium.

Back at home now, Ping is swirling around us straightening things, just like she did in my office. She served us a lot of fresh fruit when we got home, but now

Cici came in with a huge bag of potato chips. She just handed me a few and said as best she could with her mouth full, "very good."

Just another day in America.

Jun 5, 09:15 PM

Cici has assumed responsibility for feeding our Betta. I "trained" it to look for its food when I would knock on the table. She told me she tried that technique yesterday and the fish immediately dove to the bottom to hide. I told her to develop her own understanding with the fish, and she is working on that. She just ran to our home office all excited, "Papa, it worked. He came and got his food."

Ping is sitting here with me in our comfortable way, maintaining contact with each other while giving each other space. There is always something about someone that drives us crazy after a while, right? Isn't that supposed to be true in all relationships? Your mate goes from your perception of perfect, to the realization that they have little habits that annoy you, to really irritating things. This simply hasn't happened with us.

We have been together 24/7 for extended periods of time on four occasions now. We have been through what is usually a high stress activity for me, at least, which is traveling together. We have been in the rain and the cold and the heat. We have been tired and hungry. We have had work stress and family stress. Not once has any of these things affected our relationship with each other. Now that we are finally together, that greatest stress factor of all is gone - living 8,000 miles apart.

The same is true for Cici. There is nothing she does that is annoying to me. She doesn't have the bad habits that many teenagers have. She is respectful, loving, communicative, and happy. She is funny and fun to be with. She and Ping don't have the type of relationship that many mothers and daughters have, where there is bickering and jockeying for dominance. They enjoy being with each other, and they seem to enjoy being with me.

One thing for sure, we all eat the same things, almost without exception. Most of the time healthy things, but sometimes not. I just made some Coke floats with the Blue Bell cookies and cream. That was a hit with both girls. "Very delicious, Papa." They both like to mimic me, and they do a credible job of it. "Delicious", "yeesss", "unhuhhh", and more. But not in a mean way. Just part of our easy going relationship with each other. It always brings a good laugh, and maybe all these laughs are what make all of us feel so good about being together.

June 6, 08:30 AM

Last fall Ping shipped all of her and Cici's summer clothes to Houston. Before I went to Guangzhou for our interview and to bring them home, I used some of their shoes to learn their shoe sizes, and then bought some house slippers. Most of them are the ubiquitous band over the front of the foot type of shoes. At roughly $5 a pair in Chinatown, I bought multiple shoes in multiple sizes.

I noticed that Ping keeps one pair on the shelving just outside the kitchen door in the garage, so she can easily transition from garage to house. She and Cici also keep a pair by our front door for the same reason. When our neighbor Lily came to see us a couple of days after she arrived, Ping was able to surprise her with the appropriate size of house slippers to wear in our home.

Just before I left to bring my girls home, I saw some cute Karen Neuberger thong type house slippers at Costco, made of very soft cloth. They looked great with the silk pajama sets from the same designer, so I got each of them a set of the pajamas and the shoes. I put the pink pajamas on Cici's bed with the pink shoes on the floor beside the bed. I did the same with the blue for Ping.

They were oohing and ahhing when they say them that first night when we arrived. I have been very surprised by how much the girls love these little things. They even wash the shoes and put them out in the sunshine on the patio/atrium to dry. Then they go right back on their feet when they walk around our home. I think girls of any age sometimes like to feel pampered. I think some girls love to feel pampered all the time. All I know is that the shoes and the pajamas were a hit with my girls.

I made a big mistake. Actually two of them. I set a standard for myself that I can never always achieve, so there will be disappointment at some point.

I am talking about watermelon. The girls love watermelon, as do I. So I selected one using my thumping and listening to the sound method, which works most of the time. The watermelon was a perfect red when I cut it and they squealed with delight. Second watermelon a few days later. Same story. "Papa, you always pick the best watermelons."

"Leelee, Cici and I just love the watermelons you select."

Maybe in the future I should hedge against the law of averages by buying two at a time?

We heard from older sister in Guangzhou last night, and the school will fax the teacher recommendation forms to the school here in Houston today. I will therefore take a few additional things to the school today. Copies of Cici's passports and visas, a copy of Cici's yellow immunization book, copies of the envelopes that I mailed to each of them at our home address, a copy of my passport and driver's license, the white booklet containing Cici's birth certificate and translation, and the white booklet containing Ping's divorce decree and translation - which shows that she has sole custody of Cici.

When the ladies in the front office at the school asked Cici's name yesterday we told them it is Angela. We put her legal name on the application, but there was a space for her preferred name, so we also put Angela there. She will still be Cici or GeGe with us (which are terms of endearment for Cici, who is the only and very special female grandchild in the family).

Yesterday as we returned from getting the I-94's for the girls, I took a different route to our home so I could show them more of the city that they call home. I showed them two of the previous three houses that I have owned in Houston, so they could see the houses, hear some stories about them, and see the neighborhoods. To get to that part of town from the freeway, we cut through a neighborhood that most people in Houston have probably never seen.

A little two lane road bisects the community, and on each side of the road there are the little one bedroom shacks that are occupied by poor African American people. Most of the houses are very run down, and at some of them, there were people lounging on the front porch or in the yard. "Why aren't these people working Papa?" "Well, for some of them, it may be a lack of education. For some of them, it may be lack of desire. Or maybe this is their day off, I don't know." Ping used this as a motivational opportunity with Cici, telling her that this is why she should always study hard and work hard, so she would never have to live this way.

To be fair about it, I also drove them through an adjoining neighborhood, also with many African Americans, where the homes are more in the $150-200K range, although it was sad to see how run down that neighborhood has become. At one time the homes were in the $300-$500K range, an upper middle class neighborhood. But that was 15 years ago. The girls had a lot of questions about why the homes looked overrun by shrubs and sometimes grass, and I didn't have good answers for them. I remember the homes as having well manicured shrubs and lawns. Some of the yards don't even have any remaining grass in them now.

Well, we are back in our little haven, and breakfast has been sounded by Ping. Breakfast today is a delicious soup that is chock full of noodles with a little egg and onion and other things mixed in it. Ping said this is a favorite for Cici, and I have to say it is a favorite for me as well. Delicious, as Cici would mimic me saying.

June 6, 01:16 PM

Good meeting this morning with the Director of Admissions at the school we selected for Cici. I stopped by to drop off the additional paperwork and he was there, so we had an impromptu meeting. He is pretty excited about having Cici there as a student. She still needs to interview with the Headmaster, but I have no concerns on that front. She will charm him, and as the Director of Admissions said, her grades are impressive. There is definitely a space available for her in the freshman class, so we hope we have found her school home for the next four years.

I have a surprise to announce to the girls when I get home today. I think they will be excited about it. My firm was hired today to represent a medical doctor who has invented and patented a medical device that is attracting investment capital and new opportunities for her. She lives in Athens, Texas now, which just happens to be where my cattle ranch that I sold a few years ago is located. I told the doctor that we will drive to Athens on Monday and meet with her on Tuesday.

So now I have a business reason to travel with the girls into the countryside in America. Henderson County, where Athens in located, is where many of the beef cattle in America are raised, and my ranch was a small part of that business. We can visit the ranch, visit my friends who live in that area, and go see my horse and Spotted Jack who still live there.

"Hey Pingping, you know that bridle and bit you just put away for me in a special place? Guess what, we are going to need it next week."

I will see if I can book us a place to stay in a little bed and breakfast in Athens. This will introduce my girls to another slice of America that I think they will enjoy. Then we can rock the world of the farmers and ranchers who eat breakfast in the little cafe near New York, Texas, just down the road a few miles from my ranch. I doubt that many of them have met a Chinese person, let alone a beautiful Chinese woman and girl, so Ping and Cici will cause quite a stir. Maybe this is a chance for Cici to try out some cowboy boots and hat.

With a little luck I will also get the girls up on my tractor for a ride and some pictures to send to Cici's friends and former classmates in Guangzhou. This might also give Cici something to talk about in school this fall when they ask everyone the question, "what did you do this summer?" The three hour drive to Athens will also take them through some awfully pretty country. It will also be a chance for Cici to pop a movie into the DVD player in the roof of our Pilot if she gets bored while we are driving. Then there is always the MP-4 that we bought her in Guangzhou before we left. I think she will be okay.

June 6, 11:48 PM

So where is the fa? Did you know there was no fa? I never knew there was no fa. Why is there no fa? Did somebody take the fa? Or is fa an imposter? Maybe fa is hanging out with ti, because ti is also missing.

So what is all this nonsense?

We have been looking at our options for either shipping Cici's 21 string Chinese zither (Gu Zheng) from Guangzhou, or just buying one here. Apparently, it isn't easy to find a Chinese zither in the United States.

In the process of talking about the zither, we looked at pictures of the school band where we think Cici will go to school. She mentioned that they play Western music, which she can play, but that most of her music is old Chinese music. In old Chinese music, she says casually, there is no fa. No fa? I ask. How can there be no fa? She laughed and said there is also no ti. You are kidding me.

No. But I can force a fa and a ti with my zither by pressing on the strings. So there you have it. Out of the mouths of children. I am learning something new every day.

I don't like drinking water, so I find ways to encourage myself to drink water. One thing I do is buy cases of a Sports Drink from Costco and mix it with water. Ping has noticed this, and this evening I found that she has pre-mixed some for me so that I don't need to do it. Just one more little way she tells me she loves me.

One little way I tell her that I love her is to make the bed in the morning. I know she will make it, but her first priority is always to prepare our breakfast. It only takes me 30 seconds or so to make the bed, but she has noticed and is so appreciative. Another little way to show Ping and Cici that I love them is to dry the dishes and put them away when they wash them. I would feel guilty to sit idly by while they do all the work in our home. I see how hard they work to keep everything just right. They told me that the (former) housekeeper only cleaned the "face" of things, but that they clean the whole body. It shows.

We received email confirmation that the two rooms we requested in a little bed and breakfast for Monday night are available. The house is on an old horse ranch. I passed it at least once each weekend for years when I owned the ranch nearby. It will be fun to stay there, and interesting to see how Ping and Cici will react to the country breakfast that they will serve us on Tuesday morning.

Ping and Cici are working the phone and email trying to help get Cici's Teacher Recommendation Forms to the school here. Fax didn't work, and email didn't work, so they will email them to Ping who will email them to me and I will email them to the school and explain the problem. Maybe they will accept the PDF files even though they didn't come directly from the school in Guangzhou.

We will go to the social security office first thing Monday morning before we drive to Athens. It is near Cici's school, so we might also stop by the school to discuss and try to resolve the Teacher Recommendation issue in person.

Before we left Guangzhou I saw an example of how Ping plans ahead. She painstakingly transcribed the names and telephone numbers from her cell phones into a Word document, which she emailed to me. When we arrived at our home I printed it for her and she keeps her phone list on our desk so she can call friends and family and colleagues and business contacts with no problem. When she talks with family and friends on MSN, she proudly shows them our home by taking the webcam from her laptop and slowly panning the room.

At Ping's insistence we took a short nap together earlier in the evening. As we lay there I told her that I am so happy with her and Cici. She said she is also happy. Then after a little pause, she added, "Very happy!" How could I ask or hope for more? The answer is that I don't have to ask. She just gives it.

At the moment she is modeling each of her lingerie outfits for me while she shows off the black snake bracelet we bought for her today. I liked the bracelet, and it turns out that she has a black snake belt that matches it. The belt can also be worn as a necklace. It is cleverly done because the head of the snake has a wide hook behind it that fastens to the snake's round body at any point. Very versatile. And when worn with lingerie, quite sexy, I might add.

Cici and I were teasing Ping earlier this evening because she has her jewelry lovingly spread out in not one, not two, not three, but four long, wide, and shallow drawers in the dresser and chest of drawers in our bedroom. It is quite a collection. I admire her fashion sense with clothing and jewelry very much. Without me ever telling her that it would be important, she always knows when to wear panty hose. Like to Cici's school, to my office, to business meetings. Then she surprises me wearing nothing but her birthday suit in the kitchen as I walk in the door this evening. What a beautiful and loving woman.

June 7, 02:57 PM

We were awake until the wee hours of the morning working with older sister in Guangzhou, trying to get the Teacher Recommendations here for Cici's school. Ping and I still woke up at seven o'clock and she wanted to "follow with me" to Starbucks. I introduced her to cappuccino, and she enjoyed it very much.

In what seems to be a great testimonial for how far we have come in the two weeks we have been together in our home, Ping and I didn't feel the need to wake Cici to tell her where we were going to be when we left to go to Starbucks. We knew that if she woke up and looked for us, that she would know where we had gone. We also knew she could call us on my cell phone if she needed us for anything. We were literally just two minutes away, and she could have walked there to join us if she wanted to do that.

Then back to our home for a flurry of activity related to Cici's school, and to our effort to buy a Chinese zither for her. I found a website that is dedicated to promoting and preserving the zither and its music, so it is the mother lode for everything we need. We can even listen to a selection of music played on each zither, to help make a decision. Ping jokes with Cici that we are getting the zither for her so that she can play music for us in our home while Ping and I relax and drink tea together.

Our little girl paid us quite a compliment. She told us that she always wants to live with us. The odds are rather high that she will change her mind as she gets older, of course, but right now she doesn't ever want to leave us. Ping said that we want her to stay with us, but when she marries, she should live in a house next door to us. Ping said she will cook for Cici and me and take care of us, so that Cici can also become a lawyer, and then take care of us in our old age.

Ping was about to prepare breakfast for us but I told her we should go to Chinatown to eat dim sum. Really? You are welcome. So off we go to my (and now our) favorite little dim sum place. We all wanted to order the same thing. There is nothing like chicken feet for breakfast. We ordered other things too, of course, and after eating we stopped to pick up some of the Vietnamese barbeque pork sandwiches that we all love.

We saw a slick looking poster that was advertising hair styling services. There was a picture of the hair stylist, and a telephone number. Ping called the number out of curiosity and the man didn't speak Chinese, and his English wasn't very good. We think he must have been Korean. Ping said, "Here, please talk with my husband," when she saw he couldn't communicate with her very well. He told me that he charges $200 for the hair styling services she was inquiring about. We stopped in the salon where he works and Ping talked with the lady in the front in Chinese. She said that they provide the hair styling services in question for $70.

We stuck our head in the door to say hello to our dentist and his staff. They were all in a buzz when they saw Ping with me. The dentist came out to the reception area when he heard we were there. He made sure that Ping met the two dental hygienists on his staff who are from Guangzhou. We picked up a brochure about braces so we could show it to Cici. Now she is excited about what they can do to close the slight gap between her two front teeth, and help make her smile more beautiful.

Now it is nap time for mama and papa while Cici works on her English some more with the Disney Channel.

June 7, 09:58 PM

Two weeks ago at this time my girls didn't know how to do anything in our home. We were still about half an hour from landing in Houston. The next morning they didn't even know how to heat water so they could make some breakfast.

This evening, however, Cici has the clothes washer and dryer working away. She took a shower and blow dried her hair while waiting for the clothes. This afternoon Ping cooked a huge number of steamed dumplings, which the three of us devoured in one sitting. The girls know our home inside and out. Their touch is everywhere, and this house feels like a home. It is a home. It is our home.

This afternoon we did what many people in America did when we watched the Belmont Stakes. The girls are familiar with horse racing from Singapore and Macau. They said that Guangzhou shut down its horse racing ten years ago because of gambling, but it is about to allow it to start again. Now Ping and I are together in our home office making plans for our wedding while our daughter flits in and out of the room, doing little things that are enjoyable for her.

Ping is wearing the yellow silk pajamas that I bought at Victoria's Secret more than a year ago and gave to her on my first trip to see her in Guangzhou. I honestly didn't think she liked them when she opened the package, but now I see that she wears them often.

Now you can believe this or not, but Ping is jogging in circles through our home office, the sitting room, and the front entry area of our home while she is wearing those yellow silk pajamas and wearing a pair of her favorite house slippers. Cici, by contrast, is wearing the little pink blanket that I gave her around her shoulders. She has joined me in our home office while Mama is jogging.

If anyone is still waiting for some indication that we don't really have an idyllic family here, I must disappoint you once again. Every day we spend together has brought us that much closer as a family. Cici and I now have no hesitation about linking our arms together as we walk along, or touching arms or shoulders as a sign of affection. Ping and I are inseparable, yet always ready to spend more time together.

Nothing is a point of contention between us. I didn't shave this morning because we sprung into action right after we got out of bed. I told Ping while she was cooking this afternoon that I would go shave, because I felt bad that I hadn't done it earlier. She asked me not to shave until tomorrow, because she likes the way I look when I don't shave. When I drive aggressively, she doesn't make an issue of it, because she drives the same way in Guangzhou. If I snore sometimes it doesn't bother her at all, she tells me, because she sleeps so soundly when we are together.

I told Ping today that in just 12 more days she will be my wife. She looked me in the eye and told me that she has been my wife since she fell in love with me, and that she didn't have to wait for a piece of paper to make it true. When she talks with someone, she always refers to me as her husband, and I refer to her as my wife. Why confuse the issue by going through a long explanation about how we aren't married yet but we will be married soon.

We no longer dream of spending our life together. We are living our life together and enjoying every moment of it, and we wouldn't give this up for all the money in the world.

June 8, 08:11 AM

They are both eying the white VW New Beetle that is just sitting in our garage. With their high energy levels, I can imagine what they will do with that turbo charged engine once they start driving it. Ping said she will study for the driver's test after our wedding, but she is already suggesting that maybe she should practice driving the VW just in our little neighborhood. I think I would be smart to not jump the battery to get it started for a while.

All is quiet here on a Sunday morning. The girls are sleeping soundly and the house is still. We had another late night trying to get the Teacher Recommendation forms understood and filled out properly. We had older sister send a copy to us first so we could proof read them, and I am glad we did. The math teacher apparently doesn't understand English at all, but fortunately older sister's husband, who is also a math teacher, is able to help us as long as Ping helps him. That in turn means that sometimes I need to help her. At least they gave it a high priority and even worked on it this weekend for us.

Yesterday when we went to Starbucks (this one is located inside of a supermarket), Ping was eying the cakes in the supermarket. I know what she had in mind, but I was discouraging her. Some of those cakes have more than 700 calories per serving! I say serve up some fresh fruit instead. She told me what my new age will be on my birthday in a few days and I told her that she is mistaken. No, she says, I am not mistaken. We will count your birthdays backwards and my birthdays forward until we are the same age. Then we will count them forward together. Hmmm. Now if we could just get our biological systems to go along with that plan.

It took hours to find a place for us to stay in Austin when we go there for our wedding. Ping asked me to find a place where we could all stay in the same suite, but with separate bedrooms. The only major hotel that had suites like that had no availability, but I kept looking. I checked bed and breakfasts but still no luck. I finally found us a place in a suite hotel that I had never heard of, but they had photos and it looked very nice. They had a two story suite with two bedrooms and two baths and a living area. "Perfect", says Ping. "You are welcome."

Today the Whole Foods Market is on the agenda. I want Ping to be able to see the selection of whole grains that we can buy in bulk quantities. She knows millet and amaranth and barley and quinoa and buckwheat and spelt and so forth, and knows that they are good for us to eat. She also knows how to cook them, whether in congee or in other ways. I finally took the time to study the user's manual for the pressure cooker that I bought for her, so I could show her how this particular model works. What ever happened to the pressure cookers with the little metal thing that sat on top of the steam release and jiggled when the steam came out? This pressure cooker will make her life a lot easier by reducing the cooking time on some of our favorite foods.

One of Ping's favorite movies is Phantom of the Opera, in part because she loves the music. We watched it together in Guangzhou while she and Cici were packing the last of the boxes that we shipped to Houston. Yesterday morning we saw the movie on sale for $5 so we bought it. I told her that any movie that we watch over and over again is worth buying, especially at that price, and we don't know for sure that her DVD will play on our DVD player here. That got her mind off of those cakes until I got her out of the store.

The first week we were here we also purchased the entire collection of Sex and the City for the girls because they didn't want to try to bring their street version through customs. It was an investment, but it will help them learn English better, and in a way that they will enjoy. I suspect we will also end up going to see the movie version that recently hit the theaters. I know it is a chick flick, but they take such good care of me that I can sit through a movie like that with them, and even be happy while I am doing it.

Ping keeps a cup of water sitting on the short chest of drawers in our bedroom. Any time that she gets out of bed, she drinks some water. Any time she sees me get out of bed she makes sure I drink some water. She is especially diligent to make sure we drink water first thing every morning when we get up for the day. I know she is right in doing this, and I know I wouldn't do it if she didn't take care of me this way. I snuck right out of there this morning without taking that medicine. Bad Leelee!

June 8, 04:02 PM

Look, look, and look some more, and then you find it. This should be the last piece of furniture we need for our home. Ping found the king bed that she wanted to put in our bedroom. She loves sleeping on our mattresses, so all we needed was the bed. Cici also loves sleeping on her mattresses, and she loves to lie on the big white fluffy dog that I bought for her as a surprise many months ago. It is as big as she is, so she keeps it on the floor next to her bed. Often we will find her during the day lounging on the dog.

Cici stayed home while Ping and I shopped for the bed. That gave Ping and me a chance to talk about her. Ping said that she has noticed that Cici has found her cocoon with our family, so she is reverting in some ways to the baby stage. She almost always has her pink blanket with her, and she loves it when we pamper her. Ping thinks she is recapturing some of the years of her life when she wished that she had a mama and a papa. She also told me that Cici is still a little shy, but she really wants her papa to hold her in a comforting way. We will get there one step at a time, at her pace. Ping said she has never seen Cici as happy as she is here in America with us.

We stopped at a Barnes and Noble and selected a couple of English study books and a couple of math study books so I can help Cici and Ping with their studies. For now we will do ESL studies at home together, and then see if it makes sense for them to go to a school after the wedding. We will do some refresher studies and exercises in math in preparation for the evaluation tests that Cici's school will give her this summer. We will bring her back to her usual level of math proficiency prior to those tests.

Ping just joined Cici and me in our home office. Cici and I are eating apples at our computers. Ping just sat down in the leather recliner, raised her legs, and let out a big ahhhhh. "I enjoy our home so much," she said. "So comfortable in our house. Leelee, our house is very comfortable, huh? Leelee, yes? Lee, yes? Leelee, Leelee, Leelee", again and again with a big laugh, as she asked me to pull the recliner away from the wall so she could fully extend herself on it.

Now under a blanket, she will enjoy a short nap before jumping back up to continue taking care of our home. She told me from the beginning that this is the kind of life she wants to live. She isn't interested in parties or being on the go all the time. She wants a happy and comfortable home life with her family. Cici and I are only too happy to oblige her desires.

June 8, 05:38 PM

And a little more.

I went to kiss Ping's forehead as she lay in the recliner. She pulled me down beside her. But the recliner really isn't built for two, so after a few minutes she said we should go to the love seat in the sitting room. The love seat has a big wide ottoman so we were able to snuggle up together under a big pink blanket that Cici brought to us, and take a short nap.

I got up to continue preparing something for our dinner. Ping moved to the big leather sofa in the living room and I put some soft Chinese music on for her. "Welcome," she said softly with a smile, her eyes still closed.

I found some fresh creamer peas (these are like black eye peas or purple hull peas, but completely cream colored) at the store this morning, and bought some smoked ham hocks to cook with them. I boiled the ham hocks earlier in the day, seasoned the water with garlic powder and seasoned salt, and then added some onions and bits of carrots and celery for flavor. After boiling it for an hour I turned off the heat and let it sit the rest of the day.

Now I have added the peas, and I cut up a potato in the broth to thicken it. When the potato is soft enough for me to crush all or most of the pieces against the side of the pot with a wooden spoon, the ham hocks will be tender and this dish will be ready to eat.

Ping once told me that a good mood gives us a broader sky. On one more thing we agree completely since we have been together, our sky has been as broad as the horizon.

Jun 9, 07:29 AM

At the furniture store yesterday Ping was like a young filly chaffing under the bit. She wanted to roam free, but a dour looking older woman had latched onto us when we entered the store. To say she had a lack of enthusiasm for her job and trying to actually help us would be giving her too much credit. She showed us bed after bed that was nothing like we wanted to see, so we finally told her we would just look on our own.

"Well", she says very haughtily, "this is a very big store. Have you ever been here before?" "Many times", I said. "And I have learned it is impossible to get lost. You just follow the furniture back to the front door." No sense of humor either. "Okay, just give me your card and if we find something, we will tell them you helped us."

"Oh, I can't give you my card."

"Really? Then since we won't remember your name, I guess we can't tell them who you are if we find something we want to buy." Suddenly a card appeared in her hand, but I declined to take it. She had condescended to Ping a few too many times as we walked along.

Then literally within two minutes after we set off on our own, Ping found the bed that she wanted to buy. A minute later she found another one that she liked so well that she ultimately asked me to decide. I went with her first choice.

Another sales lady saw us as we debated the decision. She entered the information in the nearby computer and she got credit for the sale. When we talked about delivery I told her we would be in Athens today and tomorrow. Her face brightened considerably and she said that she is from Athens. Texas, I said, not Greece. When I saw her last name I knew I had surmised correctly. There might have been a letter or two from the alphabet missing from her name. She must be related to Uncle Adrian.

Speaking of Uncle Adrian, he emailed some pictures to us yesterday that he had taken in his home when we visited there last weekend. "Put that one as desktop background", says Ping. Done. "No wait, put that one." Done. "I can't choose, I like them all Leelee. You choose." Done.

Ping has our photos all over our home, and sometimes when she is at the computer she starts our wedding picture video, which is on a loop. Then she just lets it play over and over again. She loves to listen to the music and look at the pictures. She also sat at my computer and looked at every picture in the photo gallery one by one, and there are hundreds of them.

Many of them are pictures that I took of the inside of our home so I could send pictures to her and Cici, but of course I didn't send every picture that I took. "Where is this, Leelee?" "Oh, I gave it away."

"But I love it. Where is this?"

"I also gave it away."

"But why, I love it too?"

We went through this sequence of questions and answers many times

so I finally told her that there just wouldn't have been room for all those things after she and Cici arrived. "That is why I kept saying we should consider getting a larger house, Pingping."

"No Leelee, this is our home." No more questions.

Jun 9, 09:35 PM

"Leelee, can I drive the car?"

"Sure. Show me how to change the seat."

"Okay. Show me how to make it go."

"Okay. Now, go for it Pingping."

"Hey, this is easy. Is that a policeman?"

"No Pingping, that is the mailman. He puts a flashing light on top of his car so other cars can see him."

"What's that?"

"That is a stop sign. Pingping, a stop sign means we must stop." "But Leelee, there were no cars coming."

"This is not Guangzhou, Pingping. We must actually do what the signs tell us to do."

"Okay Leelee, next time."

So you think I have lost my mind? Not really. We are in the country. When the foregoing incident happened, we were on a country road so narrow that only one car could be on it at a time. We had come to a T intersection, and there were no cars within miles of us. But it was a training session nonetheless, so we had to learn the rules.

"What's that?"

"What darling."

"That, beside the road."

"You mean those things with numbers on them?"

"Yes."

"Those are mail boxes. That is where the mailman we saw puts letters for the people who live in the houses."

"Oh. Cici, Cici, look at all those..."

"…cows, Pingping…"

"…look at all those cows, Cici. We are in the countryside."

So we are in a little bed and breakfast in Athens. Earlier this afternoon I took the girls to New York. They didn't believe me at first when I told them we would go to New York, but when they saw the sign they believed me. It could say New York on both sides of the same sign. Really, it is that small. One store - a feed store. Owned by the descendants of the man who founded New York in 1856.

The man moved from Georgia with his wife, four unmarried children, and three married children. They traveled by wagon and on foot with a few slaves to help them. There is a roadside commemorative sign that tells this story. The sign is on the site of the feed store. This is where I bought things for my cattle ranch in Athens.

We stopped at the ranch and visited with the lady who bought it from me. The girls were wowed by the two story log house that sits in the edge of the woods on the side of a hill. A creek cuts deep into the property not far from the house. There is a 3200 square foot barn close by as well. I took some photos of my girls sitting on my tractor, and photos of them with my donkeys in the background. Well, they used to be mine. They were a little scared of all the dogs at first, but they adapted to them.

There is no Chinatown here, just down home country cooking. The girls were ravenous so I took them to a place that I knew would have good food. While we waited for the food, we ate beans from one of the big pots. The girls also ate some of the ice cream that is sitting in the big ice cream tubs, just waiting for people to help themselves.

Our food was something neither of the girls had ever seen. A deep fried chicken fried steak, and a grilled country fried steak. We ordered one of each of the available vegetables. Green beans, corn, mashed potatoes with the skins in them, and french fries. Two house salads and some Texas toast were also served. To top it all off, there were two bowls of country gravy. The steaks were huge, and I knew there was no way we could eat all of that food, assuming they even liked it.

I did the cutting and we all did the eating. The girls weren't big on the gravy, but they used the ketchup liberally. Did you know that you can make great little bite sized sandwiches with Texas toast, ketchup, and chicken fried steak?

I was wrong. Every morsel of food disappeared, and they sent me back for more ice cream!

The waitress was a local girl of about 19 years old. She has never been out of Athens, and had no idea where these exotic looking girls came from. When they said China, she got a far away look in her eyes and said she always wanted to go to China. I was glad I had cautioned Cici before we got to Athens that many of the people here have likely never seen a Chinese person.

Jun 10, 07:31 AM

This old farm house is very comfortable. I got up at daybreak and the rain started falling about the same time. They needed it badly so I am glad to hear it on the roof. It rained some last night when we stopped in the local Wal-Mart (in these small towns that is usually the place that draws the most people, and it is no different here) to pick up some fresh fruit to snack on last evening.

I took the umbrella with us as we started inside and Cici looked puzzled. There was no rain cloud in sight, but I lived up here. I could see the clouds beginning to gather in a way that I thought signaled rain. When we walked out of the store it started to sprinkle, so Ping raised the umbrella over our heads. Good thing. The sky opened up and it poured. Even with the umbrella for protection we got a little wet.

The old grandfather clock in the room where I am sitting just chimed the hour. It is two minutes fast according to the computer. The little dog that lives here just walked through the living room where I am sitting. I left the girls sleeping upstairs, because breakfast is not until eight thirty. Ping thought I was going to Starbucks for coffee and wanted to get up with me, but I told her I was sure they would have coffee ready early here. I was right, and it is good.

When we arrived here yesterday in the late afternoon, only the man was here. The woman does volunteer work with the hospital and wasn't due home until six thirty. He welcomed us and showed us to the stairs, telling us that the upstairs was ours, and that we should also make ourselves at home downstairs. When we got home last night in the rain the woman was itching to meet us. We left our shoes at the door just as we do at our home and she greeted us in the front hallway. So curious, but very nice.

The lady was fascinated to see that Cici and Ping could communicate with her in English. She asked all kinds of questions and they never looked at me for support or interpretation. They injected humorous comments, and were as charming as I know them to be. I knew we were the object of some intense curiosity when the son appeared with the grandson, and then the daughter in law appeared. They just had to meet us. Ping charmed the little boy, who with a little coaching from his father said ni hao to her.

The girls even surprised themselves on this trip. They were thrust into situations where they needed to communicate in English with total strangers with widely varying accents, and they had no problem. Ping even commented on how surprised she was that they were able to talk with everyone. This was a real confidence booster for both of them.

Cici has started calling me by the old Chinese name for father, just as she likes to use the old Chinese name for her Mama. A few days ago I asked Ping how to say pronounce daughter in Chinese. She was working away in the kitchen at the time and thought I had asked her about the word "doctor." So I go proudly to the home office to use my new found ability on our daughter. Cici looked at me very puzzled, and Ping heard me and came running. She was laughing and explained to Cici what had happened.

Well you can guess what came of that. The Chinese word for doctor has become a pet name for Cici. She rather likes it. Cici is very quick and she has an excellent memory. Ping said that the family told her from the time she was about three years old that she should be a lawyer. She always remembered things and corrected everyone, and would debate the issue with them. That topic keeps coming up in our conversations with Cici, so who knows, maybe she will follow that career path and join her Papa in the practice.

I can hear the girls talking upstairs. This is early for them, but they are excited. They couldn't believe it when the owners went to bed before nine o'clock last night. Cici and I went out to the car to get a few things after the owners went to bed. She accidentally rang the doorbell, thinking it might be the way to turn on the outside light. The woman came running in her night clothes, thinking she had locked us out of the house.

I need to end this story and start preparing for the meeting that I came here to attend. Only an hour until breakfast. I plan to leave the girls here when I go to my meeting. That will give them another chance to use their English speaking skills, and they can discover a little more about America on their own.

Jun 10, 06:38 PM

We stopped in the little gift shop where I bought so many things when I owned my ranch. The owner greeted my girls with open arms. Just as older sister says, Ping and I are just alike when it comes to collecting things for our home. We walked out of the store after a nice visit carrying two round silver chickens, one large and one a little smaller. They are a depiction of my two little chickens, mama and daughter. Ping has already found the perfect spot for them in our home.

Yes, we are back home, and these girls are such good travel companions. They talk, they laugh, and they have fun in the car. Cici watched the "Phantom of the Opera" movie on the drive up to Athens. Ping stayed in the front seat beside me, but she learned that if she leans the seat way back, she can also watch movies with Cici. They both took a short nap on the drive back to Houston. They were so happy to be back in our home that they just walked around for a bit looking at everything as though they had never seen it before. Then Ping insisted that I take a quick nap while she sprang into action.

I can hear Ping in the kitchen now. Dinner will include more of the creamer peas and ham hocks that I prepared before we left. It turned out to be a big hit, especially with Ping. Now they are requesting more of my cooking. But Ping is smart enough to know that fresh vegetables are king in our home, and I saw that she is preparing them as well.

Breakfast at the bed and breakfast this morning was presented so nicely and tasted so good that Cici said she felt like this must be the way the President is served. Talk about putting a smile on the face of the B&B owners who prepared and served the breakfast!

My meeting lasted longer than I expected, and when I got back to the B&B I found my girls lounging in bed. Cici in the bed where we slept last night, and Ping in the bed where Cici slept. But they had been out for a walk along the country roads, and they had explored the garden. They quickly packed everything, tidied up the rooms, loaded the car, and we said our goodbyes to the owners.

Ping made sure she wrote a few things in Chinese in their guest book, with the English translation beside them. They are delighted to have added some International flavor to their little place. We were delighted with the bag of fresh tomatoes that they sent home with us, especially since tomatoes have been pulled from the stores because of the health scare.

This was actually our second family vacation together. The first was a trip that we made together to Hong Kong last fall. Next week we are off to Austin for the ultimate family vacation - our wedding.

Jun 10, 10:02 PM

I don't think anything has been as gratifying to me as watching Ping putting down roots. There is a little patch of dirt near the garage where it is very difficult to grow anything. It is heavily shaded by a magnolia tree as well as by the house, and the roots of the tree tend to hog most of the moisture in the soil.

Tonight after our bike ride Ping asked me if I would help her find the light green plant with the large unusual shaped leaves that spread along the ground like a vine that we have seen several times when we walked through the neighborhood. She was lovingly spraying water on some potted trees that she had placed under the magnolia tree, and eying the bare dirt that is just begging for something that will grow on it and hide it.

My first reaction was that we would get to it in time. I told her I would take her to a nursery to look for one. My second reaction as I watched her working so diligently was to think that she should not have to wait. I told her to wait a minute, I will be right back. I hopped on my bike and rode to the house with the vine and got a strand of it for her. I know the neighbor would have given it to me anyway, and it didn't disturb the look of his yard. I brought it back to her and she acted as though I had just fought a grizzly bear for her. She couldn't wait to get it into the ground and water it. We also put several leaves with stems in water to let the roots grow.

These kinds of roots are just a manifestation of the true roots Ping is putting down in America, and those are the roots I am really talking about. When a beautiful woman is down on her haunches getting dirt under her fingernails, I believe it is fair to conclude that what she is doing is important to her. Ping does this almost every day at our home.

I lived here five years before she arrived and I never bothered to do anything with the yard. The men came every week to take care of the lawn and the shrubs and the trees, and that was enough for me. Not enough for Ping. Our home is her piece of ground in America, and she intends to give it all the love she can, just as she is giving all of her love to her family.

Tonight as we rode our bikes, just the two of us, the neighborhood was very quiet. We didn't see a car the entire time we rode. Seven and a half miles of silence except for us talking at times. As we rode up the very wide street where our home is located, Ping looked at me, rode her bike very close to mine, and said quietly in Chinese, and then in English, but using the Chinese word for husband, "You are so nice, Lao Gong."

I felt like I had been touched by an Angel.

Jun 11, 08:07 AM

Some potpourri this morning.

It looks like the big 'ole hat rack on the wall of the home office might survive. One of Ping's wide brimmed hats has been placed on it between my two cowboy hats. The baseball hats on the lower portion of the rack have been rearranged from clutter to red. That is, all of the caps that are red are the visible ones on the four evenly spaced lower prongs.

"Don't be offended," I told the lady at the B&B yesterday morning. "Your towels have not been used, since my girls bring towels for us wherever we go." Not a problem. The lady told Ping that she had saved her some work, but she did say proudly that her towels are big and fluffy. I know they were. I saw them. It doesn't matter, because Ping will take care of her family her way.

The wedding bears that Ping and Cici love just made an appearance in our home office. Ping handed the one she calls Pingping to me and told me to hold it while I work at the computer. She put the one she calls Leelee on the filing cabinet next to the laptop that she and Cici use so they can hold it when they work at the computer. She is quite romantic, and it shows throughout our home. For years she has collected pairs of things because they are romantic. Ducks, pigs, Mickey & Minnie, bears, and so forth. That is why she fell in love with the round bodied silver chickens that we bought yesterday.

The telephone with a Chinese phone number just rang in our home office. I can hear Ping's business voice as she sits here in the recliner. She is still helping her old company with the problem they cannot solve without her help.

I have listened to her handle business calls this way for more than a year. I don't understand her words, but I understand the art of persuasion. She is a master at using voice inflections, tone of voice, varying the speed of talking, and more. At times scolding, at times praising, at times being insistent, at times showing cooperation, but always moving the conversation toward her goal. No wonder they miss her so much.

I saw this morning that someone else has started a thread looking for advice about a divorce. Married just over two years. I feel for them, as I feel for anyone whose experience has not worked out well. Too often I have seen indications in posts that there were problems from the very beginning of a relationship, but the couple pressed onward, perhaps believing or hoping that the problems would go away once they were together.

I am in no way suggesting that this happened with the member who posted the message to which I referred, I am just making a comment. I am also in no way suggesting that Ping and I are the only couple who found such happiness together.

I know that there are couples who have been married for years and they have a happy and loving marriage. They are understandably too busy and happy to post about their marriage and their life together on a regular basis, but perhaps this thread about our life will serve as a beacon of hope against the less happy threads that are sometimes started when a relationship does not work.

"Yiang Qin, Fu Qin". Her calls often ring through our home. It makes me feel very special, because at first, Cici only called Yiang Qin. These are the more formal words for mama and papa that are used by older Chinese people. You can tell from the tone of her voice that Cici uses them as terms of endearment.

I am her Fu Qin, and when I told her last evening that the flat bear looking pillow that she placed in the driver's seat of our car for lumbar support had made my back feel better than it has ever felt after the drive that I have made hundreds of times to Athens, she beamed with pleasure. She does many little things to help her Fu Qin, and her love of our family makes her Yiang Qin and her Fu Qin smile at each other and feel very happy. This is our little girl.

Jun 11, 12:17 PM

"I told my husband.... Yes, my husband will.... This is my husband." Ping often uses these words when talking with people in America. I had grown accustomed to hearing her say Lao Gong when she talked with people in Guangzhou, but hearing these words in English makes me feel like she is proud of me.

Often when we are walking together in a store, Ping will put her arm around me and lean her head on my shoulder as we walk. She leaves no doubt in anyone's mind about her feelings for me. Cici seems to enjoy seeing the way her mama and papa are always holding hands or walking arm in arm. She seems to admire our easy going relationship with each other, and she seems to enjoy spending time with us.

We received a very big compliment this morning from a Chinese woman who was the single biggest skeptic about Ping's intentions. She has observed us together, read our stories, and called to apologize for her disbelief. She told me that I certainly made the right decision when I chose to believe in Ping.

My girls presented me with two birthday ties this morning. Ping is a smart shopper. Last week she saw an ad for $40 designer ties that were being sold for $9.99 if purchased within a limited window of time on a particular day. She made sure we were there, and she selected two ties that I like very much. Cici bargained with me to advance the money for the tie she wanted to pay for, saying she would wash our car in return.

They didn't need to do this, as just hearing their voices and their laughter, and seeing all they have done for us in our home, is all I could ever want. Well, there is one other important thing they have given me, which is the still consistently low blood pressure readings. They might just keep me around for a long time after all.

Jun 11, 09:58 PM

Somebody loves cake. No, two somebodies love cake. And ice cream. And watermelon. Good thing our actual dinner was only a great selection of vegetables. Ping and Cici were laughing and each accusing the other of being the one who ate most of the cake before I even got home today.

Ping said that Cici eats so much that she has made us poor. She said that all day Cici opens the door to one or both of the refrigerators and tries to decide what to eat next. Her description of Cici looking like a turtle with her tongue protruding from her mouth and moving from side to side slowly had Cici and me laughing like crazy.

I just tried to get Ping to look at a spider identification chart on the Internet but she couldn't bear to look. I was doing this in an effort to identify the spider that was crawling on her pillow just before we got in bed at the B&B in Athens. Spiders are a fact of life in Texas, especially when you get out in the country. Almost a thousand identified types of spiders, but only one shiny, small black one that I have found so far. That is the black widow.

We didn't have anything to help us turn this spider over to check for the red hourglass on the belly before I had to crush it, so we will never know for sure. Despite her revulsion for spiders, Ping still climbed right into bed after I removed the spider.

The girls have gotten real comfortable here, and they have started asking for my help to change a few things. Cici wants a mirror on the back wall of her closet, so we will lower the belt rack that holds her over sized bags, and mount the mirror above its new spot. The place where the mirror comes from will be replaced by a large picture that Ping wants to put in its spot.

Our king bed was delivered today and Ping is very happy with the way it looks in our bedroom. The headboard is so high in the middle that the picture on the wall had to come down. I wondered what in the world we could put above the headboard that would look good, since a picture really would not work. I went in the bedroom an hour later and loved what Ping had done. She had put the very large stuffed Mickey and Minnie Mouse couple so that they are sitting on the headboard on either side of its peak. So clever. So creative. So perfect.

Ping and Cici asked me this evening to show them how the Sony Dream Machine that I bought for Cici's bedroom a few months ago works. When Ping saw that it plays CD's she started negotiating with Cici to trade for the smaller Sony radio that sits in our bedroom. She told Cici that she only listens to music on her MP 4 player anyway, so it would only be fair for Ping to be able to listen to CD's in our bedroom on the Dream Machine. I know they will work this out amicably, because they never argue about things. I could offer to buy another Dream Machine but I know that is not the solution that either of them would want or accept.

I listened to Ping talking on the telephone with my younger (no longer youngest) daughter this evening, making plans for our family reunion in August. It won't be a typical step-mother, step-daughter relationship because they are too close in age. They will just be friends. Since they are both very outgoing with great personalities, they will have no problem getting along with each other. They talked and laughed on the telephone like they already know each other. One more piece of the puzzle falls nicely into place.

Jun 12, 07:33 AM

I have noticed that each day the garage is a little neater. This is a project that I should have finished before they arrived, but Ping hasn't complained. It is getting close to the time for cranking up the Beetle, because it will need a new inspection sticker next month. Ping will study for the driver's exam after our wedding next week. Because she is already a very experienced driver, it shouldn't take long. Then she can see whether she likes driving that bug or not.

When Ping and Cici first arrived I would only go to the office for a couple of hours in the morning, and then come back to our home office and work from here. I didn't want them to ever wonder or worry about when I would be coming back home. I steadily increased my time away from home, and now they know that they need not worry. I will be back. Today will be my first long day away from them. I will be in a multi-party mediation that will take two days, and everyone has already agreed that we will work late today.

We talked about it last night and Ping said not to worry, she will have dinner ready whenever I get home. Then she asked if it could be as late as nine o'clock.

"Yes."

"Later?"

"Yes."

"But also earlier?"

"Yes."

"Okay, no problem. Cici and I will take care of everything."

Speaking of taking care of everything, they worked a long day yesterday, cleaning the house and doing the laundry. They knew not to wash new red towels with yellow towels, but they thought it would be okay to dry them together. They didn't anticipate all the resulting lint that transferred from one color to the other, so they spent some time using a sticky roller and also hand picking the lint. They do that anyway with all of my clothes. I keep telling them that it doesn't matter if there is some lint on t-shirts that I just wear around the house, but it matters to them, so they do the extra work.

Our evening routine has developed so that the girls send me to shower first, and then they spend time together in the bathroom talking and laughing like college roommates. As I mentioned previously, I noticed that Cici's toothbrush and other bathroom items have slowly worked their way into the master bathroom. That is fine. Ping has two vanity areas that are separate from mine, so they share them. Then Cici likes to lie on our bed next to Ping and talk with us before she goes to her bedroom to sleep.

Ping has never met a morning she likes, and she looks so sleepy each morning, like now, when she comes into our home office for a hug and kiss. But when it has been necessary for us to get up early, even at 4:00 a.m., she has always popped out of bed and has never complained. Here in our home she cheerfully prepares breakfast for her family, and by the time she finishes that project she is wide awake. She told me again last night that she is very happy here, and that Cici is also very happy here. Still not a moment of loneliness or regret in these girls. They are right where they want to be, and loving every minute of it.

Jun 12, 09:46 PM

It was a long day today, as I had told Ping it would be. I got home a little after nine o'clock. This is the longest time that we have been separated since I arrived in Guangzhou on May 15. Ping greeted me at the door with a hug and a kiss. She always takes my work shoes and clothes and provides clothes and shoes for me to wear around our home.

I went to the living room to say hello to Cici. She got a big smile on her face and told me excitedly that she cooked a pizza today for her and Mama to eat for lunch. She was so proud that she took a picture of it to show me. She said she just followed the steps that I showed her and it worked great.

Ping said they talked with older sister on MSN this evening. She saw the pictures that were taken of us at Uncle Adrian's house, and said that we sure look like a happy family to her. Cici told older sister that her bedroom is very beautiful, and that she will send pictures to her.

When I went out to get the mail I saw that Ping had been at work again. She followed me and showed me how she had watered the plants and cleaned the walk and front entry way. She even used the hand held vacuum cleaner on the mat that is outside our front door.

June 13, 12:09 AM

"So do you want cream with that?" Sometimes I want to ask the lady if she really thinks my answer will be yes after she has asked me the same question every morning for a year and the answer has always been no. I am talking about my daily trek to Starbucks, at first to return home so Ping and I could talk on MSN. Now to return home so I can peek in at my sleeping beauty, knowing she will be awake and preparing breakfast soon.

"Can I help you?"

"Yes, Venti Bold please." I hand her three ones because I never carry change in the morning. Besides, by putting the $.89 in change in piggy banks every day, along with other change that hits my pockets, I have collected a somewhat impressive amount of change for our little girl over the past year. When the piggy banks get full I have a little machine that will sort it, and I put it in the paper rolls. Now Cici can do that by herself.

"Do you want the Bold?" she asks, after giving me the change. Yes, I am thinking, just as I said thirty seconds ago, and yesterday morning and the morning before that and the morning before that and ... . Well, you get the point. This is a small Starbucks, so it isn't like there are a million customers who show up first thing every morning.

When I was age 16, I worked as the short order cook in a busy restaurant and had to memorize every order that the typically 6-7 waitresses (no guys waiting tables in those days) came and read in rapid fire fashion from their little order pads to me, so I know it is possible to remember things. Maybe that ability goes away after a certain age. Ping says that Cici took her good memory and her good body from her when she was born. I would have to dispute at least the second part of her contention.

This lady is there at Starbucks five days a week. The other ladies who work there part time know exactly what I will order, and they prepare it when they see me coming. The lady who is there only on Saturday mornings, and the lady who is there only on Sunday mornings, had my order memorized after two weekends.

The lady who is there most of the time, however, seems to have a memory that resets every day. Even the look in her eyes seems to be one of startled surprise when I say "Venti Bold" each morning. Really, she seems to think. "Do you want cream with that? she says, like she just thought of a very intriguing question.

Ping doesn't ask, she decides how I will have things, based on what is good for me. I noticed that she even filled up the 7 cup holders in the Pilot with bottles of water and sports drinks so she can be sure the three of us always drink water when we are driving around.

Our new king bed gives the bedroom a stately look and it raises the bed by probably 4-6 inches. When I look in and see Ping snuggled beneath the white feather comforter, she looks like a beautiful princess. Her long dark hair spreads here and there in stark contrast with the puffy feather filled baffles on the white of the comforter. Her favorite pair of house slippers sits beside the bed. I know they are her favorite because she brought four extra pairs from Guangzhou. They have wooden soles with raised bumps on the top of the soles so they massage her feet as she walks.

And our life together remains the same. No tension, no drama, no sadness, no tears, no miscommunications, no anger. Our relationship has been this way for more than a year and a half now, whether we are together or apart, whether we are relaxed or under stress, whether we are rested or tired. I have never known such an even tempered and loving woman. This is my life.

Jun 13, 10:52 AM

China calling! My heart doesn't leap quite the way it once did when that phone lets out its distinctive ring. But if I am asleep or only half awake when it rings it takes a moment to realize that it isn't Ping calling.

"What's this?"

"That is a CD with my mother singing."

"Really, this is our Mama?"

"Yes."

"When did she make it?"

"When she was 82 years old?"

"Really?" I went to shave, and the next thing I knew I heard the sounds of my mother's voice coming from our bedroom. I hadn't noticed, but the Dream Machine with the CD player had made its way into our bedroom. I looked and Ping was lying on our bed with her eyes closed, listening to the music.

This was so sweet of her that I had to give her a little kiss. She pulled me down beside her and put a pillow under my head. She put her bent leg across my body, her arm around my chest and her head on my shoulder. Listen with me Leelee. To be honest I never really listened to the CD. Now I closed my eyes and listened to it through Ping's ears, and I was surprised at the strength in an 82 year old voice. My mother always sang alto when singing with her sisters or in a choir, but now she was singing soprano since she was singing solo. Wow, I thought, she can still hit the falsetto notes in a song.

This is where we were when the China phone rang. While Ping talked on the phone I took my shower, and when she helped me get dressed she started playing the CD again. I don't know that it means she liked the music, but I believe it does mean that she wanted to know more about our other Mama.

I told Ping that my mother and three of her sisters had cut some records when my mother was age 17. They sang together all of their lives, with one singing soprano, my mother, who is the youngest of the four singing alto, one singing tenor and the oldest singing bass. The oldest sister has died, one sister is a little addled much of the time, and one sister is pretty much tone deaf now.

The pianist on the CD is my uncle, who Ping will meet in August. He is a rather well known musician in some circles, and was recently inducted into the Gospel Music Hall of Fame. My mother also plays piano. In fact, in her family all of the ten siblings and their father played musical instruments. I know that those who are still alive will be fascinated if we take Cici's zither to the family reunion so she can play it for them.

In the call from China, Ping's good friend and her ten year old son, who is Ping's godson, said they wanted to chat with Ping on MSN. She signed on, and when I said I was leaving for the office, I thought I would just give her a quick kiss. That wasn't acceptable, as it turned out.

Ping quickly told her friend and her son to wait, and she walked me to the car. She opened the passenger door and leaned across to put the little flat bear pillow behind my back as I sat down in the driver's seat. Then she leaned across to kiss and hug me goodbye. She stood in the doorway as I backed out of the garage, and blew me a kiss goodbye. Have I mentioned that this woman is stunningly beautiful?

Jun 13, 05:54 PM

A coat rack, as it turns out, makes a great place to hang over sized purses and hand bags. The house coats and robes that formerly hung on it fit nicely on a hangar in the closets, thank you very much. I understand from a very good source (thank you Pingping) that hanging the bags helps them retain their shape. That coat rack looks better in the closet anyway.

That little multi colored hour glass shaped table inlaid with ceramic tile that I brought home, thinking it might hold a potted plant, turned out to be the perfect seat to have in a walk in closet so a lady can sit while changing shoes. I have to agree that it is a creative and functional use of the table, and it adds character and color to the closet.

Our ever helpful daughter is emptying all of the trash containers in the house while Ping is cooking dinner for our family. Our roles in our home have been defined quite well, sometimes by default and sometimes by design, but we still help each other so that nothing becomes a burden. It has become my role to not only select the watermelons that we eat, but to cut them, remove the meat, cut it into bite sized pieces, and put the pieces in a large covered container that can go in the refrigerator. The girls poach the pieces even as I am working on this project, because once they see the red melon, they can't wait to sample it.

"Look Cici, sqrioel."

"No Pingping, squirrel."

"Sqreil."

"No, squirrel."

"Squrreil."

"No, squirrel. This is difficult to say Leelee."

"I understand, just say *girl*."

"Giral."

"No *girl, girl, girl*."

"Girl. Girl."

"Perfect."

"Girl. Girl. Squirrel. Squirrel."

"Perfect."

"There is a girl squirrel"

"There is a girl squirrel."

"There are two squirrels."

"There are two squirrels, a boy squirrel and a girl squirrel. The boy squirrel is named Leelee. The girl squirrel is named Pingping." Overachiever.

"You got it Pingping!" English 101 in our family. Lesson number 237.

Jun 14, 08:30 AM

Someone we know suggested that our relationship is like kismet, so I looked up the meaning. I found an interesting distinction between fate and destiny. Considering how Ping and I have handled things after we met, I would have to say that destiny is a better description than fate, and destiny is the word that came up as the first definition for kismet.

Coca Cola. I can remember when it cost a nickel a bottle from the machine at the local Coca Cola bottling company in my home town. I went there once on a hot day after mowing yards and spent a whole quarter drinking coke after coke. I was so thirsty.

I haven't wandered on you here. I just learned a new way to use Coca Cola last evening. Put it on your feet.

Chicken feet, pig feet, duck feet. Also the wings. Put them all in the same pot, like a wok or another wide bottomed and deep pan, cover them with Coca Cola, and start boiling it. When the coke boils away, add some more and do it again. Wow! The meat on the bones will melt in your mouth when the feet are still hot, or it makes a great snack when they are cool or even cold out of the refrigerator. Ping didn't even use any additional seasoning.

Well that dinner earned me another job in our family. I am the official toe nail trimmer. I don't think most restaurants bother to trim the nails, but Ping had me use a pair of kitchen shears to cut the toe nails from the chicken feet before she cooked it. It does make for a little less aggravation when you eat them. So why bother eating chicken feet? It just might be that all that collagen has some health benefits, and you aren't likely to be getting it from other sources. I just eat the feet because I love the taste.

Our little girl showed me the dress she will wear at our wedding this week. She is so proud of how she looks, and she should feel that way. I had the girls select their flowers, and they both wanted to wear a wrist corsage instead of wearing one on their dresses. Then they selected a tuxedo for me after debating what color and style they like best. They selected the classic tuxedo look that I like best, with no suggestive comments from me. Ping was unfamiliar with using the word "taste" as a way of saying that we appreciate the same things, but now she knows and says that we have the same taste.

Today we will find out if the hair stylists in Chinatown can compete with the hair stylists in Guangzhou. With all the questions that Ping has asked as part of her due diligence, this should be a good experience for her. She and Cici will go together, and they seem to be excited about it.

The Disney Channel has become a favorite for Cici, and most of the content seems to be wholesome. She is fascinated when she watches American teenagers. This exposure should help her understand the lingo and the teen culture in America. Assuming she goes to the school that we have selected, there will only be 300 students total in grades 9-12, so she won't be overwhelmed.

Cici also attended private school in Guangzhou, and she was surprised that there is no requirement at this school for all students to wear the same shoes and use the same backpack. She also likes the fact that even though there are uniforms, you have choices so that not everyone will be wearing the exact same thing each day. And then there is the school lunch menu. Not the best nutritional choices, but all the things that kids, including Cici, love to eat. Pizza is on the menu three days a week. We will just make sure that the breakfast and dinner she eats will offset the lunches from a nutritional standpoint.

Saturday mornings. They sure have changed in this house. But so have all the other days. These girls have changed my life. I have changed their lives. Yes, kismet.

Jun 14, 05:47 PM

"Papa, will our TV do this?"

"I don't know, Cici, I never thought about it."

"Leelee, if our TV will do this it will help Cici and me to learn English."

"I can see that Pingping, I am sorry I didn't think of this before. We can check as soon as we get back home."

The girls had been in the hair salon in Chinatown for more than 3 hours, and there was a big screen television there. It had English captions on the screen, and Cici and Ping loved the assistance. They asked me these questions when I arrived. We are back home now, and the English caption option has been turned on for the girls. What was I thinking?

But there is more I didn't think about. Cici just asked me what 9E/8C means when they say that a program will be shown at that time. I drew a map of the United States and drew the lines for the time zones (no, not exactly, but just to demonstrate the point).

"Oh, you mean America has more than one time, not like China with just one time?"

"Yes Cici, I am sorry I hadn't thought to tell you about that either."

We have practiced with money and many other things, but I am learning that I have failed my girls in some important ways. Cici is laughing so loudly in the living room now that she can read the words to assist her in understanding what is happening on the Disney channel. She can barely catch her breath.

Bad Leelee. Bad papa.

Jun 14, 09:00 PM

Well, the girls haven't beaten me up for anything, so I guess I am still doing alright. Cici keeps me under a close watch, though. Today she joked with us that Papa can't let a day go by without spending money. When she saw that I bought a couple of small things while she and Mama were at the hair salon, she wanted to know if I had bought anything else that I hadn't told her about. I was clean.

That initial quote of $200 for the hair styling that Ping wanted done only amounted to $60 when all was said and done. I should say when Ping was said and done. She used the Chinatown yellow pages and worked the phone until she found the place, the service, and the price that she wanted. It is a very nice salon and they did a great job with her hair.

Cici was so antsy when I got there that she jumped at the opportunity to go next door with me to the Asian food market. They were still working on Ping's hair. It was fun shopping with Cici. She either okayed or nixed every purchase that I had in mind. She and I love to eat the Chinese rice crackers and she selected the ones that she said would taste best. Then we broke into them while we waited a bit longer for Ping. She shared her large green tea drink with me. Then the three of us went to our favorite Vietnamese noodle place where we were greeted with big smiles and a flurry of activity to serve us.

We walked and looked at jewelry and other girlish items for a couple of hours this afternoon, making only one minor purchase. Well, I thought it was minor, but Ping sure loves it. It is difficult to get Cici to say yes when we try to buy something for her, even when we know she wants it.

But ... she isn't bashful about everything. Ping and I found the empty Blue Bell ice cream carton in the trash this evening when I was taking out the trash. We laughed and played a joke on Cici, who was washing the dishes. I called out to Ping loudly from our home office that we should all eat some ice cream. Then Ping and I made a big production out of opening the freezer door and "discovering" that there was no ice cream.

Cici was laughing silently, her body shaking, as we did this. When she knew she was busted she started laughing out loud, and we laughed with her. She and Ping suggested we should get some more ice cream and another cake to take with us to our hotel in Austin. Which just reminded me - who ate the rest of that chocolate cake? Busted again, our little chicken ate that too. Nope, the truth just came out. Under intense cross examination, with much laughter, they accused each other of eating the rest of the cake, and then confessed that they shared in the crime.

Guess where we are going now? Yep. Gotta go get some more cake and ice cream. "Dress Mama, quickly, quickly," Cici says. Here we go.

Jun 15, 07:44 AM

"Pardon?" A look between startled and shocked! "Yes, Venti Bold please."

"Oh, would you like cream with that?"

And thus the beginning of our fourth week in America.

When I was a kid, my aunt and uncle owned "the" store in an even smaller town about ten miles from my home town. It was called a mercantile, and they sold everything from barbed wire and nails to eggs and ground beef. One thing they sold was coffee cake. You remember the packages, with the coffee cake all squeezed together, and with trails of the white icing clinging to the top and sticking to the package.

This was a treat that my family could not afford to buy, so on the few occasions that I stayed at my aunt and uncle's house overnight and we had this coffeecake for breakfast, I thought I had never tasted anything so good. I just tasted something that brought back those memories. One of the things that Ping and Cici put in our shopping cart last evening was a large round coffee cake, like a very thick pizza. I popped a piece of it into the microwave just now and the cinnamon and pieces of pecan fought with the flavor of the icing in my mouth for creating the most desire for another piece. They all won.

The girls had not had the experience of shopping in a large western grocery store yet. When I told them we could go at nine o'clock last night they were surprised that the store would be open so late. Yes, the store near us is open until 1:00 a.m., and reopens at 6:00 a.m. But we will go to the store just a few blocks further away, I told them. It is open 24 hours a day. This is a signature Kroger store, and when we walked inside and they saw what looked like a quarter acre filled with cakes and cookies and donuts and pies and other sweets, they went wild.

Before I knew it the cart contained a chocolate sheet cake, a round chocolate trio cake, the large pizza shaped coffee cake I mentioned, a nine pack of small blueberry muffins, and a four pack of large blueberry muffins. "Should we put something back?", they inquired. "Who will eat all of this?" I asked incredulously. "Okay Cici, let's put this back." And the chocolate sheet cake left the cart.

"Now let's find the ice cream papa!"

The Blue Bell ice cream was on sale, and the girls know what 40% off means, so we just had to buy two tubs of the ice cream. First the search for the elusive cookies and cream flavor, with success at last. Then the debate over all the other choices. Coffee flavor won the debate. Then a huge package of uncooked chicken wings went in the cart for something that Ping has in mind, along with a couple of pork steaks for something that I have in mind.

"Do you want to buy that, Pingping?"

"No, I just want to see what they are wearing." This was a slick looking magazine somewhat like People Magazine, but primarily pictures, and Ping was flipping through the pages as we waited in line to pay for the food. Fashion is important to Ping, so I know why she was looking. She was wearing a black dress yesterday, but not what you would expect. First it was sporty looking, with a drawstring around the hemline, and it struck her above mid-thigh.

An African-American lady had complimented Ping on her dress earlier in the day when we shopped for jewelry. We saw a couple of African-American women as we left Kroger. When we got in the car, Cici said that those ladies could not wear mama's black dress at night because no one could see them except for their eyes and their teeth. Oh my child, I thought, I can see that human relations training will be on our agenda soon before you run into trouble in America.

Jun 15, 02:09 PM

I never really wanted a pink Cadillac. I never thought I would help someone buy one either. But Ping has been putting her favorite Mary Kay moisturizer on my face every day. This bottle traveled from China, but I guess we will have to find a pusher in Houston soon.

The girls were introduced to fried cat for lunch today. They didn't know quite what to think about them but they ate them and liked them. I ordered two whole cats, butterflied and fried in corn meal, so there was plenty to share. They also enjoyed the seafood gumbo. Now you are with me. Catfish, but in the lingo of Captain Benny's, on the boat, they are known as fried cat. We even ate the bones that had been fried to a crisp.

Our daughter has learned the purpose of the TV Guide that comes in the Sunday Chronicle each week.

"What time is it now, papa?"

"Okay, Sunday afternoon, two o'clock. Oh yes, here is a program I want to watch. You are welcome, Papa."

But Papa needs to head outside to help Mama plant the flowers and yes, the ivy that she wanted. We stopped at a nursery and the girls were wowed by all the plants and trees and flowers. We came home with our fair share. Gotta go earn my keep.

Jun 15, 09:03 PM

Ping and Cici continue to amaze me not just with their ability to communicate in English, but because of their ability to say the right things from a social perspective. Ping spoke on the telephone for the first time with my son today and I was very impressed with her social skills in that setting. No awkward silences and a very polished conversation. I wish I could do so well.

We have a beautiful little flower garden near the garage now. Ping worked very hard on it today. Someone had to handle the more difficult things like driving to Home Depot to pick up a couple of things, so I volunteered my services. The neighbors around us are already falling in love with Ping. We are surrounded by older people, and they love having this vivacious, personable, and beautiful lady living next door.

Cici also has a way of warming my heart. We just spent several hours in very pleasurable company in a large and beautiful home. She walked into our home office with me and told me spontaneously that she likes our home better because she loves its feel. This wasn't a slam at the home we were just in; she appreciates its roominess and feeling of grandeur, but she is like Ping and me. She said that she likes the closeness of our furniture and our walls around her, like arms holding her close, and the warm and safe feeling it gives her.

I have the same feeling in our home now, but it wasn't that way until my girls arrived and filled the emptiness with their laughter and their love.

Jun 16, 07:54 AM

Three minute warning.

I have never known anyone who is so diligent about brushing teeth. Ping calls it washing teeth, so even when toothpaste is not available, she will have us swish water around in our mouth to wash our teeth after we eat something or drink something other than water. These techniques have paid off well for her, as she has none of the discoloration or decay in her teeth that seems somewhat prevalent in China.

She tells Cici and me that we must brush for three minutes, and she has even been known to hand a loaded toothbrush and a cup of water to me while I am in the shower. I wish she had been around when I was a kid like Cici. Maybe I wouldn't be missing a couple of my back teeth.

Ping was teasing Cici last night that Cici should have to say something in the wedding ceremony too, since we have written her into the ceremony. "Welcome", said Cici with a smile. She is looking forward to this wedding with great anticipation. As much as she sometimes likes to duck the camera, she is proud of our growing library of family photos, and she knows we will add many more on our wedding day. She puts all of them on her MP 4 player and then shares them with her friends in China, Canada, and America.

I always just point the camera and shoot, thinking that if the person or persons who I am trying to capture on film are in the picture, I accomplished my purpose. Ping and Cici are giving me lessons about how to use certain techniques to make people look taller and thinner, however, which is something I never thought about. Ping just walked in looking tall and thin as she slipped her house dress over her head, but she looks a little groggy eyed. Her former colleagues called for some help three times during the wee hours of the morning because they forgot about or didn't understand the difference in time.

In about 36 hours we will be taking photos as the sun slips up over the horizon and tops the cliff where Chapel Dulcinea sits awaiting our wedding. The noted Seer in China who selected June 19th as a good day for our wedding projected a long and happy marriage for Ping and me.

It is easy to discount her ability to foresee anything just by looking at dates and times of birth. It is rather difficult, however, to discount her ability to tell us about our past, using that same data as her sole source of information. She was uncannily accurate when telling us about our respective lives before we met. So this is why, in order to be married on June 19th China time, we have a relatively early morning wedding planned, central time.

The early time, mid week, is also why we are just having a private ceremony, but it will all be captured by a photographer, and we can share it with everyone at a later, more convenient time. As close as we have become as a family, we especially like it this way now.

We have come a long way.

Rare and Beautiful Treasure

Chapter Thirteen

Jun 16, 02:00 PM

Flowers? No problem. What kind of flowers? Well, white wrist corsages, the girls told me. I don't know about the bridal bouquet, but they will choose the flowers for it when we are in your store. "Oh, the girls are from China? Well, then we know they will insist on red flowers. Asian people always want red flowers."

Really? Have you met my girls? They have minds of their own, I am thinking. They just might surprise you.

But the important thing is that the store opens early enough on Thursday morning that we can pick up the flowers that morning and then drive to Chapel Dulcinea for our wedding. That solves the logistical concern that I had about making sure we had fresh flowers.

"Where is your daughter?"

"Well, she decided not to eat lunch today because she feels like she has been eating too much." The lady who owns the Dim Sum restaurant that we love already feels close to the girls. She was complimenting Ping about what she was wearing today, and was asking about Cici.

"Mama, I will tell you the good news! Papa is home early!" Ping said that Cici told her this when I came home to get some documents and take them to lunch today. They always make me feel so special when I come home. It also felt rather special to have a date with Ping for lunch. She can go from the beautiful housewife look to the ravishing, sexy beauty look in minutes when the need arises.

Our count down continues....

Jun 16, 06:34 PM

Now that boy can flat cook. The problem is that he set the standard so high that I likely can't beat it. The girls talked about the food all the way home. Char-grilled pork ribs with a secret recipe homemade barbecue sauce. German (or maybe Greek) potato salad. They want to know if I can prepare food like that. Sure. Thanks to Uncle Adrian I have a tough task ahead.

Someone else has fired up some delicious cooking as well. I can hear the sound coming from our kitchen. I love it when I hear her using that large, fairly deep, and thin skillet looking pan that conducts heat so quickly and evenly. I had no idea when I bought it that it would turn out to be the most used pot in our house, and we have a few of them. They hang on a heavy metal rack that hangs from the ceiling over the counter that divides the kitchen from the breakfast room. It is perfect for quickly cooking fresh vegetables, and we eat a lot of them.

The girls discovered my past today and spent hours digging through it. There are several other boxes they need to go through if they want to see it all. Pictures that date all the way back to 1925 when my mother was born. They saw both sets of grandparents and their 18 children. Well 17 children. One of my uncles disappeared many years ago, and I have no pictures of him. I never met him. My grandmother and grandfather grieved all their lives over his disappearance. He went to California to work for the singing cowboy Gene Autry some time in the early 1950's and was never heard from again. His wife raised their two children on her own.

My grandparents died in the early 1970's, still grieving. A couple of years ago one of his children, a cousin who I have never met, tracked down her long missing father. He had married another woman and lived another life in another state without ever contacting his family again. If I have difficulty understanding this kind of behavior, which I do, then you can imagine how Ping and Cici reacted to this story.

When she went through the pictures she talked about my children being beautiful, because they had a beautiful mother. Then she looked me in the eye and said "Leelee, in two days I will be your wife." Then after a pregnant pause, and with no hint of a smile, she said, "I will be your last wife."

Jun 16, 10:03 PM

One week to the day. Ping received her second piece of mail at our home, this time from the Social Security Administration. She inspected her card to see if it met her approval.

"Let's see, issued on June 9th. That is a good date. The first number is a six, also good. The sum of the first two numbers is nine. The sum of the next two numbers is nine. The sum of the next two numbers is six. The zero doesn't count. The sum of the final two numbers is nine. So let's see. The number is actually 9969 issued on June 9th. Wow Leelee, I like this number!!"

We saw that the moon is almost full in the sky as we walked this evening, so we checked when we got back and we see it will be full on June 18th, but not until the afternoon. So it will still be full for all practical purposes at the time of our wedding on June 19th. The moon will be our friend.

"I really like our neighborhood, Leelee. We will live here for a long time. We will have Cici's husband buy a home next to our home when she gets married. Then their baby can come to our home often. Okay Leelee? Then when we get old we can live in China and pay someone to look after us. Okay Leelee?"

Ping looked like a movie star as we walked along this evening. I told her that is how she looked before we left the house. She told me thank you, I guess you are lucky to be married to a movie star. No, I thought, I am lucky to be with a woman so beautiful who never gives her beauty a thought. A woman whose values are so centered on family and home and love.

This kind of story doesn't even happen in the movies. Ping gets all the credit for taking my blood pressure from 183/111 just a few months ago to 112/66 this evening. The word unbelievable doesn't begin to describe what she had done with my life and my health. And every day she works even harder to bring happiness to our home. I forget now who said it, but I think they were right. I am actually dead, and this is what heaven is all about.

Jun 17, 08:03 AM

"I believe that love cannot be bought except with love."

While Ping didn't use these exact words, this is a message that she gave to me very clearly and very early in our relationship. I believe we ended up with the relationship and the family that we have only because we were both willing to give all, trust all, love all. We did this not just when a little doubt might try to creep into our minds, but we did it when we were confronted with the ultimate challenge to our life together.

When a woman loves you enough to spontaneously put her arms around your sweaty body as she walks along beside you, with her head against your shoulder, I think you can believe that her feelings are genuine. Ping did this as we walked together last evening, speaking softly to me about how much she loves being with me, how much she loves our home, how much she loves our family.

Just now she came out of the bedroom in her altogether, eyes still fighting to open, beautiful tousled hair, slipping a red body hugging soft cotton shirt dress over her head. Each guy has his own preference in women, and my preference is a woman who has some curves. That isn't always easy to find in a Chinese woman, in my experience, but I found it with Ping. The sway of her hips when she walks is a wonder to see, and in a dress like this, even more so.

"This is just a bed dress," she tells me when I admire the way she looks.

"No darling, this is a dress you should wear anywhere we go."

"Really?" She has no idea....

Jun 17, 01:20 PM

Last minute planning. It often takes a certain amount of luck to turn out well. The stringed music for our wedding ceremony just fell into place. It will be a surprise for Ping. Some might consider it to be unnecessary for a small private ceremony, and Ping would likely take that position, but love knows no bounds. I have been trying for about six weeks to get this group to play for us, and just as we got down to the wire, everything worked out just the way we need it.

Now we will hear the sounds of soft and beautiful wedding music as the sun rises and filters through the openings in the wedding chapel, stirring our souls and our imagination as we pledge our love and our lives to each other. The description of this day, this event, accompanied by photographs, will circle the globe as it is shared by Ping and Cici with everyone they know.

This day will live in our memories forever.

Jun 17, 06:29 PM

"That one is ugly Leelee."

"I bet it will taste the same," I responded without looking at the subject of her comment. It wasn't that I was inattentive. I was 100% focused. I just wasn't focused on the dumplings Ping was making.

You see, I came home early to surprise her with a little gift. Something that a groom should do for a bride on her wedding day. Ping isn't familiar with American customs for weddings, but I won't cut any corners with her. She was so excited and she called Cici to come and see what papa had done. Like children at Christmas time they opened the three gift wrapped boxes to find the necklace, bracelet, and earrings that they contained. "Oh Leelee, these are so beautiful. I love them so much. You are welcome."

But that isn't why I was focused on something other than the dumplings. I also had difficulty seeing the jewelry. You see, Ping had removed her top to wash it in a load of clothes and hadn't bothered to go put another one on. I have never seen such perfect dumplings before in my life.

Jun 17, 10:16 PM

“But I look so Chinese when I wear this Leelee.”

“You are Chinese Pingping, which is one of the things I love about you.” Ping had several beautifully colored and patterned cheongsam dresses made for her in the last few months that she was in Guangzhou. They fall below the knee, but are slit up the thigh on each side. High collars with Chinese buttons strategically placed help complete the picture. I love the way she looks in them. She will look very Chinese at our wedding.

The girls are packing for our trip to Austin. My tux will be waiting for us there, so I have little to pack except for the important things. Like the marriage license.

Tonight we watched TV together for the first time. We laughed at most of the people who were competing on “America’s Got Talent”, but the little four year old girl who sang “Somewhere Out There” stole our hearts. While she wasn’t much of a show person, the eighty year old lady who tap danced was inspiring if not talented. As we watched the show we voted and decided that we should not buy cake and ice cream very often, since we love it, because if it is here we will eat it.

We all love fresh fruit, so we decided that is what we will eat. Cici ate some papaya tonight, and offered some to me, but Ping told her that I cannot eat papaya. Only females can eat papaya, she told us, because it causes human breasts to grow, and doesn’t discriminate between male and female. Maybe that isn’t scary enough, but when she added under her breath for me that it also causes performance problems for men, she and I decided to ban papaya from our home. You never know what you will learn from a Chinese woman.

The girls saw pictures of the hotel on the Internet and decided to pack their swim suits. They like the look of the pool, and the hotel has beautiful gardens. We took a virtual tour on the Internet, but will walk them in person when we are there. That reminds me, I need to pack the camera. The pressure for wedding photos will be on the photographer, however, and we will just take pictures for fun.

My ex and I collected a lot of artwork when we were together. Many Japanese woodblock prints and Hakata Dolls, among other things. She emailed me to ask if we would be interested in having some of them, since she has too many and wants to redecorate. Ping and Cici said yes, so the three girls have agreed that Ping and Cici and I will go together to meet my ex at her home and help pack everything in bubble wrap, then bring it to our home.

I know most everyone thinks this is insane, but it works for me, and it works for Ping. I have no doubt that my ex and Ping will like each other, and they will learn things from each other. This will also give Cici another female role model in America, especially if she wants to be a lawyer. My ex and two of her sisters are all lawyers, as was their father and their grandfather.

Ping and Cici will undoubtedly meet all of them in the coming months, and they will be welcomed with open arms. Ping and Cici can both see and learn from this family about the way immigrants to America can become successful in just one generation if they are willing to work hard. Ping has already extended a standing invitation to my ex to join us for dinner, since she knows my ex does not cook. She is smart enough not to abuse the privilege, so I am not concerned about it.

Less than 36 hours.

Jun 18, 07:42 AM

Aaahhh Choooo!! It finally happened in public, in the food market. "Bless You!!" The words from a pretty young lady who was standing near Ping. "Thank You!!" Words spoken proudly and confidently by Ping as though she had been having such an exchange with others her entire life. Later in the car she talked excitedly about how she just reacted without having to think. Thank You!! You are Welcome!!

"Two men came to the gate", Ping said. "They said they were checking the telephone lines and wanted to know if our phone was working. I told them our phone was working with no problems."

"You didn't open the front door, Ping?"

"No, in Guangzhou we never opened our door or the gate at the door unless it was for someone we know. Bad men try to come in with knives and they take the money and the jewelry, and sometimes they hurt or even kill the people. So we never open the door or the gate."

Good Pingping. Now I know that our neighbor had telephone problems. He told me about them. I therefore suspect rather strongly that these men were legitimately inquiring about our telephone. I am very glad that Ping took our conversation about safety to heart. Even if our phone wasn't working, I told her, she did the right thing.

Ping will be heartbroken, or at least sad, to see that the wind that was blowing hard yesterday evening when it rained for a while caused a limb from the magnolia tree to break and fall to the ground. I saw it there when I went to Starbucks this morning. She spends time every day babying that tree and our little flower garden that she planted. Now she has expanded her work to include all the plants and trees around our home. The ladies from nearby houses have begun to gather with her to talk when they see she is out working.

Our neighbors always introduce themselves to Ping, and Ping tells them that she is Ping, and her husband is Lee. Later in our home she confesses that she doesn't remember their names. Jessie Lee Roark Cain. Our immediate neighbor to the West. I looked in the directory. I don't think I would remember her name either. She has lived there since July 2007. I not only have never met her, I have never even seen her. I guess she feels safe with Ping. These elderly people are very careful, but she is coming out every day now to visit with Ping.

Sometimes the ladies who are out walking their dogs from elsewhere in the neighborhood also stop to talk with Ping. She told me last night that she really liked the black and white dog that we saw at the ranch last week. It is a border collie, born to a female border collie that was on the ranch when I owned it, and sired by a border collie who was also there with me. I told Ping that we can get a puppy from the next litter if she would like that, but she says no, because she likes the character of the dog we met. I tried to explain to her that all border collies are very submissive and will act the way the dog she met acted, but she isn't buying it yet.

"Papa!! What are you doing in the refrigerator?" Cici laughed as she peeked around the corner into the dark kitchen. "Mama, Papa is in the refrigerator", she called with another laugh. Dang, I will have to be sneakier with this little girl watching out for my health.

We have a date with destiny so I better awaken my girls. Nope, that will do it. The China phone just rang and I took it to Ping. Some time during the night she slipped into that body hugging red bed dress, as she calls it. Wow she looks good. And this is the woman I will marry in just over 24 hours from now. I am sooooooo very lucky!

Jun 18, 04:16 PM

Did I say last minute planning? I have been trying to reach the minister who agreed to perform our wedding ceremony since Sunday. I called him again as we left Houston this morning, without success. I called him at two fifteen, three fifteen, and no success. We checked in at the hotel after driving out to look at the chapel and I found an alternate phone number and called

it. He answered. I was about to start trying to line someone else up at the last minute. In his defense, he is a little hard of hearing.

The girls are exploring the book in our suite that tells about things in Austin. They keep talking about barbecue restaurants. That sounds pretty good after the poor excuse for Chinese food that we ate for lunch. They called it gourmet Chinese food. What a joke.

I asked the girls if they want to go enjoy the pool. They looked at me like I must be joking, and said that we can swim when the sun goes down. My bad. I always thought one should swim when the water felt the best, but this works for me. I always sit in the shade anyway. I wonder what we will do with this fireplace in our room on this hot June day.

There is a bell tower at the little chapel. There is a long rope dangling from the bell. Guess who rang the bell? Poor child, it almost scared her out of her shoes. She was standing outside the bell tower and didn't yet know that the rope was attached to the bell. She couldn't resist reaching through the barred window to pull on the rope.

We selected our flowers and picked up my tux within easy walking distance of the University of Texas campus. This is territory with which I am fairly familiar. Cici has now seen the campus that she and Ping have set as her goal for college. It isn't easy to be accepted here, but if she works hard she can gain admission.

We have decided to have some quiet time, so I will join the girls. We can share our thoughts about tomorrow. One year and eight months to get to this day. We each have our own thoughts about why it is meaningful for us. We have time. Let's let them run freely through our heads.

Jun 18, 10:36 PM

We ordered a slab of ribs and some grilled beef medallions with grilled vegetables for dinner at a steakhouse in Austin. The unanimous verdict was that Uncle Adrian's ribs were better, though there was nothing left of these when the girls were done. The beef medallions were so tender they literally melted in your mouth. I introduced the girls to fried onion strings and they were a big hit.

Good night Cici, see you in the morning. Nothing unusual about those words that I heard last night in our home. Nothing unusual, that is, unless you consider that they were said by a Chinese woman to her Chinese daughter, with no one else in the room, and the words were said in English. While the girls still have some conversations in Chinese, they mostly speak in English when I am with them. Now I know that they also speak in English to each other at times when I am not involved in their conversation.

This evening as we drove around the University of Texas, Ping told Cici about the conversation we had a few nights ago as we walked in the neighborhood. The one about Cici and her husband buying a house next to our house when she gets married. The subject came up because Cici wanted to know if she could come home every weekend from college. Three hours driving each direction Cici. Okay Papa, how about every other weekend. We told her it sounds like we will have to live in her college dorm with her.

"What about Houston, Papa. Does it have any good colleges?" "Yes Cici, Rice University is a very good university."

Now Cici and Mama have a new idea about where she might want to go for college. One thing is clear. At least the way she feels right now, this little girl is in no hurry to leave home. She told us that even when she is 25 and finished with graduate school, she will not be ready to marry. She wants to live with us. Time has a way of changing things, so we will see how she feels in a few years.

I purposely did not shave this morning, and Cici just stood by my side stroking my cheek, feeling my beard. "Papa, you feel just like the little dog we once had when I was little." Then she rubbed my shoulders as she and Ping talked with me. She told Ping and me today that in the future, we should get one big hotel room with two beds, rather than getting a suite with two separate bedrooms. She doesn't like being separated from us in a strange place.

So how did we relieve any possible tension that anyone might feel before the big day? We all sat on Cici's bed and watched the new Mr. Bean movie together and laughed like crazy. We all appreciate the same kind of humor. The truth is, though, that no one felt any tension.

I read an article in the Houston Chronicle this week that was written by one of their staff writers who had just gotten married. The focus of the article was on what she called Groomzillas. She had witnessed it personally in the weeks leading up to her wedding, she said. I think I can honestly say that Ping has not experienced any of that kind of behavior from me. I know for sure that there has been no change in Ping's behavior.

As for Cici, if anything, I believe she has been even sweeter. She waited a lot of years with her Mama for tomorrow to come. Tomorrow is therefore Cici's day as well. I cannot imagine what more she could have done to show me that she believes that her Mama made a good choice. She takes great delight in showing me that she knows every mannerism that I use, every word that I say. She has watched and listened to me intensely. She is my daughter. I am her father. We both love Mama, and we all three love our family. We are ready.

Jun 19, 06:49 AM

Yes, this is quite an adventure for us. Guess who crept down the stairs in our suite quiet as a mouse just after midnight and slipped into our king bed next to

Mama? Yep, good thing we are going home after the wedding.

The little one is sitting on the sofa here in front of me, yawning. She and Mama have never met a morning they like. There is a bride's dressing room at the chapel that they would like to use this morning, but there simply isn't time. We can't pick up the flowers until eight o'clock, and it will take us a little more than half an hour to get to the chapel office.

We must walk the remaining hundred yards or more on a dirt path to get to the chapel. Once there, we must discuss the ceremony with the minister, discuss the music with the string group, and then discuss and begin taking photos with the photographer. The ceremony, says Ping, must be at 9:36 a.m.

With that schedule, I think it is fair to assume that breakfast will be fruit in the car. Ah, but at least there was Starbucks coffee in the room. "You mean that you know how to make coffee?" asks Ping innocently. "Nope, never done it before in my life." Lazy Leelee.

One of the young ladies at the chapel office told me yesterday that it should be around 70 degrees at the chapel this morning before the sun warms the top of the hill with its rays. Even in the heat of the day yesterday, the chapel itself was comfortably cool with a slight breeze blowing through it. There is a small fountain where a pulpit might usually sit in a church, and the air on the water might help the stone columns that support the chapel roof cool the air inside.

Stone seats inside the chapel can accommodate only twelve people, though they often have weddings here where people stand all around the outside of the chapel.

We should find out if they will allow Cici to ring the bell in the tower after the ceremony. The setting, even during the heat of the day, is just as compelling and romantic as the photos show on the website. If you haven't been there yet, you can join us at www.chapeldulcinea.com.

I didn't particularly like the sample wedding ceremonies that were given to us, so much of our ceremony I wrote for us. Sometimes I modified what was already written, and sometimes I wrote the words from scratch. Ping and Cici have blessed my work, so this will be our wedding ceremony:

Words of Greeting: Lee and Ping, we have come together in God's loving presence to witness and celebrate your vows to each other in the holy relationship of marriage.

These moments we will share today are about much more than ceremony and word. They are about the beauty of relationships. They are about the deepest feelings of our spirits. They are about a covenant with one another, with your beautiful daughter Cici, and with God. Finally, they are about your commitment to each other and to your daughter Cici that you will be together as husband and wife, as mother and father, as lovers and friends, and as a warm and loving family, forever. I am honored to be part of your covenant making.

Invocation: Gracious God, bless Lee and Ping who now join their lives in marriage, that their vows will be strengthened in Your steadfast love. May their love and care for each other remain strong through trust and friendship all their days, that they may complete all the promises of their already begun journey. In the spirit of Christ's love we pray. Amen.

[BOUQUET to the Maid of Honor]

Lee and Ping, if you desire now to enter into a marriage covenant with each other, please indicate that wish by joining both hands.

Declaration of vows:

Lee, do you commit yourself to Ping, to be her life partner and best friend, to laugh and cry with her, to listen and share with her, to love and honor her, and to live fully and honestly with her, as long as you both shall live? (I do)

Ping, do you commit yourself to Lee, to be his life partner and best friend, to laugh and cry with him, to listen and share with him, to love and honor him, and to live fully and honestly with him as long as you both shall live? (I do)

Lee and Ping, do you commit yourself to your daughter Cici, to be role models for her, to laugh and cry with her, to listen and share with her, to love and honor her, to live fully and honestly with her, to provide a warm and loving family for her -- as long as you both shall live? (We do)

Meditation: The Psalmist says, "This is the day the Lord has made, let us rejoice and be glad in it." And indeed, we do rejoice and are glad to be alive, and are glad for the treasure of marriage, your own unique marriage. There has never been a marriage like that which you bond today, nor will there ever be another marriage just like it.

Preparation for your vows now brings you to these moments of covenant, and this preparation comes from different areas of your lives. The truth of all truths is this: God gave you birth into the world with the gift of life, and all that you are-- your bodies, health, intelligence, and abilities. It is God who created love itself, the way of marriage, the power of commitment, and the will to see it through. It is God who makes your relationship possible, and God sustains you in that relationship. God is the rock on which your relationship is built.

Lee and Ping, the simple truth is this: TRULY you are blessed! To you much has been given. To understand this is to know that you have been brought to this day to give all that has been given to you--to each other.

You have come together against overwhelming odds, from opposite sides of the earth where you were each born. You have chosen not to allow language, culture, politics, government, ideology, religion, distance, or age come between you and your love. No matter what else happens, you have pledged that you will never change, that you will love each other forever, and that you will always be together.

And finally, as you requested, to your beautiful daughter, I say this from each of you:

Cici, the family that your Mama and Papa brought together because of their love for each other and for you is their everlasting gift to you. They will live together with you just as you wish. Happy every day.

Prayer: Loving God, make Lee and Ping's marriage and family a great and holy adventure. May their joining be a sacred space where they may find rest and a haven for their souls. May their marriage and family be a channel for your love and healing, a passage for your grace and power. Amen.

Vows:

From this day on I choose you Ping/Lee

To be my wife/husband,
To live with you and laugh with you,
To stand by your side and sleep in your arms,
To be joy to your heart and food to your soul,
To bring out the best in you always,
To laugh with you in the good times,
To struggle with you in the bad,
To solace you when you are downhearted,
To wipe your tears with my hands,
To play with you as much as I can,
Until we grow old, still loving each other sweetly and gladly.

Pronouncement: Lee and Ping, because of the faith and love you have affirmed in each other, I pronounce that you are husband and wife, in the name of the Father, Son, and Holy Spirit.

Now may the Lord bless you and keep you; the Lord make his face to shine upon you and be gracious unto you; the Lord lift up his countenance upon you and give you peace, now and forever more. Amen.

Kiss [BOUQUET FROM MH]

Congratulations: It is my sincere privilege to congratulate you as a newly married couple, Lee and Ping. Cici, I give you your parents, and your family. To each of you I say this as you leave today: what you have found when you found each other is a rare and beautiful treasure. It is not replaceable. Don't ever let it go.

Jun 19, 03:43 PM

"Pingping, tomorrow you will be my lao po", I whispered as we lay in bed holding each other late last night. "I am your lao po today", she whispered back to me. "I have been your lao po from the time we first met in person. Xie xie lao po. Bu ke qi lao gong. Ni hen mei li lao po. Xie xie lao gong. Bu ke qi lao po. Wo ai ni lao po. Wo ai ni lao gong." Sounds of silence.

It sounded like we had an exotic dancer at the wedding, but it gave us some moments of humor. The minister is a little hard of hearing, and he never understood that he should say Cici and not Chi Chi. So our beautiful daughter Chi Chi served as bridesmaid for Ping, and our wedding went exactly as planned.

We found out about half an hour before the ceremony that there is a security camera mounted high on a telephone pole on the hillside above the chapel. The minister just happened to mention it, and he added that it is possible for people to watch a wedding there through the security camera. Had we known this in time, our friends and family in China could have joined us for the wedding. My cell phone had no signal but I was able to borrow a phone in the chapel office and make a phone call to Uncle Adrian so he could try to spread the word to anyone who might be interested.

The musicians were great, the photographer worked hard to capture the moment(s), and the minister did a great job. We learned that after the groom kisses the bride, they should pull the rope and ring the bell in the chapel tower together. We followed that tradition and the peal of the bell rang out over the hills for all to know.

There is a very nice changing room for the bride on the premises. We used it after the ceremony to change clothes. We put on tee shirts. White for Ping, black for me. The white tee shirt is inscribed with the word "Bride", and the black with the word "Groom". We both put on shorts. Ping looks a lot better in her very short jeans shorts than I look in my shorts. Chi Chi selected what we should eat for lunch, so Gatti's Pizza it was.

"Leelee, I miss our home. I can't wait to get home. The first thing I will do when we get home is check on our new flowers, Leelee." How many brides would be pining to be back in their home immediately after her wedding? We are in fact back in our home where it looks like we will finally get some badly needed rain. My beautiful bride is calling me to bed, perchance to sleep? Not a chance, I would guess. At least not until we have earned it.

Dream

Chapter Fourteen

Jun 19, 09:54 PM

Are we yesterday's news, or tomorrow's inspiration? That is a rhetorical question that only time can answer, perhaps, though surely we will play a role. It doesn't feel any different to be legally married. The feelings of love and commitment were already there. It didn't take a marriage to form a family. Our family was formed by love and commitment. The marriage license was just a necessary formality for us.

Yet we are happy to be married, and Cici is happy that we are married. When she heard her full name read today at our wedding ceremony, it included my family name. We cannot make that name change official yet, because we don't meet the requirements of Texas law until she has lived in our home for at least six months.

After the ceremony Cici told us that she does not want Tianjiao to be included in her name. While Ping and I are encouraging her to keep that as part of her name, I suspect that her wishes will prevail. We told her that we can always call her Chi Chi. She has a good sense of humor so she laughed with us.

After a dim sum dinner at our favorite little place, we stopped to get a curling iron and a hair straightening iron for the girls. These are things I knew they would probably need, but I didn't want to make the choices for them. The possible choices are too varied. Unlike the first few times we went shopping together after they arrived, they are much more involved today in making decisions about what we should purchase.

The girls are also willing to listen to my suggestion that many times a choice should not be made based on the fact that the price is the cheapest. They have agreed with me that when we are purchasing things that will be used often and hopefully for a long time, it is often smarter to spend more and get better quality. Because of the poor quality of many things in China, they were a bit into the disposable purchase attitude, but that is changing.

As soon as we got back from dinner Ping braved the mosquitoes to spend a little time babying our little flower garden. The rainstorm this afternoon had brought down leaves and twigs from the magnolia tree, so she swept everything up around the garage entrance and I helped her pick it up and dispose of it. Her pride in our home is a sight to behold.

Our daughter is back in her little nest here in our home. She also could not wait to be home again. She asked us this evening if we could buy her a pair of the white thick soled thong type shoes that we bought for Ping last week. These shoes are only $8 in Chinatown, so she thought it might be okay if we agreed.

Cici is very careful with money. I have watched her each time we have been together. Ping has trusted her with money and responsibility for money since she was quite young. In China I never saw Ping handle a purchase in a store or restaurant or taxi if Cici was with us. Cici handled everything. She also handled banking transactions and ATM transactions. She automatically converts in her head any purchase we are considering in Houston into RMB in order to assess whether or not she thinks it is a good deal. Some purchases have not been made because she says that we can wait and buy the identical item for a fraction of the cost when we are in China.

I never envisioned writing all of these things about our life together in America. But each thing I wrote lead to another, like way leads on to way, as a poet once wrote.

Jun 20, 07:49 AM

We shared our stories on a forum, thinking they might be helpful to American men who are concerned about whether a relationship with a woman from China is too fraught with problems. To hear that our stories are also read by women in China who are looking for some reassurance that a relationship with an American man can work without a lot of problems is at once heart warming and scary for us. Now I hope that the few Chinese words I have written in our posts have been correctly spelled and correctly used. Ping understands me at least.

Some of Ping's best friends were on MSN with her last evening for a while as we worked together in our home office. They asked her if we got married as planned. They asked her if I am nice to her. They could see the answers to their questions from her smiles, but she told them anyway. She told me that she told them that I am not just nice, but that I am very nice to her and Cici, and that they are very, very happy here. Ping's friends that I have met already know about me and our relationship, but her friends who live in Zibo City haven't met me yet, so they are still curious.

I have noticed that Cici spends more time in what we call her nest now, and less time talking with her friends on line. Her nest is in the middle of the big soft leather sofa with her pink blanket, watching what have become her favorite shows on the Disney channel. On the long and wide coffee table that is in front of the sofa, Ping has placed a wooden hand carved platter. In the platter Cici keeps an assortment of rice crackers and other snacks. We were laughing about it with her last night. Ping says that Cici's mouth never stops chewing something.

Ping also says that Cici has a dog nose. She can smell anything from a mile away. Sometimes she asks us about things that she smells well before we can smell them. That helps sometimes if we leave the kitchen for a few minutes while cooking something. Cici will shoot out of her nest and be in the kitchen to lower the heat just before the water boils over the top of a cooking pot of food.

The nine roses from Ping's bridal bouquet have been placed in water on the kitchen counter. They are a color that Ping says she has never seen in China, and she loved them the minute she saw them. The flower ladies didn't understand the significance of her insistence that they use exactly nine roses in the bouquet, so I explained it to them. One of our musicians was from Taiwan. She understood the significance.

"Give me twenty minutes, Cici, and talk with Papa while I sleep."

We were all tired after not sleeping very long the night before our wedding, so on the drive back to Houston the girls took turns sleeping in the Pilot. The distance from downtown Austin to our home is just less than 160 miles, so when the girls are sleeping we can easily make the drive without stopping. Ping periodically massages my shoulder muscles when I am driving, and she wishes that she could take her turn at the wheel.

When they are awake the girls are impressed with the clean and neat appearance of the roads and the houses and apartments and shopping centers along the way. Texas has a lot of wide open spaces, even in this part of the state, and they are amazed at how small some of the towns are. They also read the signs. Founded in 1871, a sign said in one of the small towns. That led to a discussion about a number of things about American history, so the subject of July 4th came up. Since that holiday is just around the corner, we talked about Independence Day. Our wedding day was on Juneteenth, so we also talked about the significance of that day in American history. This is the day that commemorates the announcement of the abolition of slavery in Texas.

We learned from a friend that Ping can study for and take the written portion of the driver's test in Houston even before she has the required identification to take the driving portion of the test. She has the study guide in English and Chinese, so with the wedding behind us she will begin her preparations for the written part of the test.

There were some important things that came up yesterday on the never ending project that Ping was working on at her company in China before she resigned her position. With a cheerful and helpful attitude she jumped in to assist her former colleagues, on her wedding day, in the buff, after she came out of the shower last evening. I think I got the better end of that deal.

Jun 20, 08:18 AM

Ok, now we are jumping with joy. Cici is still sleeping, but Ping and I just read a letter that came in the mail yesterday. It is a great wedding gift for us.

The letter is from the high school where we submitted an application for Cici. It says in part, "Dear Angela: Congratulations on your official acceptance to our High School!"

This is a great school just 2.5 miles from my office. Cici can ride to and from school with me each day. I will be close by if she ever needs anything during the day.

Our strategy about just showing up at the school, even without an appointment, so that the ladies in the school office and the admissions director could see us and talk with us, paid off. We gained admission for Cici without having to wait for the usual requirement to interview with the Head of School before being officially accepted. We had been told that he would be interview applicants for about another month before he could meet with us.

Maybe when I bragged about my son graduating as class valedictorian two years ago at a competing high school when I talked with the Head of School briefly on the telephone helped. I told him that Cici might or might not achieve the same result, but that we know she will work hard and do as good as she can. Maybe it also helped when we told the admissions director that Cici's school day in her private school in Guangzhou was from 7:00 a.m. until 10:00 p.m. five days a week. He was shocked!

Gotta write that tuition check now, but I will do it gladly for our little girl.

Jun 20, 09:37 PM

One thing about attending private school is that it is like law school in some ways. They expect you to walk into class prepared the first day of school. That means that there are reading and study requirements during the summer. Today we bought the two books that Cici must read for her English class this summer. One of them I have read. Agatha Christie's "And Then There Was One." Good book, and worth reading more than once, in my humble opinion.

The other book I have never heard of, and would never choose to read. It is "Ender's Game" by Orson Scott Card, who I have also never heard of. I couldn't even find it at the book store because I had no idea in which category of literature (assuming it qualifies as such) it would fit. I will probably get slammed by someone who thinks this is the best book ever written, but it simply isn't my type of book. The young lady who worked at the book store, however, walked straight to the book when I asked her about it. I asked her how she knew where it was on the shelves. She said it is her favorite book and she has read it three times.

This is a lot of reading for Cici, so I have tried to help her as much as I can by purchasing SparkNotes (which have apparently replaced CliffNotes, at least at Barnes and Noble). We agreed that she will first read the SparkNotes, and then read the books.

Quite honestly this second purchase was also to help me, because I will read the SparkNotes but not the books themselves (actually I might just read Agatha's book again). Then I can discuss the books with Cici so that she will be better prepared in class. I have worked with each of my children in this way for all of their subjects in school. Sometimes I feel like I am being punished for being a high school dropout, by having to study high school courses again and again with my children.

Ah well, there are worse things to do with one's life than learn something new every day. We are embarking on Cici and Papa's big adventure. But -- we won't leave Mama behind. I also bought 1000 vocabulary cards that have words on the SAT level with definitions, identification of the part of speech, and sample usage in a sentence.

Studies begin at nine o'clock each morning beginning on Monday. The girls will study on their own each morning, with a progress review in the evening with me. Cici's studies will also

include a review of Algebra in preparation for her placement tests at school.

I have noticed that Ping and Cici both read the Chinese newspapers that we pick up every week in Chinatown. They also read parts of the Houston Chronicle that is delivered to our home each day. Cici has even been reading a Bible that is written in Chinese. Uncle Adrian left it here months ago and Cici picked it up herself and started reading it.

A second language is a required part of the curriculum at Cici's school, but they only offer Spanish and Latin. Since English is her third language, I hope to broker a deal that would allow her to study extra semesters of English, and perhaps test out of Chinese to meet the second language requirement.

It isn't all work and no play. We spent time at the pool this evening early. Ping impressed me with her stamina in the pool. She swims multiple laps around the perimeter of the pool without ever touching the edge. Cici is more like me. In fact, Ping told us that next time we should bring a book to read while she works out in the pool. Then Ping did sit-ups on the wooden benches at the pool. She asked how many I could do, so I said I could do one more than she could do. She made me prove it.

June 21, 07:49 AM

Silence. No good morning. No how are you. No "would you like cream with that"?

This morning the younger, sullen one was at Starbucks. She often shows up late and doesn't have the coffee ready at 6:00 a.m. when the store is supposed to open. It is because of her that I don't arrive at Starbucks any more before 6:30 a.m. But at least she knows what I will order. She simply places a Venti coffee in front of me, takes my money, and hands me the change.

I know if Ping were there with me she would say cheerfully, "thank you very much," because that is what she has trained herself to say in English any time someone does something for her or compliments her. The other person's attitude or outlook on life is immaterial to her. With one exception. She wants me to smile. She has told me many times that when we are together, it is my smile that gives her a happy heart, and if something is troubling me, it brings her down. So she has developed ways of taking my mind off of other things, and making me smile.

"Where is Cici?"

"She went to her room to read, Leelee, let's check on her."

There she was, sitting in her bed, her legs under the covers, book in one hand and the hand held electronic dictionary and translator in the other hand.

"This is very difficult, Papa. There are many words that I don't know".

"Don't get discouraged little one. We will help you."

So we did what we believe will help her. It is the same technique I have used with the other kids. We gave her a highlighter and a fine point pen.

"Mark every word you don't know with the highlighter, and write the meaning in Chinese above or below it with the fine point pen. Then keep reading. Many words that you don't understand are often repeated in a book, so it will be faster as you work your way through the book."

There will be roughly 75 students in Cici's freshman class. School begins on August 20, and on the evening of August 21 they will go as a group to a retreat in a town North of Houston. Thursday evening through Saturday they will get to know each other and their teachers. They will engage in activities and games that will require them to learn how to work together. They need some daring and energetic parents who are willing to go along to help.

I am curious to see if Ping has any interest in doing this with the group. I think it would be a good learning experience for her as well, if she has any interest in doing it. It might also help us help Cici, because it would give Ping a chance to spend time with her teachers. I also believe strongly that parental involvement in the education of their children is one of their more important roles in parenting.

So this morning we will be at the school uniform store when it opens at ten o'clock. We planned this last night as a family outing as we sat on our bed eating blueberries and talking about things. Cici is excited about selecting her uniform items.

For the girls there are pleated skirts, pleated kilts available in navy and khaki colors. There is also a navy, red, and white plaid skirt. There are long sleeved oxford blouses in white and blue, and blouses with a 3/4 length sleeve in white and navy. Then there are pleated shorts in navy and in khaki, and flat front shorts in navy and khaki. All skirts and shorts must be knee length.

Oh but there is more, since slacks can be obtained in the same styles and colors as the shorts. There are also long sleeved knit shirts in navy or white or red, as well as a navy windbreaker jacket. There is a black and brown reversible belt and there are braided leather belts in black, brown, or navy.

Top that off with cardigan sweaters in navy or red, sweater vests in navy or red, and pullover sweaters in navy or red.

Now imagine that in the past you have been dressed in dull, drab identical uniforms that never vary, right down to the same boring shoes and backpacks that are worn by every student in the school. I know this is more than you ever wanted to know about how kids will dress at Cici's school, but this trip to the uniform store even has Ping excited!

At the moment, though, the girls are enjoying their last little bit of sleep for the night. They are ready to get back on a more rigid schedule starting next week. Yesterday Cici slept until noon, which she enjoyed, but she knows it is time to get back to work. Her future beckons.

Jun 21, 05:55 PM

"We don't need anything Leelee. Well, maybe some apples and some milk." How could we reasonably expect to get through the week without a watermelon to back up the one in our refrigerator in the garage? And the double jugs of apple juice, grape juice, and orange juice were just begging to queue up on the pantry floor.

"That 8 pound bag of Vidalia onions - Leelee, are these the sweet onions that Adrian used with his barbecue? Really? We should eat these every day. Why don't you get some barbecue Leelee? Can you really prepare barbecue for us?" By the time we left Costco the cart was full. More fresh fruit and fresh romaine lettuce. I have learned that if romaine lettuce is prepared the way A Choy (Chinese lettuce) is prepared, the taste is almost the same.

No point in going through the whole cart with you. We just happen to enjoy shopping as a family and talking about all the good things we will eat. We stopped in Costco after we bought Cici's school uniforms. Now there is a good deal. Some of the uniform items usually end up lasting for several years of school, and since the possible items of clothing that can be worn during the school year are rather limited, there is not as much need to keep buying more clothes throughout the year. Cici and Ping shopped excitedly together in the uniform store, assisted by the manager and two sales persons. We have a happy little girl with a closet that is filling up quickly.

Next up, little things like the required TI-83 graphing calculator. Ping told Cici that we have spent more money for her education in just two days than we will spend on Mama and Papa all year. It turns out that Ping is very interested in going to the retreat with Cici and the freshman class, so she will volunteer her time for that purpose. If one wants to become integrated in a community, school is a great place to start. Ping seems to recognize that, and she is eager to get involved.

The girls have been busy cleaning our home and cooking while I have been adding Ping's name to credit card accounts and utility bills, positioning us for the next stage of this process. I also downloaded, printed, and filled out the application for Ping's Texas identification card. We won't have her get it until we receive the file marked marriage certificate back from the County Clerk's office, because we will get the ID card issued in her married name. The DPS office where she will get the ID card is very close to my office, so she can ride with me when I go to the office one day.

Another afternoon thunderstorm has rolled in and Ping is excited. Our plants and flowers are quite happy when it rains. This will cool the air and it will be more comfortable when we walk or ride our bicycles later this evening. No one who looked in on our family right about now would ever guess that today is just the end of our first month together in America. We look and act like the prototypical all American family from years gone by. Unless they listened closely, someone watching us might even have difficulty recognizing that we were born on different continents and come from totally different cultures. We fit together as though it was always intended by a higher power that we would be a family.

And guess what, we have simply had no problems of any kind. No moments of tension. No flashes of anger. No brooding or loneliness or sadness. No problems communicating. No problems spending all of our time together. No problems shopping or deciding what to eat or deciding when or where to sleep. We love our family, and we love our life. We are very thankful that we trusted each other and believed in each other and took this risk to be together.

Jun 22, 08:19 AM

"Dream." The first words out of Ping's mouth this morning, but said with a smile. Cici often says this word when Ping is teasing her, and we all laugh. "Mama and Papa will go [do something we know Cici would love to do with us, for example], but Cici will stay at home." "Dream!!!" Cici will shout with a big laugh. Her version of "you are dreaming" or "you're dreaming." We all know what she means.

I had asked Ping jokingly if she wanted to go to Starbucks with me this morning, knowing it was not her favorite time to get out of bed in the morning. "Dream." But then she popped out of bed and threw on some short jeans shorts and a tank top, ran her fingers through the curls in her hair using some of the special conditioning cream we got for her a couple of days ago, washed her face and brushed her teeth, and she was ready to go. The way she looks would take away the breath of most any man who is breathing.

Speaking of dreaming, Cici told us a few days ago that she had a long dream at night. She dreamed that her closet was full of treasures, and her Mama and Papa went in and out of her closet many times, bringing more treasures each time. She said it was a happy dream, and the treasures in her dream meant that we would always be happy.

Last night we each checked our blood pressure. I check mine every day, but we check Ping and Cici each week. 106/72, 102/66, 100/64. Ping understands so well how to put the brakes on at the right time. If we have meat at one meal, it will be in very small amounts (unless of course Uncle Adrian serves up those ribs), and the next meal will be all vegetables and grains. Fish is also fair game, but even then we eat moderate amounts. Soup and congee are also regularly on the menu.

But this is the most delicious food I have ever eaten. Guangzhou cooking usually predominates, because it usually doesn't involve frying food. Any fried food that we do eat will involve using only a very small amount of cooking oil in the wok, and it will be fresh vegetables. The Pacair range hood keeps our kitchen smelling clean, and Ping keeps everything in the kitchen shiny and clean. She cleans things every day that I hadn't thought about cleaning the entire time I have lived here.

First thing every morning the patio door slides open and Ping steps outside with our plants. She has a spray bottle that she uses several times each day to spray water on the leaves on the small trees. If trees could smile, these trees would be laughing with happiness. They have changed so much since Ping arrived. She started by removing all of the dead leaves. She rotates their placement on the patio to control the amount of direct sunlight that they receive.

When I watch Ping with the plants and the flowers, I see how she takes care of her family. When I watch Ping clean and care for our home, I see how she takes care of her family. Cici and I receive the same kind of loving care. “Look at the sky Leelee”, is her way of telling me to straighten my back. Ping has a very erect posture and is determined that Cici and I will not end up with a stooped posture. “Wash your teeth”, as she hands me some water if I take a drink of juice or a sports drink. “Drink some water”, she says each morning as she hands me a glass of water.

“Cici, do you want to go to Starbucks with Papa and me?” “Dream”, she replies sleepily, but this time with the opposite meaning. We were up late last night, as we are every night (the girls have changed my living habits completely). Ping has given Cici responsibility for taking care of Infinity, our Betta. She decided to change its water around eleven o’clock last night. Help me Papa, I don’t want to hurt him. I showed Cici how to let Infinity swim into her cupped hands and lift him gently from the bowl and place him in the small travel jar that came with him from the pet store. This little project doesn’t take very long, but I would have never have envisioned doing it this late at night. These are my girls, though. They get more energetic as the night gets later.

Jun 22, 05:23 PM

It all started so innocently. We might have had high hopes when we were first introduced, but I think we knew the odds were against us. We were 8,000 miles apart, and I never really expected to meet the woman who would change my life.

Now she is my wife and I have been out in the hot sun with her, putting down roots. We have expanded her little flower garden a bit by taking down part of the hedge that was there. Every neighbor who comes by stops to chat and admire the way her garden looks.

We could tell you more of our story, day by day, but every book must come to an end. We will do the next best thing for you. We will take you on a walk through time. Shall we?

The Rocking Chair

Chapter Fifteen

The rocking chair moved with a gentle motion. Forward and back, forward and back, soothing the sleeping baby in Lee's arms. "Daddy's gone a huntin,' with his little dog and gun, sleeeep, Kentucky babe. Ammo in his pocket, walkin' thru the woods, sleeeep, sleeeep, sleeeep." Lee half hummed and half sang the little ditty in a soothing tone. It was a long ago tune and he had forgotten most of the words, so he made them up or hummed when needed. The baby didn't seem to mind.

LeePing was nestled in his arms. A little pink blanket with bears on it was wrapped tightly around his fat little body. Worn and faded now from years of use, the baby's mother loved it so much that she always wrapped him in it for sleeping. His dark round eyes were closed. The thick dark hair he inherited from his mother and his grandmother was curling on his little head already. Not quite a year old, he was the most precious little treasure in the world for Grandpa Leelee and Grandma Pingping.

In her early fifties now, but not looking anything like a Grandmother, Ping sat in the love seat close to her husband and grandchild. Her hair was still long and mostly dark. Her body still shapely and firm. She walked every day with her husband. Some days if the mosquitoes were not out they would push the baby stroller as they walked, the baby sleeping contentedly. With her left hand she kept reaching out to caress her husband's arm as he rocked their grandbaby. It was a cold night in Houston, but the soft glow of the fireplace warmed their home almost as much as she was warmed from within. Her heart was so full of happiness and love and contentment that it was almost bursting. This was the life she had always dreamed of living. She knew her husband felt the same way. After that one time, they had never quarreled again; never doubted each other. He told her every day how much he loved her. "I love you too, Da Niu Bao Bao", she would always say, holding him close.

Cici, the proud mother of the baby, sat beside Ping, holding hands with her mother. Still more like sisters than mother and daughter, they shared the responsibility for raising the sleeping baby. Her husband had gone to the store to get some Blue Bell Cookies and Cream. "Go quickly," Cici teased him, "they might sell the last of it before you get there. Then what would we do?"

The rocking chair was still now. The baby snored quietly. The singing and humming had stopped. "Get a blanket, would you darling." Ping said. "Papa's arm is so cold."

Letter to Our Daughter

Chapter 16

He dribbled the ball back and forth, working on his game, wishing he had someone to play with him. He was twelve years old now. His tousled curly hair was sweaty and dark. He had seen pictures of his Grandpa Leelee when he was the same age, and he could see where he got his curls. I wish Grandpa was here now, he thought. I wonder what he was like. Mama and Grandma always talked about how much they missed him.

"Look at him Cici," Ping said. "He is so intense, just like Papa was. He wants to be the best at everything he does." They were sitting at the breakfast table watching little Leelee play on the driveway. After Grandpa died they started calling him by that name. That was more than ten years ago now, but Ping still ached inside every day. In her mid sixties now, with mostly white hair, she missed Lee so much. He had died in his sleep, holding little Leelee in his arms that night in the rocking chair. The fire warm in the fireplace, his body cold in the chair. Ping had never felt pain as great as she felt that night. Not even sure if she could go on with life, she was numb during the days that followed.

They buried Papa and stood over his grave together, looking down one last time at the casket. Little LeePing was asleep in his father's arms a respectful distance away. Papa's two beautiful girls held each other tightly, the tears streaming down their faces. "What will we do, Mama, what will we do"? "We will do what Papa would have wished," Ping said. "We will go on living. We will still have our warm and loving family. And don't worry darling, Papa will always be with us in our hearts."

Little Leelee was so tall now. Tall and skinny like Grandpa had been when he was young. It gave the girls a lot of pleasure to watch him. "What happened that night, Mama?," Cici asked, speaking ever so softly?. "The night that Papa said goodbye. You and Papa never told me."

Ping knew what she was talking about. She remembered that night like it was yesterday. She remembered how her heart was broken. She remembered watching Cici sob her little heart out. She remembered Cici begging, pleading with her, to let her call Papa. She remembered how much it hurt to tell her no. Cici became very angry with her that night, Ping remembered. It is the only time she could remember that Cici had ever been angry with her like that.

"Go to my bedroom darling. Look in the bottom of my jewelry box. You will find an envelope with a letter inside. Papa wrote that letter to you that night but I never gave it to you. Now you should read it, and I think you will understand."

"Dear Cici:

When you read this letter you may still be angry with me, but I hope you are not. You may also be hurting or sad, but I hope you are not. You may not wish to read my words, but I hope you will read them anyway.

Sometimes life is very complicated, even for adults. Perhaps even especially for adults. Sometimes we become disillusioned, sometimes we misunderstand each other, and sometimes we don't act as we should.

The most difficult relationship for a man and a woman to live through is a long distance relationship. Your Mama and I have been living in a very successful long distance relationship for almost one and a half years. Each time we have had some misunderstanding about something we were able to quickly resolve it by just talking about it with each other.

In recent days our ability to communicate as we usually do was disrupted because of your trip to WuTai Mountain and to Zibo City. A difficult topic arose that we were unable to discuss as quickly and as comfortably as we usually do, and before we resolved the matter, we made a mistake. I will accept full responsibility for that mistake.

Because of this mistake, or more accurately because of the misunderstanding that lead to this mistake, for a very short time your Mama and I thought that we had lost our relationship with each other. I promise you that neither of us lost our love for each other, but we allowed ourselves to become discouraged and to doubt each other.

I was so worried about this that I was up around three o'clock this morning (my time) writing to your Mama. She was up until around two thirty this morning (your time) writing to me. We both realized that we hurt you very much, and we never want to hurt you. You went to sleep not knowing that we talked until we resolved our misunderstanding. When you awaken, your Mama will talk with you about this, and tell you that we still love each other very much, and that being together with you in a happy family is the most important thing in the world for us.

There is a story in the Christian Bible about how God was very angry with people on earth many years ago, so he sent a great flood that killed everything on earth except for one man and his family, and the animals and birds that God had the man take with him on a huge ark (boat). After this flood, which lasted for forty days and forty nights, God placed a rainbow in the sky as a promise that he would never again destroy everything on earth by flood. Sometimes when it rains, you can still see his rainbow in the sky today.

It is not within my power to send a rainbow to you as a promise to you that I will always be with you and your mom. All I can give you today are my words. Then one day at a time, as the sun and moon rise and set, I can prove to you with my actions that we will always be together. Your mom has made the same promise to me, and I have made the same promise to her.

I had hoped that you thought of me as your natural father, and honestly I did not think you felt that way about me. Then Mama told me how much it hurt you when you thought that we would not be together as a family. For that I want to apologize to you. I do think of you as my natural daughter, and I love you and Mama with all my heart. I felt like my world had ended during those hours when it seemed like your Mama and I had lost each other. The most important thing in life to me is to have both of you here with me in our home.

My daughter, there are good people and bad people in every nation on earth. There are also people who cause problems between other people by telling them things that are not true. I have always believed Mama no matter what other people have said to me. You know that there is an age difference between us, and you also know that the age difference has not mattered to your Mama and me. You are old enough and mature enough that I am going to tell you something.

The reason it has taken so long for our Visa application to be processed, and for an interview to be scheduled, is because some people in other countries want to come to America so much that they do illegal things to get here. In China and some other countries, some people have paid a lot of money to people in America to marry them so they can come to America. For this reason, applications for a Visa take a long time to process, even when two honest people like your Mama and I are the ones who have applied for the Visa.

While it is difficult for me to understand, some Chinese people who already live in America believe that women who live in China are willing to marry an American man only so they can come to America. They especially believe this is true when the Chinese woman is much younger than the American man. I know many Chinese people who live in America. Many of them are clients of my law firm. They see our family photo that I keep in my office, and they ask questions about our family.

At first I was proud and happy to tell anyone who asked all about our family, especially if a Chinese person asked. Now I have learned to be more careful about what I say, because I have learned that some Chinese people think your Mama doesn't really love me, and is just cheating me so she can come to America with you. Some of them have done everything they can to convince me that your Mama is not a good person and cannot be trusted.

Please don't conclude that all Chinese people in America feel this way, because they do not. We have a Chinese woman living very close to our home in Houston. Your Mama met her and her parents when they were in Guangzhou last year. She has lived in America for many years. She was at our home just a few days ago, asking me when you and your Mama will arrive. She is very excited and happy to know that we will all be arriving at our home on May 24. She is an example of the Chinese people in America who don't look down on your Mama because she wants to marry me.

What happened in the past few days is that I told your Mama what some Chinese people in America said about her. They showed me something that I thought was indisputable proof of what they were telling me, and I told your Mama that I believed them because of what they showed me. Your Mama was very insulted and angry. I couldn't keep talking with her about it because you and she were traveling. Then your Mama and I had a serious misunderstanding about it and each of us had hurt feelings. That is why for a very brief time we were so discouraged that we thought we had lost our opportunity to have the warm and loving family that we both want to have with you. Our trust was broken, but our love was still strong.

Cici, I hope you can understand and forgive both of us for causing you pain. I want you to look at me as your natural father, and allow me to treat you as my natural daughter. I cannot send you a rainbow so I will send you pictures of your Hello Kitty bathroom. For lack of a better symbol, this will represent my promise to you that I will always be there for you, will always love you, will always comfort you, and will always treat you proudly as my natural daughter. I love hearing your voice when you call me papa. I hope you will do that again.

My daughter, I have given you as much information as I can in this letter. Mama and I think it is best if we don't tell you any of the specific details about what happened. What we did decide, and what we promised each other as we set aside what we believed was an insurmountable problem, was this: to protect our family, to protect our daughter, to protect our love for each other, to always be together, we would do anything. There is No Price Too Great.

From your papa, who loves you and never wants to disappoint you or hurt you again."

"Mama, why are you crying?," little Leelee asked. "Give her a minute, little Leelee," Grandma said, giving him a hug. "She just read a letter from Grandpa." "Grandpa? But Grandpa is dead." "Let me tell you something, little Leelee, Grandpa tried very hard to think of everything. He always tried to do the right thing. He wrote this letter to Mama before you were ever born, because he loved her very much. I saved the letter and showed it to her today."

No Price Too Great

Chapter 17

"Why didn't you get married again, Grandma"? You always seemed to be so lonely. Little Leelee was not so little now. Even taller than his Grandpa had been, he was a handsome young man, fresh out college. He spoke Chinese and English equally well. He loved it when they traveled to China with Grandma. It was such a big and wonderful country. No wonder she and Grandpa had spent so much time there after they were married.

Ping rocked slowly in what had been Lee's favorite rocking chair while she thought about his question. The chair had been covered and recovered several times over the years. She loved to sit in it. Lee always seemed to be there with her. Stroking her hair. Kissing her forehead. "I love you so much, Pingping," she could still hear his voice whispering those words in her ear after all these years. It sounded just the way it had sounded every night after they were finally together in America.

Her body and mind were still strong. She was a proud and still beautiful woman, now almost eighty years old, but anyone would think she was still fifteen years younger. "I always called your Grandpa "Da Niu Bao Bao". Did you know that little Leelee? He was born in the year of the ox just like you. Just like my father. The three men in my life have always been strong as an ox.

There will never be another man like Grandpa. No one could have ever replaced him in my life. Besides, he has been with me every day. I saved every letter he ever wrote to me, and he loved to write. I loved him more than I loved life, little Leelee." Very quiet now, the rocking chair still.

"I read some of Da Niu Bao Bao's letters every night before I go to sleep, then he joins me in my dreams." Sitting quietly, waiting for her to go on, a tear slipped down Leelee's face. Mama walked into the room and sat quietly beside him, listening to Grandma.

"I can only tell you that I loved Grandpa with all my heart. One of his greatest concerns was that he would die too soon and leave me all alone for many years. I knew that was possible, but I told Grandpa that I would take that risk. I felt exactly as Papa felt in the letter he wrote to your Mama so many years ago. I have never forgotten his words, and tonight in his letter he came back to say them to us again: to protect our family, to protect our daughter, to protect our love for each other, to always be together, we agreed that we would do anything. There was No Price Too Great."

--The End--

Printed in the United States
133945LV00007B/9/P

9 781598 588408